"MARS IS JUST A MEMORY NOW, AT-TANIO, AS LOST AS OLD EARTH."

She paused and once more seemed to evaluate him.

"A new empire has risen in the Pleiades. It's a human-based civilization, but they are allied with a very unpleasant bunch of aliens. Their power has been building for centuries, and less than one standard year ago, they struck the Solar System and sacked Luna and Mars. The devastation was brutal, pointless, irrational...

"And now they're headed this way..."

THE BROKEN WORLDS

RAYMOND HARRIS

ACE SCIENCE FICTION BOOKS
NEW YORK

This book is an Ace Science Fiction
original edition, and has never been
previously published.

THE BROKEN WORLDS

An Ace Science Fiction Book/published by arrangement with
the author

PRINTING HISTORY
Ace Science Fiction edition/August 1986

ISBN: 0-441-08143-6

Ace Science Fiction Books are published by
The Berkley Publishing Group,
200 Madison Avenue, New York, New York 10016.
PRINTED IN THE UNITED STATES OF AMERICA

This book is dedicated to my parents.

I. Poisonous Leisure

Two men and a woman carefully made their way through the slums of Ashbeck just as dusk settled in. A light drizzle was falling and wisps of fog swirled up from the pavement. Now and then a sickly biolume flickered on as they passed, and brief shadows stalked them through the dingy glow: otherwise their passage went unremarked.

Still, they walked slowly, with many backward glances, and their hands never strayed from the weapons all three carried: needleswords and nullbeams of the finest design. When they spoke it was in guarded tones, using the clipped cadences of Middle Galactic. Though common enough in the Home Stars, this tongue was rarely heard here in the clustered worlds beyond Antares.

"We know who it is we must deal with, and where to find him." The woman spoke. "But as for how . . . I confess my ignorance."

"No mystery there." Her companion frowned. "We move in secret, strike hard, and cut deep."

"Then that leaves us with when." The woman smiled sidelong. "And the more secrecy and the less violence we use the better we'll fare, that I guarantee. If only we could find one good informer! As it is we're probably making all the wrong moves."

"Unfortunately," the man replied, "the natives are less than friendly." His companion remained silent: in fact the two men resembled each other so closely that it seemed one could do the talking for both. "We learned all we could at that spacer's dive last night; there's no point in returning."

"Oh no!" She winced at the thought. "And our interview with the port authorities was just as useless. They won't tell us a thing. No one will! They're all too afraid of that Ypousef Makhlouf. He's the man we need to see, yet he's impossible to approach without the right introduction. We do seem to lack credibility as wandering robot merchants."

"Everyone thinks we're here to buy drugs." He shrugged helplessly. "Too bad nobody believes we're just innocent star-farers."

"Hah! These people suspect the very air they breathe."

They turned onto one of Ashbeck's main thoroughfares, Canopus Avenue. The lighting here was more constant but so was the garbage. Since it chiefly contained abandoned and decaying buildings Canopus was almost deserted: most of Ashbeck was the same. Even inhabited structures sometimes gave the appearance of ruins, all bricked and boarded up, with perhaps a concealed entrance around back. This was indeed the home of paranoia.

The woman caught sight of a solitary wanderer approaching them and murmured to her companions. The stranger was female, swathed in a voluminous robe that left her head uncovered; they could see that she was shaven bald. Over her shoulders balanced a wooden yoke from which dangled four covered baskets, two from each end. She was young and delicate.

When they drew abreast of her, the bald woman seemed to notice them for the first time—though of course she had only been feigning indifference before. She barked a single word in the local argot: "Offworlders!" Her tone was an odd mixture of awe and condescension. She reached inside her robe, whereupon all three of the so-named offworlders put their hands on their weapons. But the young woman merely withdrew a slip of paper, gravely presented it to them, and continued down the avenue. A sinister musty odor hovered in her wake.

"Charming," was the offworld lady's only comment. The printout she now held was tissue-thin and contained the following information:

Tonight: Succubarium: Cabaret by Attanio Hwin and Skiff Welt: *alto relievo* by Farelus Delice: *danse du ventre*, Kpuhdeh Kafu: Poisonous Leisure.

"So many words from the dead languages," remarked the young man. "The natives are more erudite than I expected.

Succubarium—that would be 'Place of Nightmares,' I think."

"And *cabaret,* and *ventre?*" the woman asked eagerly.

"Something to do with wind, and drinking liquor in a . . . a kind of wheeled carriage."

The woman squinted as if trying to picture anything so bizarre. "This Succubarium sounds like the place to go in Ashbeck. Now we need only find it." The prospect of a new environment cheered her.

"But first our dinner," the man insisted, and for once his silent partner chimed in. Without further ado they headed for the all-night snackpit they had discovered the day before, tucked away on the Street of Obscure Interiors. Soon they were seated in the dingy cafe over bowls of pods-in-broth, plates of steaming buckwheat, and skewers of roots drenched in hot sauce.

Among their fellow diners—a shifty lot of no particular stature or quality, sallow, mouse-haired, and ill-dressed—these three Galactics stood out like aristocrats of the starpaths. The two men were very tall and muscled like greyhounds, without a gram of superfluous weight. Their proportions were elongate and their chests deep, testifying to an origin on some low-gravity world with relatively thin atmosphere. Both were clean-shaven, with chin-length silver manes and wide obsidian eyes set in finely sculpted faces. The metallic luster of their hair contrasted sharply with their coffee-brown complexions, evidence of years spent under fierce ultraviolet light.

They answered to the names of Momozon and Tutunchi and could only be brothers. Tutunchi was the quiet one.

The woman was Sringlë, but they knew this was an alias. She claimed origin on Phayao, a minor planet in the Maung Cluster, but again this was open to speculation. She concealed her true hair color under a luminous violet dye, and spoke so many languages so fluently that her accent was no clue. She had the body of a warrior-goddess: lean rippling arms, a taut narrow waist, firm conical breasts, and the powerful legs of a dancer. Her beauty was a weapon every bit as potent as the gun she carried, sparkling in green eyes and laughing out of heavy lips.

"I don't think I can finish this." Sringlë pushed her plate away with a grimace. "I have this strange feeling that all the food here is poisoned."

Momozon went on chewing. "Suspicion breeds suspicion," he said between mouthfuls. "The wise man ignores distractions and cleans his plate."

She rolled enormous eyes and turned to one of the other patrons, trying to make conversation. But though she spoke the local dialect, a bastard child of Englesce and Romansce, quite flawlessly, most of her questions met with smirks, shrugs, or stony silence. She was used to it by now.

Finally, with much patience and perseverance, she managed to get some information out of a hollow-eyed boy in tattered leather overalls. Though barely in mid-adolescence he already sported the yellow bruises of a flicker habit.

"The Succubarium, yeah," he mumbled. "That's where all the trendies go. It's too expensive for a loser like me. Just follow the crowds on the Flicker Circuit—and watch your backs."

She relayed the directions to her companions, who had finished eating and were sipping cups of hot *shekk*. In a few more minutes they were ready to hit the streets again.

Outside, it was full night. No hint of moon or stars lit the coal-black sky, but at least the rain had stopped. They turned off Canopus Avenue and started down the Flicker Circuit girdling the starport.

Shadowy hulks of warehouses and gantries loomed over them; from the middle distance came the soft blue glow of runway lights. A dozen or so shuttlecraft of various descriptions, including their own, were scattered around the landing field. Hundreds of locals strolled or lounged about the area.

"The ship is quite secure, isn't it?" Sringlë asked absently. "This is a fine collection of cutthroats here."

"Strictly small time," Momozon assured her. "Our ship has automatic defenses that could pulverize half the port. Not to mention our friend on sentry duty."

"Yes, Fsau of Myint," she said, relishing the alien syllables. She loved anything new and exotic. "He seems deadly enough."

At least a quarter of the crowd thronging the circuit were drug peddlers, each chanting the list of substances he or she sold. Another quarter might conceivably be prostitutes. Most of the rest were drunken spacers and bored young people of fashion, all with the animation of zombies. Finally came a sprinkling of grotesques, poor wretches who probably slept in back alleys and refuse dumps: hunchbacks, eggladies and hermaphrodites, whispering cultists, pinheads, and pale, pale children. ("Infant whores," murmured Sringlë. "Ashbeck isn't so backward after all.") There were very few offworlders and no nonhumans in sight.

The Succubarium proved difficult to find. Nothing in Ashbeck advertised itself openly, of course, so their only recourse was to follow the crowd as they had been told. They passed arcades that purported to offer live combat and little shops that sold cheap shatterguns. They smelled meat frying in an unbelievably filthy snackpit. At length, they came upon a knot of reasonably well-dressed people hanging around the cavernous door of a warehouse. "This must be it," Sringlë decided. "Shall we?"

And they did.

2

Within the Succubarium's huge entrance four bouncers in black vinyl and tarnished steel stood guard before a second door, this one closed tight and flanked by chrome pillars. An amiable dwarf stepped forward and said, "Park your weapons with me. They'll be quite safe."

At this the two men grumbled—after all, they were professionals. But Sringlë merely shrugged and said, "Let's be realistic."

As they handed over their small arsenal the dwarf kept up a friendly chatter. "This is Ypousef's place, of course, so there's nowhere more secure in town. Your death toys are guaranteed while you're inside misbehaving, and all the other patrons are at the same disadvantage."

Sringlë thanked him and accepted an itemized claim ticket. Then Momozon presented his plastic for the appropriate deduction and they were admitted into the main hall.

"By my bloodline!" The tall warrior groaned in disgust. "This is a cattle pen!" They were immediately engulfed in a mass of jostling bodies.

But Sringlë was undaunted. "Just think of all the opportunities this crowd represents!"

Though the crush really was outrageous. They struggled through the maze of tables, couches and bodies to a relatively calm corner and ordered something relatively harmless to drink. Synthesized music blared at them from all directions, while overhead a phalanx of holographic projections carried on a dream-party of its own, in the form of skeletons, golems, and unlikely aliens. Sringlë wondered what next.

There was so little time left, and the two muscleboys seemed to be losing faith in her, as if they could do just as well on their own. She'd have to show them. She relaxed into receptive mode, casting about among the possibilities. There certainly were a lot of them. They wriggled through her mindnet like clever fish, too slippery to hold on to. She cast down a little deeper—

Without warning the houselights began flashing and exploding like a miniature space war and the crowd broke into spontaneous applause. There was a blackout. Then a single pink ray focused on a transparent platform suspended from the ceiling, illuminating the figure of a young man. He waved his hand and the show began.

Enveloped in light the young man gestured, danced, cavorted. It was impossible not to be riveted by his display. His costume Sringlë recognized as a variation on the ancient trappings of the harlequin of Old Earth, done here in black and white and shades of grey rather than the riotous colors of the past. He performed solo, but there was much use of holograms projected rather shakily from some obsolete equipment. Sometimes the clown-figure was accompanied by a legion of mirror images, sometimes he was obscured by a phantom chorus line, sometimes he was alone in perfect stillness. Always his energy was a palpable thing.

"Look at him—he's like a stream of electrons, or a flame burning," Sringlë murmured. "A conflagration of flesh."

"Really?" Momozon replied, with a show of indifference. "I'm not much interested in popular theater. I suppose I've been spoiled by the classics." On his homeworld there had been a contemporary school of Nō-drama.

In one piece the performer danced gently and quietly, each of his movements tripping a photocircuit to produce musical tones. Gestures and countermoves called forth harmonies and dissonance; footsteps generated polyrhythms. Behind him appeared sinister figures of spiders and cockroaches, but he danced on unaware. They began an absurd multilegged variation of his steps and he began a quavering song. His voice hovered at the breaking point, wailed on and split in two, simultaneously soaring to impossible screams and plummeting into moans and growls.

"A laryngeal implant?" Sringlë wondered.

"In underground Ashbeck?" Momozon puzzled.

Then the insect figures collapsed onto their backs and wiggled mad legs in the air. The harlequin levitated and babbled to a mechanical beat, allowing only an occasional word to come through clearly. The insects shrivelled away into dust and were replaced by naked women and rotting corpses, who pranced hand in hand to the patterns the clown was now coaxing out of a small keyboard. The music accumulated. Melody layered on melody, texture on texture. Tiny bugs appeared and devoured the dancing grotesques, then faded in a swelling crimson radiance generated by the sonic field.

So it went—an undisciplined romp, conceptually shaky and crudely executed, yet still compelling. The force of the young man's vital energy penetrated his audience's disbelief and held them mildly hypnotized. He was supremely resourceful. Although the technology at his disposal was antique and recalcitrant, and certainly everything he attempted had been done before, nonetheless he shaped it all to one design and made it speak his own language.

As a grand finale he vanished in a shower of green sparks.

"So this must be *cabaret*," Sringlë concluded. "I wonder which one he was—Skiff Welt or Attanio Hwin?" But her companions showed little interest in the distinction.

They decided to split up and mingle through the crowd separately, engaging likely candidates in conversation. As Sringlë moved off a new act announced itself overhead. The performer now revealed in shimmering colors was none other than the bald girl of Canopus Avenue, accompanied by four enormous snakes. All undulated in a sensuous manner to some saxophone melodies, as the woman slowly stripped off her costume. Sringlë glanced up from time to time during her circuit of the club; the quintet finally reached its climax, *illa serpentibus penetrata*.

What foul spirits the natives have, she thought.

For a few minutes she chatted with a gaunt fellow who insisted that he had met her before. Since he was too drunk to speak coherently, she shook him off. Then she encountered an extremely beautiful woman and posed as an exile who wanted to pawn some valuable jewelry. But this woman turned out to be a courtesan, and took her leave as soon as she realized Sringlë wasn't interested in her wares.

After a while she saw an older man of striking appearance, leaning against the dispensary console as he spoke with a few others. He wore a cylindrical cap, an armored jacket, and loose trousers. His eyes were as hard as granite and his face was deeply lined. Most interesting of all, he was accompanied by a large bland fellow carrying a gun.

Sringlë turned to someone nearby and asked the man's name. As she suspected it was none other than Ypousef Makhlouf.

Should I approach him? she asked herself. He might just put me off and that would spoil my chances later. Her training could find no integration.

Before she could decide he was gone, passing through a very private-looking door. Just as well, Sringlë thought, because now she recognized one of the master's recent companions—a lithe, sharp-featured youth who could only be the cabaret performer.

And this one was definitely approachable, oh yes. The chemistry was all there. Smiling slightly she adjusted her robe and went over to him.

"Great show," she began. "Can I buy you a drink?"

He had been standing pensively, smoking something out of a long tube. When she spoke he turned without really looking at her and seemed about to wave her off. Then his dark eyes opened wide and finally saw her.

"Why yes—I mean, no—I mean—I'm not drinking tonight." Already he was floundering. "But I'll get you one, if you like." When she held up a full glass he flushed deeply.

"You're a stranger," he said, trying to cover his embarrassment. "An offworlder. You know, I rarely see people I've never met before."

"And I too rarely meet people I'll ever see again. Are you Welt or Hwin?"

He laughed. "You must have been reading one of those fliers. Skiff isn't even performing tonight—he got beat up yesterday. Call me Attanio."

"And I'm Sringlë of Phayao." They clasped hands in a gesture much older than starships.

"What brings you to Ashbeck, of all places?" The young

man's face was returning to its normal color.

"Business."

"Naturally. But what kind?" He made a vague gesture. "I suppose that's a dumb question. There's only one business here and my boss controls it."

"So we've discovered. But actually we're not in the poison trade at all. We sell cybernetic technology."

Attanio laughed again. "Then you're in the wrong place, my friend. On Parmenio human labor is a lot cheaper than robots or androids. We do use computers but they're all antiques—we just keep fixing them up until they disintegrate."

Sringlë frowned. "That's what I keep hearing. No one in Ashbeck wants to invest in anything new."

"It's just a measure of our faith in the future—everything looks too bleak. But see," and here he changed tack boldly. "This place is dull. Would you like to step out, go to some other club? I spend too much time here."

Sringlë's eyes were like an afternoon at the beach. "That sounds wonderful! But I'm here with two friends that I can't lose. Could you—would you like to sit down for a few minutes and wait for them to pass by?"

This answer seemed to bore Attanio and for an instant she was afraid she'd lost his interest. But only for an instant. He shrugged, agreed, and led her to a nearby alcove set halfway up one of the walls. There they punched in an order for gillybud nectar and settled back into a low divan.

"Phayao," he mused. "I didn't think there was any high-tech industry there."

"There isn't. Like most other worlds in the Cluster we depend on Viharn for just about everything, from biotechnology to perfume."

"Then where do your toys come from? That is, if I may be so bold as to ask."

"The White Bear."

Attanio was amazed. "You haven't been back there, have you? To Sol? Even Makhlouf's ships never go that far."

"No, I've never been out of the Reach of Antares myself. But right now I'm working with a few gentlemen who've come all the way from Mars." Then they both had to laugh, because in this part of the galaxy Mars was an even more mythical place than Old Earth.

"Real Martians! I can't believe they'd travel all this way

just to peddle a few robots. If it's not drugs then it has to be politics."

"In a way it is politics. They're exiles, so naturally they're short of cash. They're trying to pawn some spare androids and cryptoelectronics."

"Too bad I can't help you." But he didn't seem too much put out; his initial fascination was slowly giving way to caution.

"Oh, but you could. Without any effort on your part. I could lend you one of our imaging boxes to use onstage—the one you had tonight didn't do your act justice."

"Ha! She tries to win me through flattery. You mean I'd be advertising your product?" He pulled an earlobe thoughtfully. "That could be fun, I suppose."

"Yes, couldn't it. Do think about it. We could work together on adjusting it to your act." Sringlë's charm was near its maximum setting.

Attanio weighed the prospect. "But how long will you be here?"

"Only a few more days, I'm afraid."

"That could be enough. After all, my act is half improvisation—too often I forget what I've programmed into the imager and I have no idea what's coming next."

"Well," she said smiling, "it must keep you in good mental fit."

"It makes me wild. Listen, in two days there's going to be a big party in Makhlouf's quarters. Maybe I could use your imager then, and whatever other gizmos you think appropriate. It would be great exposure for you. We'd only have tomorrow to work on it, though. Let's think about it some more, and meanwhile we can get to know each other better."

"I suppose that's one way of passing time in this dreary place," she said archly.

He winked at her and ordered more nectar from the console. Neither seemed to have any taste for intoxicants.

"By the way," he asked, sneaking an arm around her shoulders, "what's your interest in cabaret anyhow? Are you some kind of performer too?"

"Obviously you know nothing about Phayao." She chuckled and moved closer. "On that peculiar world the ruling passion is music. Everyone plays at least five instruments, and I don't mean synthesizers. We—they—go in for all sorts of acoustic oddities: harmonicas, balalaikas, rebecs, and so on ad nauseam. I sang before I could speak."

"Then I'm sure they'd hate me there," said Attanio, shaking his head. "But you said you liked my act—either you're very polite or you're a renegade."

"Oh, definitely a renegade! But I still love music, especially when it breaks the rules."

"There are no rules in Ashbeck. Maybe we could use a few." He leaned back and yawned. In repose he looked younger rather than older, and Sringlë realized that in fact he was scarcely out of adolescence. She had intuitively responded to his youth by conjuring up a much earlier version of herself, one who might honestly fall in love with a young man at a party. The reality was a good deal colder.

Attanio's looks teetered on the edge of beauty. His features were finely modelled and regular, but nature had added a touch of the bizarre to prevent him from being conventionally handsome. His whole face was long and thin, dwindling to a pointed chin; his eyes were narrow and glittering, his nose straight, and his cheekbones prominent. Only his mouth departed from the overall sharpness; it was sensuously full. He had striped his hair black and white, zebra-fashion, and it stood stiffly on end as if in caricature of shock.

After a moment he blushed under the lady's scrutiny and spoke again at random. "You say your companions have come all the way from Mars. That means they're traveling in a private veilship, doesn't it?" She nodded. He whistled. "That's unheard of! At least in this part of the Reach. They must be very powerful men."

"Well," she said slowly, "they certainly could upset a few things around here. But with one ship they can't do much against Makhlouf and his bullies, and as for the Viharnese fleet—believe me they're treading softly."

"I wonder where you fit in." But he didn't ask and she merely gave him a quizzical glance. "Anyway, just think of the freedom, the mobility! On Parmenio only one in a thousand, one in ten thousand ever travels in space."

"Do I detect a yearning for wider horizons?"

"You certainly do."

Sringlë nodded, saying only, "Time holds many secrets." But to herself she thought, I've found his lever.

At that moment she caught sight of Momozon and Tutunchi

in the crowd; she leaned over the balcony to signal them. "Now you can meet my associates," she said with relief.

They climbed up and suffered themselves to be introduced to the Parmenite. There was a language barrier, though, since Attanio only spoke the local dialect, plus a smattering of Ptok Prime, while the Martians were limited to Middle Galactic and their native Nippo-Martian. Attanio was nevertheless eager to communicate with these exotic visitors from the White Bear, so with Sringlë's translations and his own expressive panto-mime he succeeded pretty well.

To Sringlë Momozon said privately, "I found a few locals to talk to—some business folk and poison traders know the old Galactic tongue. I pretended to be high, even bought a few cheap pillules to get them talking freely. And so I discovered that there's to be a party in Makhlouf's quarters in two days. That sounds like our opportunity." He was well pleased with his success.

"Oh yes, the party," Sringlë yawned. "This charming young man has already invited me."

In spite of himself Momozon was impressed. "Excellent. While you're inside Tutunchi and I can be outside, and with the right plan we can pull it off."

"It may involve taking Attanio into our confidence. In fact if I could manage that we'd be much better off, because he commands so much valuable information."

"But can he be trusted?" Momozon was dubious.

"He must have a price, and I'm well enough acquainted with Lord Teoru to know how high I can go."

Momozon stroked his jaw thoughtfully. It plainly disturbed him that this foreign woman, little more than a stranger, was so deep in his liege lord's counsels. And now she proposed recruiting yet another stranger into their band of desperadoes.

"You'll do as you see fit, I suppose," he concluded. "Greater men than I have put their faith in you, so I can do no better than to follow them."

It was a small triumph; but Sringlë was far too wise to let her satisfaction show. Instead she gathered them up and led them all to the Succubarium's exit, there to collect their weapons and return to the Flicker Circuit.

Conspicuously enough Attanio had nothing checked with the dwarf and his henchmen. Obviously he must be high in Makhlouf's confidence, to be allowed inside under arms.

"Only Makhlouf himself never carries a gun," Attanio explained when they were on the street. "He always has at least one bodyguard close by, so he has no need. But all the rest of us play with our little death toys night and day. This city is full of murder."

II. The Pinkflash

By this hour the Flicker Circuit was positively clotted with people, almost as many as inside the Succubarium. Their former listlessness had given way to a feverish energy, and now many voices were raised in exuberance or anger, with here and there a hand flying to sword without quite drawing it forth. Attanio himself was in an exalted mood, jabbering nonstop and showering Sringlë with all manner of cryptic observations on his fellow citizens. Even Momozon made some effort at conviviality, joining in the chatter occasionally, while Tutunchi quietly guarded their backs.

They stopped in a tiny cafe to suck tubes containing several different bitter potions. "Just a mild stimulant," the Parmenite assured them. Here they met Kpuhdeh Kafu, who had finished her set and was on her way home with her four pets coiled snugly in their baskets. She had that post-performance flush of well-being and spoke pleasantly with Sringlë. "I always stop here after my show," she confided. "The owner is so kind, he saves the vermin he catches and gives them to me for the snakes." She held up several packets containing excited mice. "A true patron of the arts, that man."

Braving the concourse once more they witnessed the aftermath of a quarrel. A corpse sprawled on the cobblestones, smoking slightly and exuding the aroma of freshly barbecued meat. Its killer was still at hand hurling scatological imprecations at the dead body; apparently the victim had no friends nearby to seek vengeance.

Most of the crowd just stepped over the corpse without a backward glance.

Presently Attanio led them into another club, the Pinkflash. Here there were no requests to check their weapons. Nor did they have to pay any cover, since they were guests of the famous Hwin. The interior was dim and reeked of piss and disinfectant and worse.

On a small stage a live sex show was being enacted under ghastly yellow lights. There were three participants but it was impossible to determine their gender, at least from any distance. All had undergone extensive surgical modifications.

They sat in a private booth with the sculptor Farelus Delice, who was inhaling vapors and sweating profusely. He was nevertheless quite willing to discuss his work with Sringlë. It developed that he sculpted with his own hair, nail parings, and excrement. "In this way I maintain the most intimate relationship with my material," he explained. "Nothing is wasted, nothing lost." He told them about the individually tailored diet he followed. Sringlë made all the correct noises, Attanio looked bored, and the two Martians watched the sex show with mingled awe and revulsion.

When the charming Delice left his place was taken by Silk Effanse, a noted beauty. Her face and body were painstakingly etched with a pattern of self-inflicted scars. Excessive artifice, Sringlë thought. But she did speak intelligently.

"So you've come from the White Bear!" she marveled. "I'm sure it's been centuries since any ship has visited us from so far away. Does this mean there's new prosperity back there? Can we expect more contact with your worlds?"

Momozon replied through Sringlë's interpretation. "Our mission is a diplomatic one, dealing with delicate political issues. Unfortunately I can't discuss them in much detail. Also unfortunately our presence here is no result of prosperity; the Home Stars continue in genteel poverty."

Silk Effanse found the last phrase amusing. "Genteel poverty, as opposed to the revolting mess you find here? Ashbeck is a rough town, I suppose, though I've never known any other. Tell us about Mars."

And so, for some time Momozon discoursed about the cold beauty of his homeworld, with its pink skies and wan sunlight by day and its millions of unblinking stars by night. About the blue-green fields crisscrossed by canals (for human technology had of necessity transformed Mars into the image of an old dream). About the arid geometry of its quiet cities with their slim pyramids, piled cubes, empty plazas and sky-piercing obelisks. About the round of daily life with its thousand degrees of etiquette, and the sublime formality of its rituals. About the scores of noble houses with their polite rivalries and regulated feuds.

"To have known all that, and then come here," Attanio mused. "I wish I could say as much for myself."

Silk agreed; both felt locked away on Parmenio, when there were so many worlds of man to see.

"And now will you sample the unclean pleasures of Ashbeck?" the young woman asked coyly.

For the first time something like mirth showed on Momozon's face. "No, no!" he managed, in tones of choked hilarity. "I'm working!" But he was still amused by this pert gamine, so unlike the porcelain maidens of Mars.

"How sad," Attanio sighed. "You're in a libertine's paradise. No child prostitutes? No necrophilia? No flicker spasms? Oh but flicker's much too low-class for a Martian lord—perhaps your pleasure is *nong khla*, the death-by-living?"

"I've heard that mentioned so often," Sringlë broke in. "And yet I'm not sure what it actually is." She wore a mischievous smile now.

"It's not really a drug at all," said Silk. "It's a parasite. Imagine, it must be Parmenio's chief natural resource, the most valuable thing this world has to offer. *Nong khla* is a parasite of the *qualla*, those little beasts who eat the *porvro* mushroom that only grows on this planet."

"*Qualla* were the highest form of life here before humans arrived," Attanio added.

"When the *nong khla* is introduced into a human body," Silk resumed, "it becomes entwined with the nervous system. It proceeds to integrate the organism into peak function. It doesn't produce the instant orgasm of heroin, or the slow euphoria of blood crystals. It just puts you in a state of perfect mental and physical health. It heals all diseases, lights up the darkest sorrows, floods the organism with creative vigor, like an elixir of life. I suppose it could make an artist produce her masterpiece, if she worked fast enough."

"Because there's a catch, of course," Attanio said. "*Nong khla* has a short lifespan and can't reproduce itself in a human host. With *qualla* there's no problem, but with humans the consequences are fatal. After about ten days, the *nong khla* becomes feeble and dies, and the host does too, horribly, unless a new *nong khla* is injected."

"And they're very expensive," Silk said with wicked glee.

"Imagine what it's like catching those little *qualla* out in the bush, and then bringing them to the laboratory to have the *nong khla* extracted."

"But don't people breed the little monsters commercially, on a farm or something?" Sringlë asked.

Silk wrinkled her scarred forehead. "That would make sense, wouldn't it. Maybe they bite. Or . . . maybe the poison barons want to limit the supply and won't let anyone do that. All I know is that *nong khla* is rare and expensive."

"It's only used by people who are near death anyway, or by madmen as the supreme form of suicide," said Attanio.

"With an unlimited supply of *nong khla*," Sringlë said slowly, "a person might theoretically be immortal. How old is Ypousef Makhlouf, by the way?"

The two Parmenites laughed. "Clever," said Silk. "He's probably the only man in the Galaxy with access to that much. But I do think there are drawbacks. There would always come that dreadful period when the old *nong khla* began to wear out—a day or two of anguish, I'm told. And the new one can't go in until the moment of the previous one's death. I think there would be too many hills and valleys. But who knows. People are crazy enough to try anything."

All agreed except Momozon, who argued, "It doesn't sound very tempting to me. On Mars we have dispensed with euphoriants, and we have our own scientific methods of prolonging life. For sensory stimulation we meditate."

At this Silk and Attanio positively howled with laughter. Momozon, however, couldn't fathom their amusement, which of course made it even funnier. When he had recovered Attanio said, "I find it interesting how often people's minds turn toward immortality. Almost nobody wants to have babies, but almost everybody wants to live forever."

"Yes, and there are so many strategies for life everlasting," said Sringlë. "Religion was the first. Now we have *yuthex* treatments, and the mysteries of Lumiphat, and the milk of the Imagoes of Xuun. And then the Martians are always tinkering around with genes, growing clones and near-clones." This last she said with a glance toward Momozon and Tutunchi. "Cloning is in a sense just another striving toward immortality."

"And now we have your own bizarre idea with the *nong khla*," Silk concluded. "I consider this whole preoccupation a sign of the senility of our race. In a few millennia we'll be reduced to a handful of sterile immortals who will eventually suicide out of boredom."

"Don't worry," Sringlë reassured her. "If that day ever came, the Queen Mother of Viharn has a huge bank of egg and sperm cells with which she could repopulate the whole galaxy."

Both Attanio and Silk appeared disturbed by that idea; they shared the Homeworlder resentment toward the bugmen and their proteges. "Imagine a galaxy enslaved by Xuun," Attanio said. "We'd all be faceless worker-units in a great buzzing hive."

The rest nodded soberly, but Momozon, when these remarks were translated, said only, "There are worse masters than the Xuun, I'm afraid."

By now everyone had had his fill of the Pinkflash and the group seemed disposed to break up for the night. Silk Effanse made her farewells, and then Sringlë turned to Attanio and whispered a few words. He stared her full in the eyes for several heartbeats before nodding.

Thereupon she addressed Momozon. "You can go back to the hotel without me. Attanio has offered me his hospitality for the night, so I'll be staying with him. I'll call you when I arrive at his place."

Momozon raised an eyebrow but made no comment. They all left the club together, and then the two Martians headed for their nearby hotel, the Panspermia, while Attanio and Sringlë went down Cold Street toward the outskirts of town.

By now the city seemed deserted again. Though dawn was near the sky gave no sign of it; there was a heavy fog which obscured even the upper stories of nearby buildings. Sringlë and Attanio walked in the silence of exhaustion, accompanied by fitful shadows.

Before long they reached the Parmenite's house, a grand old edifice which rose twenty stories in a series of elaborate setbacks. It was deserted except for Attanio's apartment in the penthouse. Apparently, it had once been a public building, since it had a huge lobby decorated with broken sculptures and many faded frescoes depicting civic life in an outdated, idealized manner. Sringlë was amazed to discover a working elevator; it responded only to Attanio's palm, however, and whisked them straight to the top floor.

"Home," he announced as they stepped into a large echoing chamber. He took his guest on a quick tour of the place. There were a dozen sizable rooms: all the walls were cracked, all the ceilings were water-stained, and what little furniture there was obviously came from the garbage dump. But though it was in poor repair the apartment was clean enough, as Sringlë noted with relief.

"To bed?" he suggested.

"Of course," she replied.

The chamber was dimly lit by green fixtures; the bed was enormous. They undressed and got in.

"When I'm with people from around here I always know what they want," he said softly. "But you're a mystery."

"That's how it should be." She drew him close and their flesh ignited.

Sringlë was whiplike and supple, at once hard and soft; with her there was no such thing as active or passive. Their bodies began moving without any conscious direction, like figures in a dream of passion. She pulsed with more electricity than any ten local girls or boys that Attanio Hwin had ever known: her very skin was hot to touch, feverish really, a memory of the deserts of Phayao. Her mouth was like a fruit, her sex beyond metaphor. She was an artist of pleasure and fulfillment.

They played and rested, played again. In repose they were like tired children after a fierce game of tag. Just before sleep claimed them Attanio whispered, "Will you carry me off to the stars with you?" Her only response was a bite on the ear.

2

An insistent ting-ting-ting heralded the new day. Sunlight poured in through tall windows; it was shortly after noon, and for a change the weather was clear. Sringlë jumped out of bed and fumbled among her scattered clothing for the chiming communicator.

"Momozon?" she queried, instantly wide awake. "Yes, everything's fine . . . okay . . . no news . . . sit tight and I'll give you a report in a few hours. Out." Turning to Attanio, who was peering groggily at her from a mound of sheets, she explained, "Just a routine check. They wanted to make sure I was still alive."

He nodded and she climbed back into bed to sit facing him. They examined each other in the harsh light of day, companionably enough but for the moment without lust.

"Well," he finally said, "you're terrific. And you want something from me. My cooperation, I think, since I've got nothing material to offer."

A slow smile was dawning on Sringlë's face, so he continued, "I'd guess you're about to commit a crime."

Instead of answering him directly she asked, "Is there anyone in Ashbeck you feel attached to? Anyone you feel you owe something?"

He shook his head. "I didn't think so," she continued. "So I can feel safe trusting you. Anyhow, it's very simple. The Martian boys want to rob Ypousef Makhlouf and I'm helping them. And I want you to help me."

"My reward?" he asked grinning.

"Passage to the Cluster world of your choice, and this." She reached into a pouch and pulled out a large faceted jewel, teardrop-shaped and pale pink. As she turned it in the light, it seemed to spit violet sparks. "This one I can give you the moment you agree to help us—that is, provided you do—and you can have another of similar quality when the deed is done."

"It certainly sounds attractive," he said. "But what makes you think I can be of much help? I mean, those muscle boys from Mars are probably a lot handier with a particle beam than I am. Though I must admit I'm no slouch."

"Actually we're about to discover just how useful you can be." She rested her chin on an upraised knee and regarded him steadily. "First, can you get me into Makhlouf's stronghold within the next few days?"

"Fortunately I can—there's that party we talked about."

"That's what I've been counting on. Second, how much do you know about the layout of his warehouse and of his private apartments?"

"Enough, I think." And Attanio launched into a detailed description, based on hearsay as well as on his own visits to the master's home. Makhlouf lived in a large warehouse—his goods were stored on the ground floor and his living quarters were above. Rumor had it that a secret passageway connected his bedroom to the storeroom beneath.

"What in particular do you want to lift?" Attanio asked at length.

"That new shipment of a hundred vials of *nong khla,*" she blithely replied.

Attanio wrinkled his brow, rolled his eyes, and laughed all in one instant. "You're well informed, aren't you!"

"Well," she said modestly, "we *have* been here three days now. One does find things out."

"But *nong khla!* Are you mad?"

She sighed. "A little, yes, or at least one of us is. You see, our intention isn't to sell it, but to use it. Of course I was just playing dumb last night when I asked you about it. *Nong khla* is the only reason we're here."

"It's—it's not for you, I hope."

"By the venom of Xuun—no. It's for the captain of the Martian veilship, who happens to be a prince and philosopher of incredible attainments. I don't need to go into his motives right now; it's enough to say that he's no ordinary man."

Attanio sat back and let it all sink in. In a moment he said, "I suppose it's obvious that I'm going to help you. I don't feel like I have much to lose."

Sringlë responded by putting the jewel in his hand—a Suutish sparkler, worth a year's wages for the average citizen of Ashbeck, though it wouldn't purchase even one injection of *nong khla.* Attanio had the feeling that it was her own personal possession rather than a bribe from the Martians.

"If you don't mind telling me, just how did you get mixed up with these characters?

"Coincidence," she said airily. "As you know, I'm from Phayao. A few years ago I became guilty of certain indiscretions—"

"Singing off key, perhaps, or stepping on your grandmother's violin?"

She pursed her lips, nodding. "Something like that. In any event I decided to leave home in a hurry. I had the opportunity of obtaining passage to Lumiphat, so there I went, claiming asylum."

Attanio's pale face paled a little further. "You didn't eat the fungus . . ."

"The *dwedo* fungus, you mean?" Her eyes held a mysterious light. "The sacred mushroom of Lumiphat, whose spores grant immortality to the chosen few? And cause the unfortunate many to die in agony?" She laughed merrily. "No, I'm not one of those immortals, old enough to be your great-grandmother but still looking like this year's model. I never attempted the *dwedo* ordeal. But I do happen to be an Initiate of the Outer Mysteries. You see, the Lumis maintain a sort of spiritual college up on Mount Zoz, where they hold the ordeals. Among other things they teach you the futility of physical immortality, which is nevertheless the very coin they trade in. The Lumis love a good joke. They're short hairy creatures, a bit like the ancient chimpanzees of Old Earth, and they're always laughing. *Laughter is the heart of wisdom*, they say. Their Hierophants eat the *dwedo* fungus for breakfast without even a bellyache, and then die at a hundred and fifty just like the rest of us.

"Anyhow I spent my exile learning the Lumi mind-body discipline and waiting for my next opportunity. I saw a lot of eager offworlders come to Mount Zoz and die, and heard the Lumi priests giggling about it afterward. Then one day a Martian veilship arrived full of young candidates for the Mysteries. Their master was Lord Teoru, the philosopher-prince I mentioned. He had visited Lumiphat in his youth and enrolled in the school just as I had, and now was returning for some crucial advice from his old teachers."

"What sort of advice?" Attanio's tone betrayed impatience. "Everyone is so vague about the real reason why these Martians have come to the Antares Reach."

She paused and once more seemed to evaluate him. Then, with a shrug, she continued. "I may as well tell you — it doesn't make any difference here on Parmenio because no one can do anything about it. A new empire has risen in the Pleiades. It's a human-derived civilization, but they're allied with an unpleasant bunch of aliens, the Pa-chwa. Their power has been building for centuries while the Home Stars and the Polity of Myint have declined. Less than one standard year ago they struck the Solar System and sacked Luna and Mars. It was their first foray out of the region of the Pleiades, so the Homeworlders were completely unprepared. The devastation was brutal, pointless, irrational.

"Mars is just a memory now, Attanio, as lost as Old Earth. The whole planet is in ruins, and what few survivors there are have been enslaved. You don't know how well Momozon was acting last night when he described his homeworld in the present tense. The new ruler of the Solar System is a certain Appucc of Xil. He has a powerful starfleet and a whole coven of Pa-chwa advisors."

To Attanio his home planet seemed a universe away from Earth and Mars. But for a moment he managed to achieve a more galactic perspective, and he realized that Parmenio—and the Maung Cluster—could almost be called the White Bear's next-door neighbor.

"Are we next?" he asked.

"That seems to be Lord Teoru's idea. You see, he belonged to the Martian ruling house; in fact he was one of its senior counsellors. He managed to flee the catastrophe in a small starship with some other refugees, and headed straight for Antares. They hope to drum up support for a local alliance against Appucc and his bloodthirsty hordes."

"Do you believe all this?" Attanio asked skeptically. "Or better yet, do you think any planetary governments will? And even if they find allies—what can they possibly accomplish here? This region of space is completely decadent. No one builds starships anymore, except the Viharnese, and they turned their backs on the rest of humanity long ago."

"I wouldn't be too sure of that. The Antares Reach is in fragments—who knows what's been happening on planets like Suut and Loei. Maybe a new military alignment is possible here. Maybe even Viharn would come to the rescue, if the Home Stars really are at their last gasp."

"And maybe it's all fabrication," Attanio suggested. "Maybe Momozon and Teoru are spies; maybe they're scouts for a Martian starfleet that's about to swoop down and enslave us all."

Sringlë smiled and ruffled Attanio's zebra mane. "I love your imagination. But there are some things I'm sure of, and one of them is Lord Teoru's basic honesty."

Attanio grinned and suggested a recess to the bathroom. While they splashed around in the shower he continued with his questions. "You still haven't explained how you yourself became a member of this Martian conspiracy."

She rubbed soap on his belly and thighs. "When they first landed on Lumiphat, the Hierophant assigned me as their guide and interpreter. Languages have always been my specialty; I know just about every single one spoken in this sector. Lord Teoru and I got along quite well—"

"I can bet—"

"—so when they left he asked me to come along and continue interpreting for them. The Lumis were agreeable and I was delighted at the prospect of a diplomatic tour."

"I guess I am too." And he gathered her into a slippery embrace.

She endured it for a moment and then directed a jet of cold water where it would count the most. He shrieked; she scolded him playfully.

"Now Attanio—remember we have work to do. You still haven't earned your prize."

III. Makhlouf Entertains

Sunset was a gaudy orange smudged with purple. Angular
silhouettes of spacecraft loomed overhead as Attanio and
Sringlë trudged across the landing field. They took turns carrying the Martian imager.

From the outside Makhlouf's main warehouse seemed dark
and derelict. They shuffled up to the front door, pressed a
buzzer, and faced a pair of taciturn security guards. The uglier
of the two checked off their names on a list.

"You're okay, Hwin, but who's the female?"

"Technical assistant, pal," Attanio replied. "The old man
always lets me bring a guest if I want to." For her part Sringlë
appeared completely relaxed, almost bored.

"Guess it's all right then." But the guard bit off his words
belligerently. He motioned to his sidekick, who frisked both of
them and tapped curiously on the imager.

"It don't look much like a bomb," he concluded. And so
they were allowed in.

They were an hour or two in advance of the other guests;
even their host was nowhere to be seen. But the security people on hand made no objections when they explained they
needed the extra time to install a new gadget. Attanio was
well known and mostly admired, and Sringlë herself already
had a certain recognition factor from spending the past two
nights at the Succubarium in his company.

She had assumed a new role for the evening. Gone was the
alertly competent warrior-woman; somehow she had even
managed to soften the lines of her body. She giggled and
flirted with the two burly guards, bemoaning her confusion
over how to hook up this fancy machine. Soon the floor
around her was a mess of cables and tools.

"This imager is state of the art," she explained to one of the
guards, who was already indulging in a little angel's tears.

27

"It's not really compatible with Makhlouf's housecomp so we're just kind of faking it."

No one realized how deftly she was using the imager to key into the house security program. A little holodisplay showed her the building's layout, indicating all alarms and checkpoints; then, armed with the proper codes and passwords, she rewrote the program to her heart's content. This much took her maybe fifteen minutes. The rest of the time she spent fooling around with connections and using the machine to produce a few dramatic squawks and flashes.

"Watch out you don't fry us all, sister," one of the guards called. He laughed uproariously as she cringed in mock despair.

Finally she announced that they were finished, which brought more laughter. She and Attanio rode up to a fenced-in roof terrace to smoke and wait for the party to start.

"It's amazing how people see only what they expect to see," Sringlë said, gazing up at the pitch black sky. "Stupid people, that is. And except for you and your friend Silk the only Parmenites I've met have been idiots."

"All the more reason to leave," Attanio replied softly.

When they went back downstairs a while later the merrymakers had begun pouring in. It was a typical Succubarium crowd; in fact the whole party was like a night at the club, except that it was smaller and more cramped and there were a lot more drugs.

For of course that was the whole point of a party at Makhlouf's. Already there were a dozen or so demimondaines lying in a circle passing a glimmerbug from hand to hand. This was a silvery beetle whose bite induced hallucinations. Murmurs of amazement came drifting up, and a few gasps of horror.

In another corner a young girl had a tank full of Gnyshan swamp gas strapped to her back. Her companions sucked on the hose and then went into an odd convulsive dance. It looked so funny that Sringlë was tempted to try it, but Attanio cautioned, "Excessive cortical burnout," so she refrained.

There were blood crystals on almost every tongue, and actual fountains of wine and liquor. Sitting in one sculptured niche was an elegant bronze vessel, a spoil no doubt from Suut, which at the turn of a spigot sprayed fine mist into the air. "That's the sex sprinkler," Attanio said. "Aphrodisiac."

And in a dim carpeted pit nearby several guests were busy working off its effects.

So they shuffled along, mingling with the crowd, engaging in a series of minute-long conversations about nothing in particular. All at once Sringlë found herself face to face with a tall granite-eyed man with heavy jowls. She hid her surprise behind a sly grin and a wink. "Why you must be Lord Makhlouf! What a pleasure!"

He smiled gravely. "And you must be the doxy of those mysterious offworlders who've been skulking around my city."

"Doxy?" She pealed with bright laughter. "That's all past tense, love. I've hooked up to Attanio here." She turned to point him out, but he had disappeared.

"You move fast, don't you, my dear." He was attempting to sound sinister but Sringlë had a clear fix on him. At the moment he was quite intoxicated and far more amorous than threatening.

Taking her by the arm he guided her to an alcove and produced a vial of shen-dust. "Be so kind as to give your opinion on this, won't you?"

It was impossible to refuse. She took the proffered spoon and dusted each nostril delicately. "Exquisite," she pronounced. She felt a wash of euphoria spread over her; nothing her training couldn't handle.

For himself Makhlouf took a generous dusting and said, "Now why don't you tell me a little bit about yourself. Just what are you doing in Ashbeck?"

"Why, I'm having the time of my life!" And with that falsehood for starters she rattled on about her adventures on scores of planets throughout the galaxy, inventing the most ridiculous lies and filling her tale with absurd inconsistencies.

"Really? Really?" Makhlouf barked at intervals. He laughed in spite of himself and repeatedly dipped into the dust.

"Yes," she went on, "and since those Martian characters had rescued me from a fate worse than death—and you can imagine what that means to a girl like me—I thought I'd stick around for awhile and see what else they could do. So we all hopped into Parmenio to try to raise a mercenary army. You're surprised? I gather they have plans to seize Viharn, an incredibly rich world, I'm told, and carry off the Queen's treasures. I'm surprised you haven't caught wind of their scheme because they've been trying to hire your own men away from you. Hah, I guess I shouldn't have said that but I think they're lifting off tonight anyway and you don't look a man who'd hold a grudge. But then I met Attanio and we . . ."

So she babbled on, with scarcely a pause for breath, until she glimpsed Attanio again. "Oh, there he is! Excuse me darling but we have to do the show, I know you'll understand, so look for me afterwards!" And she gave Makhlouf a quick kiss, squeezed his arm a little longer, and dashed over to Attanio's side.

2

Momozon and Tutunchi had spent two restless days in their hotel room at the Panspermia. Attanio thought it safest if they stayed out of sight, since they were such obvious offworlders, and they had agreed. But in spite of their caution they quickly discovered two of Makhlouf's thugs watching their hideout around the clock. As long as they were inactive this posed no problems; but tonight was the night to move.

"I suppose we'll have to deal with our friends now," Momozon said, speaking cultured High Martian as he buckled on his weapons.

Tutunchi acknowledged him with a grunt. "This has been a voyage from death to death," he reflected. But he made it a simple statement rather than a bleak lament. "When we were children in the Halls of Combat, who ever dreamed that we would know anything but the ritual vendettas of our ancestors? Now we live like common fighting men of the dawn ages. No formal challenges, no eight-degree swordplay, no juried duels. Just kill or be killed."

They helped each other don hooded black robes. "Still there is a certain nobility in sending our opponents off to solve the great mystery of death."

Momozon answered with a warrior's grim smile and they both stepped over to the open window. There they mounted a tiny gravity disc and sailed out, floating groundward as lightly and silently as a feather.

They landed and Tutunchi slung the disc over his back like

a shield. In that instant they were confronted by one of Makhlouf's men with a leveled nullbeam.

"Freeze," he said softly. "Now where do you think you're
going in that get-up?" He called out to his companion and
moved his free hand toward the communicator at his waist.

Momozon responded by feinting in three directions at
once. The nullbeam spat out in a brutally wide arc but managed only to singe his robe. Simultaneously, Tutunchi drew
and fired, disintegrating the Parmenite's weapon and his right
hand along with it. Momozon leaped for the wounded man's
throat, stifling his scream with a quick fatal chop.

Now the other Parmenite was at hand, weapon drawn, mo-
mentarily confused by the Martians' shadowy figures. Tutunchi fired again and he fell dead.

Without a sound Momozon knelt to gather up the two com-
municators. Though ignorant of the necessary codes and passwords he would at least know if the dead men's compatriots
tried to call them.

They left the corpses where they lay, just as any Parmenite
would, and resumed their shadow-hugging walk to the Flicker
Circuit. Taking back alleys, they met nobody but a few sleeping bums.

3

The main salon of Makhlouf's flat darkened. The guests
buzzed in anticipation, and then a green spotlight picked out
the figure of Attanio Hwin quietly juggling three balls. Within
seconds his balls began to multiply, until it seemed as though
he were handling at least twenty at a time.

Then one by one the brightly colored globes escaped from
him and began orbiting the room like planets and moons.
Empty-handed he intoned a funereal chant, using his implants
to produce ringing *basso profundissimo* notes that chilled the
bellies of his audience. His song was like the cry of a veilship
being ripped apart by intolerable dimensional stresses, excruciating in its forlorn majesty.

Hideous leather-winged creatures appeared, their faces like
hungry rats, flapping noisily through space and gobbling up
the toy planets. Attanio's metallic song slowly acquired delicate overtones, as of shimmering banks of violins and bamboo

flutes. He danced and waved his hands pleadingly, and his gestures produced a swarm of dragonflies that did battle with the flying rats. Each insect flicked out a long pink tongue to disintegrate its adversary.

Triumphant, the dragonflies withdrew into a swarm in the center of the room and hummed jubilantly. Suddenly, they exploded outward and flew into the faces of the audience—whereupon they vanished. The crowd screamed approval.

Now Attanio was singing an old song, "Harmless Pleasures," as he convulsed in the Gnyshan swamp dance. Enormous babies materialized in the air around him. The audience laughed; some had Attanio's features, some Makhlouf's, the rest other well-known characters of Ashbeck. The babies drooled profusely and dribbled excrement so realistically that people ducked and dodged in spite of themselves.

Abandoning his song Attanio recited a nursery rhyme dating from pre-colonial times:

> Swing the spoon, ring the moon,
> 　　pinch the baby's nose—
> fun slice, buns twice,
> 　　Daddy's dirty clothes!

The babies leapfrogged madly and the harlequin launched into a series of variations on the original rhyme.

> Sling the goon, sting the wound,
> 　　wring the baby's neck—
> two mice, so nice!
> 　　Dad will give you heck!

The crowd was vastly amused, especially since the subject matter was so kinky. In Ashbeck babies were as remarkable as virgins.

Sringlë kept watch from her post by the imager; since the machine practically ran itself she had nothing to do. Things were going well. Everyone, including Makhlouf and his security force, was so high that they couldn't possibly cause any trouble. It was only a matter of an hour or so now.

As the set ended she silently pulsed her communicator and was rewarded by an answering chime, which went unnoticed in all the applause. Excellent; that meant that Momozon and Tutunchi were outside and ready.

She joined Attanio. They killed time until his next set, dancing, drinking a little, sharing smiles over what lay before them. Around them the party reached new heights of abandon.

Suddenly Makhlouf reappeared. His eyes had lost their usual stony fixity and now were as melting as sherbet on a summer day.

"Hilarious show," he told Attanio in slurred tones. "Keep up the good work. And now, if you'll allow me a moment with your friend. . . ."

Sringlë smiled and leaned over as if to give Attanio a good-bye kiss. Quickly she whispered, "Start your set and meet me in his room in ten minutes." He nodded and sauntered away. Then Sringlë turned to Makhlouf and tickled his ample stomach. "What was it you were going to show me?" she asked, in her huskiest contralto.

"Show you? Oh yes, my collection of singing crystals . . . they're in my private laboratory. . . ." And conversing disorientedly they moved toward the corridor that led to Makhlouf's personal chambers, Sringlë half-supporting and steering him on the most direct route. There was no need to entertain the man with bubbleheaded chatter; he was babbling enough for both of them.

As they left the salon Makhlouf nodded to one of his guards, who smiled broadly and gave a jaunty salute. Then they were alone in the hallway a few steps from his bedchamber.

Makhlouf ran his hands over Sringlë's body, his voice a rumbling alcoholic blur. "Who needs privacy? Who needs a bed? Let's do it right here, I'm ready." And he grabbed her hand to press it to his groin.

Still she laughed, saying, "Do you realize just how disgusting you are?"

As he sputtered in outrage she reached into her belt and pulled out a tiny glass dart, which she jabbed once into his arm. Without a sound he slumped and would have fallen, except that she caught him and half-carried him to the door.

The door was protected by a battery of particle beams, and its lock sported an anti-tampering mine. But by virtue of her earlier sabotage Sringlë merely pressed her hand to the plate and it opened for her as obediently as it would have done for the unconscious Makhlouf. Heaving his body before her she stepped in and closed the door.

The room was large and tastelessly furnished, which came as no surprise, and was dominated by a huge bed that looked vaguely like a spaceship. In one corner stood a gilt cage with florid ornamentation—undoubtedly the lift connecting with the warehouse.

Then she saw it. Right next to the bed, on a low table, was a pyramid of tiny crystal vials. The whole stack was enclosed in wire mesh for convenient carrying.

"This certainly saves me a lot of searching!" she said aloud. Of course—as his prize treasure, Makhlouf would keep the *nong khla* close at hand. With one bound she was next to it, peering through the mesh at the little bottles and their contents.

Each vial held a clear fluid in which floated a long translucent filament, coiled and twisted to fit the vessel's confines. They looked glossy in the light; she was reminded of rice noodles. Then she realized that each filament was slowly writhing. It was mildly repellent, wormlike, and she drew back, involuntarily picturing one of those tenacious threads wrapped around Teoru's spinal chord.

If only she could take him—but no, she banished the thought. Abruptly she heard Attanio's voice softly calling her name from the corridor.

"Help me with this old walrus," she said as she let him in, and together they picked up Makhlouf and laid him out on the bed.

"Star's blood!" he swore. "You didn't kill him, did you?"

"No, why bother? But look, Attanio, I've already found it." He glanced quickly at the stack of vials. "We're home free!" And the Parmenite crushed her in a jubilant embrace.

Then Sringlë reached into her boots and pulled out three small pieces of apparatus. Piecing them together she had a miniature nullbeam, which she lost no time in focusing. She spoke into her communicator. "Momozon? Come immediately to the north side of the house and wait for a blast. Then get us out of here."

A few minutes later Momozon confirmed his position. Sringlë aimed her weapon at a large boarded-up window; there was a flash, and then cool night air came rushing through a neat hole. Presently they saw the empty gravity disc bobbing outside to carry them down.

The hundred vials of *nong khla* proved awkward, but still they managed to muscle them onto the disc. Sringlë sent it down alone; she and Attanio followed on the second trip.

He held her tightly. She could feel his body trembling with anticipation. "What a joke!" he laughed. "Everyone thinks I'm still inside performing—they're watching about 50 simulacra of me doing high kicks. That imager of yours is as good as the real thing."

"Yes, too bad we have to leave it behind. I guess that will be our trade-in for the *nong khla*." And they both laughed in delight.

Then all four of them were running softly across the landing field to the Martian shuttle. A lithe alien figure met them at the airlock, and minutes later they were lifting skyward on the silent pulse drive. Ashbeck dropped away like a video simulation. Well, Attanio thought, here goes nothing.

IV. Cold Master

There was time only for a fleeting glimpse of the great Martian veilship before they docked. The Parmenite was amazed by its apparent delicacy. It had no external shell: instead its various components were exposed to the vacuum. Command modules, habitation cylinders, shuttle hangars, and Cluj-pulse drives were all arranged in a roughly conical pattern. A lacy network of struts and passage tubes strung them all together, and a refractive haze surrounded the whole with a subtle aura —apparently the Darabundit field. Overall it called to mind the skeleton of some leviathan of the void.

"Not like the old adventure cubes, is it?" Fsau of Myint jived, in oddly accented Ptok.

"Not a bit," Attanio replied. "So insubstantial!"

The alien's face held a peculiar expression. "Yes, my friend, it can be that."

Docking was imperceptible. They stepped out into a vast echoing hold, as chilly as Attanio had imagined space would be. He didn't have time to puzzle over the presence of gravity. Immediately the whole crew jumped into an umbilical and became weightless again, propelled along on a jet of air.

Sringlë took his hand and guided him gently. "Welcome aboard *Samuindorogo*, love. You're about to have your first audience with the captain."

"*Samuindorogo?* Is that supposed to mean something?"

"Cold Master," she replied. Attanio wondered what those words implied for his future.

They emerged in a fragrant garden under illusionistic rose-colored skies. This much at least was typical of all the old stories—the paradox of a natural setting in the heart of a starship. They followed a mossy path that wound among lilacs and wistaria toward the sound of a waterfall. Folding screens set off a sizable area next to the cascade, and there on a wide

37

tatami, attended by an elegantly sculpted robot, sat Lord
Teoru.

All bowed casually and exchanged greetings. Momozon
began conversing with him in sonorous High Martian, undoubtedly briefing his lordship on the mission, while Attanio
stood by in momentary confusion.

For the instant he had laid eyes on Teoru he felt an electric
charge burn through his body, making all his insides knot in
shock. The man's presence was overwhelming. He was a
study in pain—excruciating pain held at bay by sheer force of
will. Attanio cringed away from the agony in his eyes, the
anguish in the rigid set of his mouth.

Yet the man was handsome enough, and his seated posture
seemed relaxed, and his words were smooth and well-
modulated. He bore a close family resemblance to Momozon
and Tutunchi, with one major distinction. Starting at the hair-
line a broad white scar ran down the left side of his face,
disappearing beneath his ample robe. This twisted an otherwise pleasant visage into a mask of suffering, most obvious in
the lines deeply incised around his eyes. His age was not
apparent; pain can make even young children seem withered
and old.

Attanio had begun to understand Lord Teoru's interest in
nong khla.

Sringlë spoke briefly, mentioning his name. Then Attanio
found himself addressed by the philosopher in fluent Ptok
Prime.

"I owe you my gratitude for your invaluable help. It must
have taken great courage to become a fugitive from your own
people merely for a stranger's sake. You are welcome on this
ship for as long as you choose."

"I'm pleased to be of service," he managed to reply.
(Though he was unaware of any bravery in his actions, knowing that his deed was prompted far more by curiosity and
boredom than any desire to serve these mysterious offworlders.)

Somehow Teoru seemed to sense his thoughts, or at least
his embarrassment. He actually chuckled softly. "Excuse these
formalities, Attanio Hwin. They are merely old customs of an
even older world. In a watch or two I believe we can speak
again under more relaxed conditions."

"I'll look forward to that," he replied, bobbing his head in an attempt at courtliness.

A few minutes later the audience broke up. Teoru rose carefully, his every movement under strict control, though it was more like a dancer's control than anything stiff or constrained. Followed by his robot servant he disappeared behind a cypress grove; the robot carried the pyramid of *nong khla* with effortless grace.

Sringlë led Attanio away in another direction, to a door concealed in a tree trunk. "Quaint, isn't it? This leads to some vacant rooms."

They dropped a short distance to a vestibule onto which several more doors opened. "Here's where I've been staying," she said, indicating one, "and here's one for you." The panel slid aside to reveal a series of austere-but-comfortable rooms, including the luxury of a private bathroom.

"So much space just for me, on a veilship?" It was indeed an unexpected extravagance. "I feel like royalty."

"The ship is practically deserted." Sringlë sank crosslegged onto a fat cushion. At a gesture, a small automaton emerged from the wall and gravely served them tea. "It can carry fifty comfortably, but right now there are no more than ten of us on board, not counting a few sleepers stashed away in the stasis pods."

"Sleepers?"

"Yes, these Martians have funny ideas. Teoru has a couple more versions of Momozon on reserve in case he needs them. Meanwhile they're in stasis for safekeeping."

Attanio cocked his head to one side. "I've already guessed that Momozon and Tutunchi are clones. Does that mean there's a whole series of them?"

"In a manner of speaking. They're not exact duplicates. But the Martians don't leave anything as important as conception to chance. For millennia they've pursued an elaborate program of genetic manipulation, particularly among the ruling families. Sort of like breeding show dogs."

Attanio looked blank; his knowledge of primitive customs wasn't quite that extensive.

"In other words, they breed people to enhance certain qualities they admire—fine bone structure, fighting ability, loyalty, occasionally even intelligence and creativity." She laughed wickedly. "Teoru is an example of someone who was designed to be a strategist and administrator. Some of the same genetic material went into Momozon and his brothers, but with the emphasis on the good-soldier syndrome."

"I suppose that's why they're so dull." He stretched and ran fingers through his zebra mane. "I need some orientation, Sringlë. I must confess I never realized what I'd be getting into. Three hours ago I was at a typical party in Ashbeck, the kind I've been going to all my life. Now—I'm not even sure where I am. Are we under way yet? And where to?"

Sringlë reached over to a nearby console and keyed in several questions. "It seems we are—we're headed on a course perpendicular to the plane of this star system. In two days we'll be set to Puncture. But I don't know our next port of call—Teoru must be in the process of deciding that now. The general idea is to visit several technically advanced worlds in this sector, ultimately stopping at Viharn, which is the richest and most powerful."

"And I'm to decide where I want to be dropped off. Too bad I'm completely ignorant of my choices."

"Well then, here's a quick tour." And she caused a series of animated glimpses of a dozen worlds to appear in the air before them. "Here's Rayong—Impasp—Suutt—Chengathrati —Loei—Viharn itself...." Attanio was bewildered by the kaleidoscopic array; by visions of jungles, deserts, icefields, underground cities, collections of thatched huts, clusters of delicate spires, blocks of massive stone houses, natives in fur coats, matrons in tailored suits, children in flimsy tunics or nothing at all.

"I think I'd like a more or less civilized place where I could eat well, play music, and maybe see the sun once in a while," he said after a moment.

"That does narrow it down a little." Sringlë consulted a color-coded directory. "But my advice to you is to stick with this mission for a while. After all, I like having you around." She pinched his nose and they shared a smile. "Figure out a way to make yourself useful to Lord Teoru. I'll help."

Attanio sat up with a start. "There's something I've been meaning to ask you. What *is* the story with his lordship? You haven't told me everything, not by a long shot."

For a few minutes Sringlë's face was an inscrutable mask. "You will discover, Attanio, that I never tell anyone everything. But since Teoru seemed to like you I suppose I can let you know a little more about him."

"Once I described Teoru as no ordinary man. That was, shall we say, a gross understatement. In fact he is close to three centuries old. Toward the middle of his natural life, some two-hundred-odd years ago, he chartered a Myint veil-ship to carry him to Lumiphat. He was the first pilgrim from the White Bear in generations. As he was already an adept at the Martian discipline of Za the Lumis allowed him to proceed to the Inner Mysteries at once. And he survived, Attanio. He ate the Flesh of the Gods and did not die. He stayed awhile longer as a disciple of the Hierophant and then returned in triumph to Mars."

"Then he's an immortal! But he looks like someone on death's door."

"Yes, I know. I'll explain all that in a minute. As I was saying, he returned to Mars, where oddly enough—or perhaps not so oddly, if you understand the prospects of immortality—he never sought political power for himself. Instead he served his brother Prince Izama, then Izama's son Churunga, and finally the ill-fated Prince Myobu, biological father of Momozon and the rest, who met bitter death at the hands of Appucc of Xil.

"In his lifetime Teoru raised his ancestral clan of Shinjuku to the place of honor among all the feuding houses of Mars; then through his counsels Mars became preeminent among the worlds of the Solar System. He built long and well, only to see his work destroyed in a night of horror by the invaders from the Pleiades. In that raid the warriors of Xil used Pa-chwa shock tubes. Teoru was hit by a charge that would have fried ten men, but by virtue of his *dwedo*-altered body he survived. He escaped in *Samuindorogo* with a Myinti crew, a few refugees, and the thirteen clone-sons of Prince Myobu."

"But that scar—"

"Horrible, isn't it. The Pa-chwa weapon did irreparable damage to his nervous system. So we have the paradox of an immortal man with an incurable ailment. Teoru voyaged to Lumiphat hoping that the Hierophant could help him somehow, possibly with another dose of the fungus, but his injuries were beyond the Lumis' powers. And then on Mount Zoz his clan sustained another blow.

"Teoru and his kinsmen reasoned that since they all pos-

sessed very similar genetic structure, there was a good chance
that one or more of them would survive the *dwedo* ordeal.
With several immortals in the clan they would have infinitely
more staying power in the projected struggle with Xil; they
could outlive Appucc and have their revenge on future generations. So nine of Myobu's progeny braved the mysteries, and
all nine were struck down."

Attanio held his head. "Talk about hard luck. Where's my
synthesizer? This story is inspiring me to write some very sad
music."

Sringlë regarded him critically; finally she sighed. "Yes, I
suppose it's good to keep a sense of humor even about the
most terrible tragedies. But you realize I saw those nine men
before and after. Corpses are never pretty and theirs were
among the worst."

"I don't doubt it." He shrugged apologetically. "So from
Lumiphat the Martians came to Parmenio, and here we all are
now. I suppose Lord Teoru decided to try *nong khla* as his last
resort."

"Yes, and we'll soon find out how good a solution it is."

Conversation lapsed shortly thereafter, and since by now it
was the equivalent of dawn on Parmenio, they both felt the
need to sleep. In Attanio's bed they made half-hearted love
before unconsciousness claimed them; but when he awoke
hours later Sringlë was gone.

2

Attanio hardly slept for the next few shipdays. *Samuindorogo*,
with its crew, its gardens and its incredible data banks, was a
whole new world to explore. His next meeting with Sringlë
occurred beside an ornamental goldfish pond.

She had undergone yet another transformation. Her hair,
which in Ashbeck had been a hovering violet cloud, was now
Martian silver and caught up in countless tiny braids that stood
out from her head like wires. She had shaved her eyebrows
and redrawn them high on her forehead like two antennae. She
wore a black gown figured with lavender crests, wide and stiff
across the shoulders, cinched tight at the waist, and flaring to
a starched triangular skirt.

He hid his surprise and sketched a mock bow. "Have you

become a Martian princess, then?"

"My new role," she said demurely. "Teoru will see you tonight in his quarters at the beginning of the fourth watch." And with a formal bow she strolled away, covering her face with a painted fan.

"Wait, Sringlë!" he called after her. She turned without lowering the fan. "Why this distance?"

Now she did relax and show her face again. "Attanio, my love, surely you realize that life is full of complications."

"Yes." Expectantly.

"Well," she shrugged, "this is one of them." And then she departed in earnest.

At the appointed hour he went to see Teoru, in a fine state of anticipation. A cascade of chimes announced his arrival, the polished ebony door slid aside, and he was face to face with a changed man—changed from the inside, and profoundly, where Sringlë had merely changed her clothes.

"Sit down," Teoru said cheerfully. "I'll thank you again, for I owe my present condition to you and the excellent Sringlë of Phayao."

The dutiful robot offered him wine and then returned to its post, standing like an exquisite titanium statue, child-sized and smoothly streamlined.

"We have decided on our new destination." Teoru's voice was rich and vibrant. "I will personally go before the court of Ixim Cuy, monarch of the Loei system, and make my proposals. Ixim Cuy sets great store by courtly ritual, so it has occurred to me that you might be included in the landing party. Sringlë has told me what a gifted musician you are; you can help me win the king's favor by playing some of your synaesthetic compositions."

Attanio's throat closed up. When he could speak he protested, "But I've only played in cheap dives for a bunch of perverts. To represent a prince, and entertain a king—"

Teoru made a dismissive gesture. "There's no need to worry. You'll have three or four days to rehearse." And that disposed of all arguments. He went on to inquire about his activities on board ship, and gave him some paternal advice on how he could most profitably spend his days—studying, practicing music, and learning martial arts. For the first time in his life Attanio felt like a pupil in the presence of a master: apparently this was the way of things on Mars.

As Lord Teoru spoke and gestured Attanio imagined that he had grown larger since their first meeting. His face was clear and unlined, free of pain and restored to a semblance of youth. The scar had almost vanished. His body seemed muscular rather than frail, and his eyes sparkled. It was hard to believe that he owed it all to a sinister writhing worm.

Soon they were laughing over their fourth cup of wine, and Teoru had introduced the Parmenite to the Martian pastime of capping verses. Although they were forced to use Ptok Prime, a birth language for neither of them, their natural verbal skill overcame most barriers and they achieved some passable poetry.

Then in mid-verse the chimes rang and Sringlë swept in. She had discarded her formal gown of the previous watch and now wore only a soft kimono. "I see you've become friends already!" she sang out, picking up the scraps of paper on which they'd scribbled their poems. "How gallant of you, Teoru—you've been treating Attanio like a grown-up, teaching him cultured Martian games. But really, he's just a boy. I'm sure he'd rather hear about your space adventures. Do spin us a few yarns, you're so good at it." And she floated down onto a cushion in a swirl of silk, smiling expectantly.

Attanio clenched his teeth in an answering grin that was at least half grimace. What a bitch she was being. "Have a drink, Sringlë," he suggested. "You sound like you need one."

Teoru of course missed none of the undertones. "Yes, do. Why not join our game—you speak Ptok like a native."

"Oh no, I'm in no mood for poetry. Actually, I was just getting a lesson in Veil theory from Fsau, so my head is spinning: the implications are terrifying. Now I just want to be entertained."

Always the gentleman, Teoru acquiesced, gesturing for Ningyo the robot to bring another round of rice wine. And he launched into a tale about his mission to Delta Pavonis. This was a former colony of the Fujiwaras, which he had scouted with a Martian crew, only to find the colony in ruins and the settlers long dead. It was a classic galactic whodunit.

Attanio was game. "So what killed them off?"

Teoru cleared his throat. "It turned out that the water of Delta Pavonis II contains trace elements, which over a long period of time prove lethal to the human organism. The colonists knew this, of course, and used sophisticated purification systems. But when interstellar trade broke down they were unable to get crucial replacements, and their systems failed. Within two generations they were gone."

"Is that sort of thing common—the failure of colonies, I mean, situations where humans get killed off by hostile environments?" Again Attanio posed the question; Sringlë sat curled up in a feline posture, green eyes watchful and amused, biding her silence.

"We have yet to see how common," Teoru replied. "Earth was the cradle of our race, the only planet in the galaxy where we were ever really at home. But with childish clumsiness we smashed our cradle and scattered our seed among the stars. Since then we've managed to survive well enough in completely artificial environments, such as orbital cities and veilships. But this kind of existence is like living pickled in a jar. Humans need to feel the wind in their hair, the sun on their skins; they need the wide horizons that only planets offer. And as we know too well Earth-like planets are rare. A world might seem benign, like Delta Pavonis, only to prove deadly after a few millennia. Remember that the human race took millions of years to evolve on the homeworld. Our galactic diaspora has lasted only five thousand. That's not enough time to say what the long-term prognosis will be.

"True, some worlds have proved hospitable—Beta Hydri is one, Xil perhaps another. But take for example your own homeworld, Attanio. It seems Earth-like enough: a good ratio of land to ocean, an oxygen-rich atmosphere, temperature well below the boiling point of water and at least a little above the freezing.

"Still the colony is clearly in decline. For example, what is the average life expectancy in Ashbeck?"

Attanio shrugged. "We don't keep records. But I do know that a lot of people die in their teens and twenties, either from overdoses or injuries. And I've never known anyone who claimed to be over seventy."

"This is depressing!" Sringlë cried out. "Can't we change the subject?"

"But my dear," Teoru said affably, "you did ask for starfaring yarns. They don't usually have happy endings." Turning back to Attanio, he continued. "When Parmenio was settled the average lifespan among Galactics was 165 standard years. So you can see how far your people have fallen."

"Oh yes. But where does the fault lie?"

"In your ignorance and isolation, I'd guess. You've forgotten too much of the ancients' medical science, and without any contact with more advanced worlds, you're sinking rapidly into barbarism. Long ago your population dropped below the point needed to maintain an advanced civilization, and it continues to sink. This is the chief problem with Galactic empires: their lifeblood is a long-distance communication. Once that breaks down, as it did when the Fujiwaras committed mass *seppuku,* the individual worlds begin to die like organs cut off from the bloodstream."

Attanio studied the veins in his forearm and imagined Ashbeck as a severed hand, flexing convulsively. "What about Viharn?" he asked suddenly. "The Maung Cluster's old capital."

"Yes, Sringlë," Teoru said. "Have you ever been there?"

"Yes and no," she answered with a dreamy smile. "There are two Viharns, you must realize. First is Luo Viharn, the Viharn of the Sky. That consists of three cities circling the planet itself, in the same orbital plane as the moons. Those I have seen: they're great glittering beehives, jammed with people, full of factories and nightclubs, habitation modules and palaces. That's where all the industry of the Maung civilization happens. The great veilship-yards are in auxiliary cylinders a little distance away from Srasuri, the chief city, and the Maung fleet follows an independent orbit in the same zone.

"Luo Viharn is the only area outworlders are allowed to visit. The actual surface of the planet, which they call Phra Viharn, the Viharn of Land, is strictly off-limits. But I'm told it's paradise. A vast world-ocean, misty green islands rising out of the waves, summer all the time. I think you could safely call it a benign environment for humans. It's been settled for three thousand years now and shows no signs of decline."

"Then why the secrecy?" Attanio wondered.

"Who says it's secrecy?" she shot back. "Perhaps it's just a natural desire for privacy."

"They certainly sound like an arrogant lot, these Maung," said Teoru.

"Such is their reputation," Attanio assured him. "On Parmenio, and I suppose most other planets in the Antares Reach, mothers frighten their children by saying that if they don't behave the Maung will carry them off into slavery."

Sringlë laughed. "On Phayao it's the same. Except that the Maung don't keep slaves—what starfaring race would? They have *saei,* biological robots from Xuun."

So they babbled on, Ningyo refilling their cups at regular intervals. Very quickly they became a relaxed and convivial trio. Sringlë abandoned her airs and warmed to Attanio, but it was plain to see the electricity which crackled between her and Teoru. Attanio's suspicions were confirmed: she was clearly his mistress, and probably had been since they first met. Almost, almost he was jealous. Then it dawned on him that Teoru had even more reason for jealousy, and yet he had done his best to make Attanio feel welcome.

He studied an antique lacquered box and wondered if he had lost her forever. His heart shrank at the thought. She was a pearl without equal, she had all the stars in heaven in the palm of her hand. In spite of her games he could never resent anything she did.

He looked up to see Sringlë and Teoru leaning over a go-board, rapt in concentration. The room's soft lights played over the rich silks of their robes and the exquisite planes of their faces. He felt superfluous. Abruptly he stood up and began saying his farewells.

"Ah! My dear Attanio! I'm being slack in my hospitality." Teoru was the picture of well-bred courtesy, apologizing for nothing. "But if you must go, you must. First let me make you a present, though." And he uttered some rapid syllables in Ningyo's direction. The little robot scurried away, returning a moment later with a large bundle wrapped in fabric.

While unwinding it Teoru explained, "Earlier I asked you to be my musical ambassador, so to speak. But now Sringlë has told me that you left Ashbeck in such a hurry that you could take nothing away with you. So, like a good patron, I'll provide you with the means to serve me." And he handed Attanio a beautiful stringed instrument, somewhere between a harp and a guitar.

It was a pleasure just to hold the thing. Teoru named it a *chiwara:* it was an exquisite example of Martian craftsmanship, carved of rare wood and inlaid with ivory. It was fully a meter-and-a-half long, with a large oval sounding box and two curving necks. Between them were stretched eighteen strings of fine bronze. Attanio ran his fingers over them idly, produc-

ing a mournful scale whose notes lingered in the ear long after
they were struck.

"I have no way of knowing whether this is in tune or not,"
he said apologetically. "I've never heard Martian music."

"We use many possible modes," Teoru explained, "but
don't worry. Tune it however you want, play whatever pleases
you. I wouldn't want you to imitate Martian forms when you
have such a fertile imagination of your own."

Attanio thanked him profusely and wished them both a
good night. Then he retreated to his own suite and played with
the *chiwara* for a quarter of an hour. But he was too restless to
sit still. He wanted companionship, diversion, something to
take his mind off Sringlë. Putting aside his toy, he went on a
prowl through the great dim passageways of *Samuindorogo*.

On a whim he entered the umbilical leading to the bridge.
He had no idea what he would find there, or even if he would
be allowed inside, but as a first-time star traveller he was
curious to see how veilships actually worked.

The sphincter opened and he gasped in shock. For an instant he had the horrifying impression that he had somehow
gone down the wrong tube and ejected himself into space. He
was surrounded in all directions by a dazzling starfield. Then
he realized that he was still breathing, that his ears hadn't
exploded from decompression. He had simply entered an
enormous planetarium.

From above came wild hooting noises: could it be laughter? An alien voice called down. "There's a ladder there,
Master Hwin. Climb up and join us."

"Excellent idea," he yelled back. Apparently a Myint crew
was on duty, which suited him fine. He had seen very little of
these aliens since boarding ship, but they seemed friendly
enough, and a good deal livelier than the Martian boys.

As he ascended he managed to orient himself. He was in a
sphere with holographic projections of surrounding space on
its entire inner skin. In the center, mounted on gymbals, was a
circular platform holding couches, more visual displays, and
various machine interfaces. Like the other living areas of *Samuindorogo* it was artificially maintained at a steady one gravity, regardless of the ship's acceleration or lack of it.

The overall luminance was dim, with a touch of purple in
its hue, and the alien faces of the Myinti were underlit by
LEDs so that they seemed even more bizarre and unfamiliar.

A pair of velvety hands hoisted him up the last meter or so and guided him to an empty couch. Attanio greeted Fsau, who introduced him to three more Myinti, all of whom bore names he could only approximate—they were something like Kkrih, Yaaish, and Hsseu. The last two seemed to be female. They passed him a silver flask in short order.

He choked heroically on one swig, which inspired another explosion of hoots. "Water of Life!" Fsau explained. "It will loosen your tongue so you can pronounce our names better."

"Are you sure this behavior is strictly regulation?"

More hoots. "We're still flying in normal space. Myint pilots can do that sleeping. It's when we pierce the Veil that the true art is needed—then we're sober enough."

"Show me Parmenio's sun," Attanio asked after a moment.

Fsau obligingly indicated a muddy yellow star beneath them. Although they were only at the edge of its planetary system it no longer showed a disc, barely standing out against the general background of stars.

"Give me some more of that *aqua vitae,*" said Attanio in awe. "Parmenio is all I've ever known, and now I can cover it with my thumbnail."   .

Fsau handed him the flask. "Don't think of where you've been, friend Attanio—think only of destinations. See that whitish point there? It's actually a double star, primary to the planet Loei. We'll reach it in four more shipdays. Exciting, no? In fact I'll be part of the landing party, along with you and Sringlë."

That was good news—Attanio had taken an immediate liking to this Fsau of Myint. "I heard we'll be visiting a king— have you ever seen one before?"

"Hundreds," he replied airily. "I've even helped depose a few. See that constellation over there? It contains the world of Chittagong. I went there with a shipload of Martians when I was no older than you and claimed the whole system for Prince Myobu. Now that was a fight!" And the alien went on to point out various places in the heavens, naming system after system he'd visited in Lord Teoru's service.

"The Martians were just beginning to reconquer some of the old empire when the Xillians struck. Before Teoru's time, there had been no interstellar reconnaissance for centuries. But he sent out the ships again. He called in pilots and engineers from my homeworld and we helped him forge a new starfleet for Sol. It was a great irony, you see. The humans themselves had taught us the secrets of Darabundit fields and Seals of Trismegistus some four thousand years earlier. But by the reign of Prince Izama practically everything was forgotten. Maybe a few old memory cores had the information stored away somewhere, but computers can't pilot veilships."

"No? I thought computers did everything."

"Hardly, my friend." The Myint hooted scornfully. "No, it takes an Adept—actually, a team of Adepts—to guide a ship through the Veil and navigate the translight realm. It's an art, not a science at all."

"Then a veilship is useless without its pilots."

"Exactly. And of all beings in known space, we Myinti are the most skilled at *pandiculari* and *labi*—the arts of rending the Veil and squaring the circle. We had founded a new academy on Mars to train human pilots, but that's all gone now." He sighed in a most human-like manner and swigged on the flask.

"Is there any hope, Fsau? Can Teoru find a way to stop this Appucc of Xil?"

The alien made a gesture with his ears that Attanio couldn't interpret. "We'll all die someday. Even Teoru. I don't think it matters how." Not the most encouraging words, but perhaps this was just the Myint's style.

Conversation passed to lighter subjects. Yaaish, with Fsau interpreting, began telling tales of the Myint homeworld. It was a temperate place with dense forests and five moons. The Myinti were nocturnal, which explained why they always took the graveyard shift on human veilships. They had evolved from primitive arboreal hunters, from fierce carnivores whose descendants were still a scrappy lot. On Myint they engaged in a great deal of ritual combat, somewhat like the pre-conquest Martians, but whereas the Martians were cold and formal, the Myint were spontaneously passionate. Their language had a dozen common words for "pleasure" and as many again for "anger."

To Attanio they looked something like a cross between a cat and a monkey. They were stocky humanoids, a good two heads shorter than the willowy Martians. Their bodies were solid muscle and so flexible that they seemed boneless. Down covered them from head to toe, lengthening to a soft shag on the legs. This resembled feathers as much as fur; in fact the

Myinti defied terrestrial taxonomy. Their young were born live, but fed on regurgitated food from both parents. Sexual dimorphism was at a minimum.

By the time the silver flask was empty they were singing their favorite drinking songs, and they had voices to match their enormous upcurving ears. Even Attanio joined in. His implants allowed him to duplicate the Myint screeches and howls, which endeared him even further to this drunken crew.

Then, in the midst of the cacaphony, the main sphincter dilated and two young Martians emerged: it was Yencho and Momozon coming to take over the first watch of the new shipday. They waited stiffly, surveying the sprawling revelers with impassive eyes.

"They're scandalized," Fsau whispered, his ropy arm around Attanio's shoulders. "Though I can't imagine why—we're always like this."

Attanio made an extravagant bow to the two silver-haired warriors. It was all he could do to stay on his feet, and he reeked of Myint liquor.

Haltingly, in his newly acquired Ptok, Momozon addressed him. "I advise you to sober up quickly, Master Hwin. My lord has directed me to supervise you in weapons practice during the third watch. Also he wishes you to play your latest compositions for him at the middle of the fourth watch."

Attanio passed rapidly from dismay to hilarity, throwing back his head and hooting like a Myint. "Certainly, certainly, Lord Momozon. I'm all eagerness."

The Martian bowed, his face a mask of courtesy, but in his eyes there was just a twinkle of amusement. Myinti and Parmenite noisily wished them a good watch and departed.

3

He slid his hand down Sringlë's thigh, a fallen pillar of polished teakwood. Her nipples were like chips of onyx pressing into his chest. His own flesh seemed as smooth and sleek as chrysoprase, on which her teeth left a persimmon trail, the spoor of a wounded animal. The tank surrounding them took on the aspect of a sculptured shrine, or possibly even a forest clearing, and the shimmering field seemed no more than marsh mist.

"Attanio Hwin," came her voice out of the clouds. "You've gone cross-eyed. Yawn and exhale, it will help."

He did so. Slowly he became aware of the fact that he and Sringlë were cramped together in one coffin-like stasis tank, that they were aboard *Samuindorogo* and not wandering together in some jungle paradise. In a moment more he could speak.

"As soon as I learned to activate a cube, I read one called *The Lost City of Angkor Wat*. It was a legend of Old Earth, about a dream-city built by saints and then destroyed in a terrible war with nullbeams and liquid fire. I felt like I was reading that cube again, except with my tongue, and the letters were stuck between your teeth."

"Such a poet!"

"We're very drugged, aren't we? I feel so gone. I remember drinking that potion and climbing in here with you. I don't remember losing consciousness, but all of a sudden it's *now.*"

"We've rent the Veil, my friend. That's what it's like. We can never feel it happening—only the Adepts can experience that. And it's not the drug that's making your brain all cloudy, it's our physical presence in this impossible dimension. Translux, my dear, toiling among the tachyons."

Attanio blinked rapidly; each eyeblink produced a new color of the spectrum. "I'm glad I'm not a computer," he decided.

Sringlë's laughter was a shower of leering imps. "I'd guess that the ship's mind is rewriting the *Pornographies of Tulvio* at this very moment, or perhaps producing new commentaries on the *Revelations of Qat*."

"So it's that bad." He rolled over on top of her, supporting himself on his elbows. The movement created waves of purple goo. "Tell me about the Adepts."

"Well, you know some already. All the Myinti are, and even some of the Martian boys. They work in pairs. Their training must begin at the onset of puberty, because what they do has everything to do with sex," and here she made a coy undulation, "except that it's like fucking with the mind instead of the body. Their discipline is a great-grandchild of Tantra— perhaps you've heard of that? Only it's called *pandiculari*, from an Old Earth word meaning 'to uncoil.' They store up individual psychic energy, winding it up inside like a spring, and then the partners unite via neural link and release the charge. It's been compared with a cobra striking. The fangs, which are the two Adepts, puncture the Veil, which is the velocity of light, and the particles of the starship shoot through like venom."

"That sounds catastrophic. Are you quite sure you're making sense?"

"Under the circumstances, no. But let me proceed a little less metaphorically. We have starships traveling through normal space at almost the speed of light, propelled by the waves of the gravitonic alternator. Darabundit fields contain and direct this fatal energy, and a Seal of Trismegistus surrounds the ship. It is this hermetic seal which makes Puncture feasible.

"When the starship is close to lightspeed, by its very existence it has stretched the boundaries of space/time. At this point a pair of Adepts plugs into the ship's nervous system. They stroke themselves up to a truly cataclysmic orgasm (apologies for the metaphor) and when the haze clears the ship is on the other side of C. The Trismegistus Seal maintains the molecular structure of everything inside it, so that we aren't dispersed across infinity."

Attanio whistled. "So right now we're riding on a blaze of glory that Fsau and Yaaish cooked up for us. They're a pretty hot item!"

"Vulgar!" Sringlë primped her braids a little, but they were in a hopeless trans-dimensional tangle. "I should have realized how a Parmenite lowlife would react to Veil theory. Do you still want to hear my explanation?"

"Of course! It's getting better and better."

"Very well then. Now we're in the tachyon dimension, but our troubles are far from over. This is a whole other universe with some extremely peculiar correspondences to the one we evolved in. A second team of Adepts must now take control to guide us through Veil-space to our proper point of reentry. Navigation beyond the Veil is an art unto itself, known as *labi*, or 'gliding.' The ship travels with the momentum of Puncture and in fact accelerates without any means of propulsion. The starscape it passes through can be described only with equations that baffle everyone except the Adepts. It's been known to drive some would-be Adepts mad, and reduce others to smoking corpses. Over the millennia hundreds of ships have vanished forever beyond the Veil.

"But if there are no mishaps, if our navigators manage to conquer their nightmares and achieve clear vision through blind eyes—"

"Sringlë!"

"—then the original pair hooks up and blasts us back to normal space, within a light day or so of our destination. From there the ship can practically pilot itself."

"Are all Adepts insane?"

"By some definitions. Certainly the best ones are. Kkrih is the best on this ship, and he's a certified lunatic."

"Oh yes, he's the one who just hoots all the time . . . I begin to understand why." Attanio settled back into his daydreams for a timeless interval, glad of Sringlë's companionship. It was more usual for a passenger to lie alone and under sedation while the ship was in translight passage; but Sringlë herself had suggested this diversion, since it was Attanio's first venture beyond the Veil.

He contemplated her disturbing new persona as the elegant Martian princess. The porcelain maidens of Tharsis indeed! Fortunately he still caught a few glimpses of the woman he'd known in Ashbeck. He turned to speak to her . . .

. . . and in the same instant an indescribable discontinuity occurred.

A tiny speaker near their feet roused them from bewilderment. It was the voice of the ship's cybernetic unit, throaty and sexless, announcing, *Samuindorogo* has emerged at the edge of the Loei system. Normal ship functions resume. Individual isolation fields for non-hibernating personnel are terminated."

A bit stiffly they climbed out of the tank. "That was fun," Attanio said as they dressed. "When do we do it again?"

"One step at a time!" Sringlë laughed. "You still have your first alien world ahead of you."

They were in one of *Samuindorogo's* ellipsoidal life-pods, arranged in a ring of ten aft of the central garden. Each pod contained six stasis tanks, empty now except for one containing a sleeping Martian warrior.

Attanio hadn't paid him much attention when they'd entered the pod, excited as he was by the impending Puncture. But now he stepped over and gazed through a shimmer of haze at the still form.

"Which one is this? He looks a little more like Teoru than Momozon."

"I'm not sure," Sringlë answered over his shoulder. "He's definitely one of the Momozon series, which would make him Prince Myobu's thirteenth son—Chuban? Yukio? I suppose Teoru will only awaken him in an emergency; he waited until after the first nine had succumbed to the *dwedo* before he pulled out the current crew."

Attanio studied the angular planes of his face, the silvery eyelashes and the parted lips. Even in stasis there were signs of character lingering there. "Somehow I think this one has a sense of humor," he concluded. "Maybe they're saving the best for last."

V. Speaker for the King

It was cramped quarters on the lander falling through Loei's turbulent atmosphere. The officials back at the starport had been very sticky about regulations: no outsystem vehicles were allowed to touch down unless piloted by a native Loeyo. So Fsau sat by grumpily as one of the locals guided them in.

Teoru and Sringlë were practically in each other's laps on one couch, Attanio and Yencho on another. Ningyo the robot had the advantage of being collapsible—he was bracketed to the wall. These six beings, human and otherwise, constituted the White Bear's embassy to the court of Ixim Cuy.

"How are you feeling?" Sringlë murmured.

"Quite well, under the circumstances." Teoru shifted his weight uncomfortably. "I estimate two or three more days before I need another one of those creatures." They exchanged a rueful glance and switched to the Lumi dialect; now only longtime residents of Mount Zoz could follow what they said.

"I'm not sure I care for these Loeyo." Sringlë gazed out the port as if admiring the view.

"I hope to spend as little time here as possible," said Teoru just as amiably. "The general feel of the place should tell us if they're really capable of maintaining high-level starflight technology. The photographs we saw could very easily have been faked. In fact maybe the Loeyo themselves circulate them as a bluff, to make other starfarers show them more respect."

He was referring to a series of old-style, two-dimensional images, quality fair to poor, which he had been given on Lumiphat. They showed a whole squadron of starships parked in a huge hangar-like structure, apparently under planetary gravity. Fsau had pronounced them battleships of antique Terrestrial design. His speculation was that they were relics of the fleet sent by the Sun Company, 2700 years earlier, in an unsuccessful bid to reconquer Viharn. If properly maintained they could be just as deadly now as the day they were launched: and naturally Teoru and Fsau imagined them under their own control, flying against the Armada of the Pleiades.

But there was no guarantee that these buried ships were actually on Loei, rather than some other world in the Antares Reach, or that the photographs were of recent date. They were merely pursuing rumors and their own curiosity.

"The boys at the starport seemed to be hiding something," Sringlë said. "My guess is that they're not on the best of terms with Viharn; they may even be cooking up some resistance. We know about the unequal treaties, about the Viharnese mining rights in the local asteroid belt. Our arrival here could complicate things."

"Yes. They might think we're spies from Viharn, or alternatively that we're a possible ally. I'll encourage that second speculation, of course. But unfortunately we have nothing backing us up; Loei would prove a far more valuable reinforcement to the House of Shinjuku than the reverse."

Their little craft was suddenly buffeted by rough winds, and they were forced to climb back up almost a thousand meters. Plainly Fsau itched to be at the controls; contempt for the native pilot was obvious in the twitching of his whiskers and the set of his great ears.

They were flying westward across a steaming ocean toward the diamond-shaped continent they had observed from space. It was in the middle latitudes, but on Loei this was no indication of temperate climate; a world-ocean and a moderate axial tilt kept temperatures fairly uniform all over the planet. Given the heat of Pacal, the yellow-white primary, this meant that surface temperatures averaged around 75°C. Human settlements were possible only at high altitudes, on the mountain faces and *altiplanos* of the highest cordilleras. In spite of the Myint's disregard the Loeyo quickly had them arrowing downward again. A narrow coastal plain emerged from the vaporous sea, mottled red and brown by bizarre fungoid growths. Then came the foothills of the cordillera, and finally the jagged black cones of the mountains, thrusting their summits ten kilometers into yellowish clouds. There was no such thing as glaciation, not even on the highest peaks.

Once more it was rough going as they crossed the mountain chain. "Now you understand, Attanio, why I made you skip breakfast." Fsau spoke as much for the pilot's benefit as for Attánio's; the latter was beginning to look a bit grey.

Very soon the turbulence was past, and they were flying through clear air over a rolling emerald-green plateau that filled the gap between two mountain ranges. Though narrow, it stretched away to the north and south farther than the eye could follow.

"Moyo," the pilot grunted. "The king's city is very close now." They dropped to within a few hundred meters of the surface.

Every centimeter of the land beneath them was under cultivation. Owing to the absence of seasonal variation both plowing and harvesting could be under way in adjacent fields.

"Those tractors look battered, and not especially effective," Teoru observed in the Lumi dialect. "They could be centuries old."

"And see, there on the mountainsides." Sringlë pointed to fields terraced into the slopes like a stairway for Titans. "Those people are actually hoeing. They're working like peasants from the prehistoric era."

The pilot noticed her attention without understanding the words. "Those are the king's fields," he said, indicating the central plateau. "The terraces are clan holdings."

Silver heads nodded at their first lesson in Loeyo sociology.

Moments later they descended to a wide terrace cut into the cliff. One other surface-to-orbit vehicle was parked there, of local manufacture and very old. All except Yencho disembarked gratefully; to him fell the unenviable first shift of guard duty aboard the shuttlecraft.

Before them, carved into the mountains like a reclining sculpture, lay the pinnacles, terraces, and caverns of Tzuin. It was the king's city and capital of this whole world. Depending on how far into the mountains its galleries stretched, Teoru estimated its population at about a million—a small place by galactic standards. Still it had charm, hovering there over the emerald fields, surmounted in turn by lofty peaks and a clear, clear sky.

Pacal was inclining toward the west, but tiny Kokob, the orange companion-sun, was still near its zenith. In its direct rays they felt quite warm.

Naturally there was a welcoming party; the starport officials would have radioed ahead with all particulars. Two dignitaries in a dazzling array of golden ornaments awaited them, attended by a handful of lesser officials in silver, plus a small detachment of soldiers. They were all short sturdy men with bronze skins and aquiline profiles. The soldiers, oddly enough, wore masks of polished steel, all sculpted to the same design: a heavy stylized face with disturbingly placid features.

"What barbarians they look," Attanio breathed in Fsau's generous ear. "Now *this* is like the fantasy cubes."

"No fantasy of mine," the Myint answered shortly. "I've already decided I don't like these people."

They were standing to one side with solemn Ningyo. These three carried the group's burdens. Teoru had wanted to distinguish the Martians from the rest of the party as beings of higher status, to impress the Loeyo.

But Ningyo obviously impressed them most of all. Robots in android form seemed a novelty to these mountaineers.

The two golden men now spoke in an odd chorus, using the secondary Ptok dialect that was current here. "From Ixim Cuy, Overlord of Moyo, Lord Protector of Ilpa and Shuz, sole monarch of Loei, greetings. His Majesty sits in judgment until the setting of Pacal and will receive his supplicants at once. You visitors from the outer worlds will kindly accompany us to the palace."

Teoru assumed equally dramatic tones for his responses. "Teoru Mashibara of the House Shinjuku, Exemplar of the Round of Mars, is pleased to accept His Majesty's welcome." With that the little party of Galactics proceeded to the two gravity sleds parked nearby. One of the golden men accompanied them—with a few of the masked soldiers—in the larger of the sleds, while the rest climbed into the other.

None of the outworld visitors failed to note how precisely these soldiers conducted themselves, marching, turning, and kneeling in perfect unison.

"Well trained, aren't they," Teoru muttered.

"For men, yes," Fsau replied. "But are they really men?"

"This one at least seems to be breathing." Attanio spoke out of the side of his mouth, indicating the warrior a few centimeters away from his right shoulder.

"And this one," Sringlë confirmed. "There are mysteries here, but I trust we'll solve them."

Looking down they caught a brief glimpse of the outer gardens and terraces of Tzuin. Where there were buildings

rather than excavations the architecture was frowning, mono-
lithic, softened only by frequent plantings of flowers and fern-
trees. Instead of proper streets there were stairways cut into
the cliffs, traversed now by stocky men and women in fringed
kilts and striped mantles. Most of the city was invisible to
them, carved out of the mountain in a maze of tunnels and
chambers.

Their destination was the highest peak within the city
limits. Artifice had completely transformed it into a many-
tiered ziggurat, whose squat skyline was relieved by several
narrow lookout towers rising a hundred meters and more
above its roofs. Almost half this structure, including a monumental gateway and all the highest pinnacles, flashed in gilded
splendor.

"Tasteless display," pronounced the Martian lord. Nevertheless they walked with the dignity of princes through those
glaring portals. Flanked by their Loeyo retinue they emerged
in a vast hall. Shafts of light fell fifty meters through incense-
laden air. Pillars carved with coiling vines and grinning skulls
dwindled upward to vanish in scented mist. Throngs of bejewelled noblemen and a whole army of masked warriors lined
the central aisle, and at the far end, seemingly kilometers distant, rose the royal dais.

For Attanio this was the threshold of dreams. Never mind
what the jaded Galactics thought, his heart swelled within him
and his head was dizzy with the opulence of it all.

Ixim Cuy himself was invisible beneath a mass of electrum
plate. To his right three well-decorated ladies knelt, swathed
in brilliant tapestries, their heads bent humbly over their laps.
To his left stood a hatchet-faced man in relatively plain garments. He held what appeared to be a musical instrument, a
sort of harp-lute with a huge sounding-gourd and at least
twenty vertical strings.

At Teoru's cue his embassy performed an elegant obei-
sance, appropriate for the most solemn occasions in Tharsis or
Olympus Mons. The hatchet-faced man replied by striking his
instrument once, producing a ringing chord that echoed and
reechoed in the cavernous hall.

One of the golden dignitaries whispered, "This personage
is the king's *odop*, Cziu Tae. You may now state your identities and your mission, addressing all remarks to the *odop*."

Accordingly Teoru recited the most long-winded list of

names and titles he could imagine, including noble pedigrees for everyone in his company. Sringlë translated it all into flowery Loeyo dialect.

"We represent the Premier House of Mars and the Sovereigns of the White Bear," they continued. "Our liege lord wishes to reopen friendly relations with the Polity of Loei, which has so long been a stranger to us. If His Majesty wills it, we will discuss matters of mutual advantage. We also offer His Majesty gifts in the name of the first Prince of Mars."

Ixim Cuy inclined his glittering head toward the *odop* and the two conferred in an undertone. Cziu Tae then announced, "The Master of Rebirth is pleased to accept these offerings, and will consider the Martian lord's friendly proposals." He struck another chord in emphasis.

Now Ningyo moved forward from the shadows of Teoru's voluminous robe with three caskets stacked in his arms. Every eye in the hall watched in fascination as he lay them one by one before the dais and then withdrew in a crouch.

In unison the three caskets opened. From each one stepped a replica of the delicate Martian robot, and all bowed low before Ixim Cuy. Gasps and titters, quickly stifled, revealed the courtiers' surprise and amusement: apparently this spectacle held some meaning the Galactics failed to grasp. The first automaton presented a priceless antique brocade; the second, an heirloom vase filled with pearls; and the third, a living rose, maintained in perpetual bloom inside a crystal stasis sphere.

Heads craned for a glimpse of these curios from another world, but Cziu Tae merely struck his harp-lute and uttered a few ritual responses. He closed with an offer of the King's hospitality for the offworlders. It was impossible to tell his reaction to such Martian subtlety, so at odds with the ostentatious manners of Loei. Nothing changed in the sharp lines of his face. At his command a party of courtiers came forward to show Teoru and the rest to their quarters.

"We'll know how well they liked the gifts by the kind of rooms we get," Sringlë remarked caustically on the way out.

"As long as they don't throw us in the dungeons, I'll be satisfied." And Fsau cast many a sidelong glance at their masked escort, military and precise.

Attanio merely looked over his shoulder at the receding

dazzle of the audience hall, wondering what it would be like to put on a show for these gilded barbarians.

2

Their suite was spacious and well-lit. It opened onto a garden shared with another official residence, occupied now by the delegation from Shuz. On its wide terrace the Galactics were served a sumptuous buffet by the palace staff, silent domestics who delivered the meal and then disappeared, leaving them to their privacy in Kokob's apricot half-light.

"I think I've figured one thing out." The rest of the company paused in their earnest mastication and regarded Sringlë expectantly. "Those masked soldiers," she continued. "They're corpses. I remember now some old rumors about the *kzeo* of Loei, the reanimated dead who serve the royal house. Each detachment has a handler, so to speak: did you notice those little boxes that some of the silver-crowned nobles carried? I watched a few of them fiddling with dials, and always their hand movements brought some response from the soldiers."

"That's why they laughed at our robots!" Attanio exclaimed. "It must have looked like a parody of their own system."

Teoru groaned. "Fine diplomats we've been. It certainly makes sense, though—one of the king's titles is 'Master of Rebirth.' They're not keeping it a secret."

"But the technology required to turn corpses into automata must be even more advanced than that used in making robots like Ningyo." Fsau stroked his feathery whiskers and shook his head. "What kind of culture would have those priorities? We've already observed how primitive their agriculture is."

"I begin to see a pattern." Teoru nodded slowly. "The zones of human settlement on Loei are highly restricted. Their intense cultivation shows how thin they've stretched their resources—there must be severe population pressures. That can typically give rise to a strict hierarchic society, and we've seen plenty of evidence for stratification in the single day we've been here. Food, as well as information, is rationed—the peasants receive the least and the king the most. Thus, to reinforce his status, he is surrounded with mystique, including the resurrected dead as his servants."

"All that from looking at a few hoes and tractors," Attanio said softly.

"In some ways Loei is a rich world, though," Sringlë countered. "Certainly in metals—and remember the asteroid belt, the so-called Banaen Zaoi we scanned on our way in? That was full of heavy elements."

"You can't eat platinum and thorium," Fsau said, taking another bit of fried bread.

"True enough." Sringlë toyed with a silver goblet. "But those things are valuable trade items. And yet we know that the Maung space fleet has extensive mining rights in this system. So apparently the starfolk of Viharn exploit the ruling class of Loei, who in turn exploit the poor peasants."

"Even to the point of demanding labor from them beyond the grave," said Attanio. "I wonder if that could be worked into a holoflux. . . ."

"I'm sure it could," said Teoru. "Meanwhile, we've come no further in our search for a strong ally."

"But those beautiful old Terran battleships. . . ." This was Fsau's daydream.

"We'll see, we'll see," Teoru murmured. "We'll learn as much as we can in as brief a time as possible. On our way here from the throne room I chanced to exchange a few words with the Prefect of Shuz, a certain Lord Pzil. He seemed more open, more human than the other officials we've met. In fact, he was summoned here to the capital to defend some reforms he had introduced in his prefecture. Perhaps he would be willing to discuss this matter of Loei's secret starfleet."

"That's encouraging news." Sringlë rose and surveyed the majestic cordilleran skyline, fading now into dreamlike indigo shadows as twilight deepened. "But in the end, you know, you must negotiate with the Maung." She turned back to face them. "I'm a native of this sector, and while there may be a few unknown quantities here and there, I'm forced to conclude that the alliance of Xuun and Viharn is the most powerful entity in the Antares Reach. What you, Teoru, have to offer them is your intelligence on the Xillian invasion fleet, and that does give you a certain bargaining position. Oh yes, I realize how wary you are of bugs and bug-men; I realize that a starflung empire could swallow up *Samuindorogo* in half a bite. But you're a realistic man. You know that you can't treat with our local starlords as an equal, now that the Martian fleet has turned to dust. You have your wisdom, your wits, and your honor. I think you'll find a way to serve Shinjuku even at this late date."

Fsau and Attanio were amazed at her forcefulness. She seemed to be reopening a subject that she and Teoru had discussed before, and her manner mixed respect with the slightest hint of impatience.

Teoru stood slowly, echoing her last words. "'Even at this late date.' Perhaps you're right, Sringlë. Perhaps our next planetfall should be Viharn."

"Or even Xuun," she said, plainly teasing. "I know I don't have many impressions to work from yet. But I begin to glimpse an integration, and it holds no advantage for us."

Teoru was silent, but in his face Attanio thought to detect a twinge of pain, as if the *nong khla* had begun to fail him.

3

Morning dawned bright and clear, like all the mornings in the Loeyo highlands. Mighty Pacal rode alone in a turquoise sky. The Martian embassy had scarcely finished breakfast when a chime at the door announced unexpected guests.

Without any ceremony, without even a corpse in attendance, a Loeyo man and woman entered the sitting room. They were Cziu Tae the *odop* and one of the king's three female attendants, the Princess Chei.

"Forgive our intrusion," the *odop* began. He carried his harp-lute but made no dramatic noises. "Courtly ritual serves certain purposes but it also gets in the way of real work. His Majesty has directed me to begin preliminary discussions with you, Lord Teoru. I trust you have time to spare?"

Teoru said he did, extremely pleased with this informality. At the *odop*'s suggestion the rest of his party stepped out to accompany Princess Chei on a tour of Tzuin. "I do like my privacy," Cziu Tae explained, and since he obviously spoke excellent Ptok Prime there was no need for an interpreter.

Settling into a three-legged chair the *odop* immediately went for the heart of the matter. "According to our records here on Loei, no emissaries have come from the Home Stars for 573 standard years. The last official contact we had with the White Bear was in the form of a trading mission from Zeta Reticuli, a consortium of mining interests who desired license to work in the Banaen Zaoi. The reigning monarch of the time referred that mission to Viharn, since such licensing falls under their jurisdiction and not ours.

"We never heard from the Reticulites again."

The two men exchanged polite smiles; then Cziu Tae continued, "My point is that legally our government has little or no power to negotiate with foreign interests. In fact, 573 years ago there was even a Viharnese garrison in orbit around Loei. By the letter of the law nothing has changed since then; Viharn could still send warships and declare martial law. I mention all this to stress the delicacy of our situation. In point of fact, however, Loei has now become much more independent, and would like to consolidate its position as a sovereign world.

"I wonder how our aspirations relate to your mission, and how closely our interests coincide." He paused expectantly, but Teoru let the implied question remain rhetorical. Unruffled the *odop* went on. "Our intelligence about the Home Stars is hopelessly antiquated. Old sources tell us that your worlds are fragmented, depopulated, and short on resources. Perhaps you can bring me up to date."

This one at least is no barbarian, Teoru thought. Self-assured with more than a little arrogance.

"What you have just described still applies to most star systems within the White Bear sector," he replied. "But during the last two centuries Mars has rebuilt its industrial base and extended its political influence throughout the Solar System, and beyond.

"You must be aware of the power vacuum that has existed since the Sun Company's demise. Mars was beginning to fill it when a new force suddenly appeared on the scene—a war fleet from the Pleiades, whose equal hasn't been seen in a thousand years."

The *odop*'s eyes narrowed till they were hardly more than slashes in his bony face. "The Home Stars invaded? What was the outcome?"

"Inconclusive, at the moment. Sol is well defended by ships and fortresses." The lie came easily from Teoru's practiced lips. "It seems obvious that the invaders were merely testing us. They've moved on to easier targets, striking other systems nearby. But of course they'll be back, and Mars needs strong allies."

Cziu Tae pondered. "You do have documentary evidence for your tale, I suppose? Holograms, statistics?"

"Awaiting your inspection."

"Again I stress the delicacy of our position. You've come to us rather than the Maung: I think I understand why. But what can Loei offer Mars?"

"At the very least, resources and manpower. At the most —we do know you have some starfaring potential, certainly a few functioning veilships."

The *odop* nodded, his face revealing nothing. "And what can Mars offer us?"

"Technical assistance in the construction of starships. Cybernetic and robotic technology. Military assistance in any future struggles you might have."

"Interesting. Possibly attractive." Cziu Tae steepled his fingers and directed his piercing gaze at Teoru. "I'm curious about your own ship. Its design is unfamiliar to me, but it doesn't look like a fighting ship. Also you have come alone, without a military convoy. If I were a skeptical man I might think you were almost anyone coming from almost anywhere with almost anything in mind."

Teoru smiled broadly. "Mars can ill afford to spare warships right now. But I assure you that *Samuindorogo* is well-shielded and well-armed, and that I am in fact who I say I am."

"Without doubt," the *odop* replied calmly. "I spoke only in hypothesis." All at once he rose and sketched a gesture of respect. "Time presses, Lord Teoru. Ixim Cuy's audience will soon begin. You have given me much food for thought, and we can continue our discussion tomorrow at greater length. Meanwhile your attendance is desired at this evening's banquet; the servants will explain everything." And with that he was gone.

Teoru remained motionless for a long time, remembering Sringlë's words of the night before. No advantage, she had said. This Cziu Tae was a cold distrustful man, consumed by ambition and probably unburdened by any scruples. He saw no reason to stay in Tzuin more than one day longer.

A little later the sightseers returned with tales of the city's nighted labyrinths, of deep tunneling thoroughfares lit by neon and filled with thronging crowds. There were markets, work-shops, theaters, and temples of the peculiar Loeyo cult of resurrection.

"What were the factories like?" Teoru asked.

"Dark satanic mills," came Sringlë's prompt reply. Only Teoru caught the antique reference. "Miserable wretches working under the most primitive conditions—almost no au-tomation. But of course we saw only what we were meant to see."

"Yes, that Princess Chei had us firmly in hand." Fsau's whiskers twitched in contempt. "I'm sure she prefers corpses to living people. She tried to find out as much about us as she could, and she *is* a shrewd observer."

Attanio shrugged. "I thought it was all very interesting. But then I'm just a Parmenite."

The day passed. Pacal descended, marking the onset of halfnight. The humans prepared themselves for the banquet; Fsau was about to relieve Yencho on the lander and so could not attend.

By chance Teoru took a turn through the twilit garden, and there discovered Lord Pzil of Shuz, sitting quietly on a mas-sive stone bench. "How are your affairs progressing?" he called out; in his tone there was just a touch of sarcasm, mixed with cheerful good fellowship.

"Ah, well . . ." Teoru temporized until he was seated next to the prefect. Then, in a very soft voice, he continued, "I've had my first interview with Cziu Tae the *odop*. He doesn't appear to be the kind of man I can work with easily."

"You or anyone else."

"So I gathered. Tell me, Lord Pzil, who exactly decides policy in Moyo?"

The prefect grinned sardonically. "There are various lords and princes, close kin to Ixim Cuy, who hold councils and issue directives, but as far as I can see Cziu Tae makes all the decisions at court. Ixim Cuy merely sits on the throne."

Teoru nodded. "The *odop* is Speaker-for-the-King, I as-sume. Is his office an ancient one?"

"Oh yes, and traditionally an influential one, too. But dur-ing the current reign the *odop*'s scope has increased enor-mously. It is really a very convenient situation, because Cziu

Tae is by birth only a lesser noble and so can dispense with the cumbersome formalities of court life. Also only a minority of citizens in the capital are aware of the true power structure, which gives the *odop* even more flexibility. He is practically invisible."

This merely confirmed Teoru's suspicions. "What about yourself, Lord Pzil? How has your reception been?"

"Cold." He made an empty gesture. "I've been chastened and reeducated in the principles of good government. My land reforms, all my innovations have been nullified by royal decree. If I didn't come from an old and powerful family I don't think I'd even be allowed to return to Shuz. As it is, I count myself lucky to be leaving tomorrow morning."

Teoru stared idly into the distance, breaking his silence only after a minute or two. "Are the mountains of Shuz as grand as those of Moyo?" he asked.

"Grander, and wilder." Pzil regarded the Martian quizzically. "Do you have any intention of travelling there?"

"It has occurred to me." Nonchalantly Teoru drew forth a square of paper from his sleeve-pocket and handed it to his companion. It was a photograph of the antique battlefleet.

"Ah!" Light dawned in Pzil's quiet exclamation. "I don't suppose you showed this to the *odop*, did you? No, of course not. Just tell me one thing—what is your connection with Viharn?"

"Nonexistent. I am exactly what I claim to be."

"A rare bird, then. All I know about this picture is where it was taken. I've never been there myself."

Teoru had some difficulty hiding his elation, Adept though he was. "Could you show me this place?"

"I could. Though what it will accomplish you I don't know."

"Nor do I, yet," Teoru conceded, though his mind raced with plots and counterplots. "But I can assure you that I have only friendly intentions toward Loei, and that my true interests lie outside this region of space entirely."

This seemed to satisfy the Prefect of Shuz. He continued in an elaborately casual tone. "I have just received some information which might interest you. Then again, it might not be news to you at all. In any case five Maung ships of the Scorpion class have just appeared in the Banaen Zaoi."

Teoru's eyebrows shot up. "That *is* news. News I'm not

sure how to interpret. Are they scheduled ore-ships or is this something unexpected?"

Pzil chuckled softly. "You pass the test. I can tell you're a good actor but I can also tell that you're not working with Viharn. To be honest, I'm not privy to the details of the Maung presence in the asteroid zone. But my guess is that this is a normal visit—possibly a bit ahead of schedule."

"And do you think the *odop* knew about them this morning when he spoke with me?"

"I'm sure he didn't."

Teoru's face was now set in calm confident lines. "You've helped me a great deal, Lord Pzil. I'll do what I can to repay you. Can we speak again before you leave Tzuin?"

"Certainly," he answered as they rose together. "And perhaps we can talk at even greater length during the long journey to Shuz. You will be joining me, won't you?"

Teoru smiled without replying, and they clasped hands in the ancient manner. With a few polite bows Lord Pzil departed.

The Martian lingered in the garden several minutes longer. Things were going very well indeed: he had identified an enemy, he had won an ally, and most important of all he had located the Terran battlefleet. It seemed Sringlë's pessimism was unfounded. Of course there was this matter of the Maung ships, but he was confident that they could be dealt with somehow.

Then the *nong khla* grabbed at his vitals and he wasn't quite as sure.

VI. In the Palace of Zombies

Attanio was disappointed that the banqueting hall had no windows, since the spectacle of Kokob skimming over the mountaintops would have lent an eerie grandeur to the scene before him. As it was the hall managed to be sinister and magnificent all at once. Its ceiling was lost in shadow; floating prisms, suspended no doubt on invisible wires, provided light. Its eight walls were covered with tapestried figures in a severely angular style, depicting alternating scenes of feasting and funerals.

Ixim Cuy, his three wives, and the *odop* sat by themselves at an elevated table along one wall. The other seven each had tables at floor level, with a large open space left in the center, from which the domestics served. This was where Attanio himself now stood. Holding his Martian lute, he sized up the audience in the last few minutes before beginning to play. A mosaic of glittering alien faces looked back in polite expectation. Only Teoru and Sringlë were familiar in all that crowd, but the philosopher-prince seemed strangely distracted: Sringlë alone gave him an encouraging smile.

He struck a lingering note and the lights dimmed. A rose-gold haze and a far-off scent of cardamom settled over the room. He began a slow descending melody, piercingly clear and simple in its upper register and then swelling into sombre chords as it dipped into the bass. The modified lute sang almost like a voice, full of yearning and regret, questioning and receiving no answer. In the light there was a hint of mauve sunsets and high speckled clouds, of shifting dunes and lonely Gothic towers. He was singing the ancient song of Mars with as little artifice as he could manage, without posturing or costumes or holoprojections, without even moving his lips. His melody kept returning to a sustained high note, a long sigh whose only resolution was the dark swell of night. At length it

71

simply faded in echoing fragments, like shards of glass swept across a temple floor.

The last notes died away. He bowed and returned to his seat.

The Loeyo weren't quite sure what to make of it, but they shook their applause-rattles anyway. Teoru touched his face almost in benediction. "I never tried anything like that before," Attanio confessed. "I hope it wasn't too sweet."

"Only as sweet as good Cimmerian wine," Teoru assured him. For a moment his face was relieved of its uneasiness.

The tables were now cleared of the leftovers. The Galactics had not been very pleased with local cuisine, since for their palates it tended to be overcooked, unpleasantly saccharine, and far too rich in meat dishes. This last was incredible ostentation on such an overpopulated world.

Cziu Tae's instrument signalled for their attention. A procession of servants entered carrying trays of liqueurs, followed by another parade of diminutive old men, comical in their hunched postures and long wispy beards. Each one held a cluster of tubes almost as long as he was tall. They were the Magepipers of Tzuin.

For their performance the prism-lamps were turned completely off. In the darkness it was apparent that the pipes themselves glowed, shimmering with a bluish phosphorescence. They lifted their instruments and began.

Once launched, their music sounded more like a natural process than anything phrased and arranged, as it did not develop or alter in any way; it simply continued. Attanio divined that all of the twenty pipers were playing the exact same sequence of notes. But no two were playing in unison, or even in any recognizable canon—they were all simply a split-second out of phase. The result was a torrent of bright sound, like a waterfall or a hurricane or a vast conflagration. It suggested no particular mood, but inclined its listeners to trance-like introspection, sending each one into private dreams.

Attanio looked up and saw that the roof was gone. Or was this just his own hallucination? Above him it was full night, preternaturally clear: Antares burned like a huge red ember, the Maung Cluster sparkled like a diamond necklace, the Sorceress cast her spells. He heard long lonely winds scouring bare mountaintops and felt closer to heaven than earth.

He remained at these lofty altitudes until little by little he realized that the music was over. The prisms flared again and the banqueters turned to each other with blinking eyes. The pipers had disappeared.

"Heady stuff," said Sringlë.

Attanio drained his previously untouched goblet and made a wry grimace at the taste. "I see they've closed the ceiling again," he said absently.

"Are you joking?" she asked—then saw he wasn't. As they followed the other guests out of the hall she realized that the Loeyo were even more dazed than Attanio. Perhaps the piping had a cumulative effect. . . .

Back in the privacy of their quarters, Sringlë announced her latest discovery. "Did you notice that the king never ate? He rearranged his food but it never diminished. He raised his glass to his lips but it was never refilled. And the Princess Chei and her companions were always busy with something in their laps. Prayer beads, maybe, but I think not."

"What do you think, then?" Though Attanio was following her drift.

"Ixim Cuy is just as much a *kzeo* as those masked soldiers. A walking corpse; the perfect empty figurehead of state. His three so-called wives control him like a marionette. And Cziu Tae certainly controls them."

"Do you think the Loeyo know?"

She made scornful noises. "Their whole social system conspires to make them ignorant cattle. Not to mention those Magepipers! They wouldn't dare suspect."

Teoru had been listening without showing either interest or surprise. "Of course Sringlë is right," he said. "But has she noticed something else, something even more pertinent to our situation?"

Her eyes widened. "Yencho hasn't come back."

"He signalled me, even while I was at the banquet. Fsau never appeared to relieve him. Yencho is still safe on the landing craft but Fsau has vanished."

Here was clear evidence of foul play. Abduction seemed the most likely explanation. As the bad news sank in, Teoru called Momozon on *Samuindorogo*, still docked at the orbiting starport; he informed him of their dilemma and asked for an update on the situation in the Banaen Zaoi.

"Stable. The five Maung ships show no sign of changing their present orbit." Momozon's voice rang from the tiny transceiver as if he were in the same room with them. "I've intercepted a few messages passing between them and Loei starport, and everything seems routine. They haven't reacted to our presence here, at least on any of the normal channels."

"Which is conclusive of nothing," Teoru murmured after signing off. His face was steadily reverting to the same mask of pain it had been when Attanio first saw him.

"Is it time yet?" Sringlë asked quietly.

He grunted. "By morning, I think. *Nong khla* goes out slowly but not gently. You know, I was immune for so long to the frailties of mortal life that I forgot what it was like. This past year has reminded me too well."

2

They all slept in the same room out of an unspoken insecurity, with Ningyo on guard all night. Only Teoru's mastery of Za allowed him any rest during the death throes of the *nong khla*.

Hours passed. The little robot stood motionless, probing the darkness with parahuman senses and finding nothing threatening. Sonar revealed a few anomalous cavities behind the chamber's walls, information which he had filed away after his first scan as possibly significant but currently irrelevant. Even when one of those cavities became filled with something very much like a human form, he saw no cause for alarm; no electronic or mechanical devices of any kind were in operation, no sonic vibrations intruded, nothing changed in the room's temperature or lighting, and the air remained untainted by any toxic fumes.

But Attanio's restless dreams slowly passed into nightmares. At first there was nothing specific to explain his mounting dread. There were no scenes of atrocities or menacing bogeymen, just an overwhelming sense of horror at the very fact of existence. He pictured a sunny garden and the garden made him want to scream. He saw a rosy sky and felt forebodings of annihilation. Then a narrative crept into his vision. Out of the sky fell a thousand needle-shapes like bright spears, and the air crackled with actinic fire. Violet rays sought out the invading spearships but were impotent to halt their advance. Thunder and smoke and the stench of death overwhelmed him.

Hovering before his dreaming eyes was a twisted corpse, charred by flame and still burning, constantly burning but never consumed. Its face was frozen in a rictus of agony. It was the image of Teoru.

Attanio knew he was dreaming and struggled wildly toward consciousness, thrashing his body around in an attempt to shock it into waking. His eyes opened onto reality, onto the shadowy chamber in the palace of zombies. He saw Teoru and Sringlë writhing just as he was. Ningyo stood by making abortive gestures, a robot's parody of confusion.

Then Teoru seemed to gain some control over himself. He and Ningyo exchanged a few rapid phrases in Martian machine-speech, and Ningyo extended an arm toward a spot on the opposite wall. Attanio felt the sudden shudder of a sonic bolt passing through the air, and abruptly his sensation of dread was gone.

Now a visible beam pulsed out of Ningyo's right hand, tracing a rectangular outline on the wall. A moment later he lifted away this neatly cut panel and the body of a woman fell out onto the floor.

Sringlë was immediately kneeling by her side, arranging her comfortably on her back. "It's Princess Chei," she announced.

"Then she was the source of our nightmares?" Attanio asked in bewilderment.

"Evidently." Sringlë searched through the unconscious woman's gown, to find a small control box covered with gauges and dials. "This must be what she uses to direct Ixim Cuy's movements. I suppose each one of the three royal ladies concentrates on a different area of the body, like the puppeteers in the Martian *bunraku*. But I think she was using pure psionic force on us—otherwise Ningyo would have detected some discharge in the normal energy spectrum."

"And of course a robot would be immune to her sending," Attanio said. "But by Xuun's venom, her power is immense. Why use it just to give us bad dreams?"

"Testing us, I suppose," Teoru answered. His voice sounded as ancient as the galaxy, and his face looked an eon or two older. "I don't think Cziu Tae is ready to do us violence yet. He's still studying our reactions."

"Did we all have the same nightmare?" Attanio felt compelled to share his vision. "I saw the invasion of Mars, and what looked like—what looked like your dead body, Lord Teoru."

"No, it wasn't mine," he said wearily. "It was my kinsman Prince Myobu in the moment he was incinerated by Pa-chwa shock tubes."

"I saw the same thing," Sringlë confirmed. "It had the quality of a memory—yours, Teoru?"

"No again. We were seeing that scene through the visual recollection of Fsau of Myint."

Sringlë nodded sadly. "At least that confirms our suspicions. Cziu Tae has kidnapped him, and Princess Chei must have assisted at his interrogation."

"And she broke him very quickly. Her psionic power is frighteningly strong—by now they must know everything that Fsau knows." Teoru seemed to be fading fast. His skin was grey and his powerful frame seemed attenuated and deformed. His eyes were two windows on the void. Turning to Ningyo he spoke a few commands, then said, "You must excuse me now, my friends. I'm afraid this will be distasteful."

He lay face down on his sleeping rug. Ningyo stood solemnly over him, and from the robot's hand came a tiny cutting beam, tightly focused to make a precise incision at the base of Teoru's skull. Attanio and Sringlë watched in morbid fascination as the robot drew forth the long threadlike *nong khla*, opaque and motionless in death. Then he opened a small vial and held it close to the incision. Like a string of handkerchiefs from a conjuror's sleeve the new parasite emerged, writhing in a loathsome caricature of volition, burying itself in Teoru's waiting spine.

All the while the Martian lord made no sound. The discipline of Za served him better than any anesthetic, and indeed, the pain of this operation was trifling compared to what he had already endured.

A few minutes more and Ningyo sprayed the incision with various disinfectants, coagulants, and adhesives. Teoru sat up and took a few sips of tea. His face was flushed, his eyes glittered, and his breath came quick and shallow.

"Well, good as new," he chuckled. "I've survived my first

replacement. But it's not a course I'd recommend for either of you." He was genuinely in exalted humor, ready to joke where ten minutes earlier he had been lamenting.

"What do we do with her ladyship?" Sringlë asked quizzically.

"Give her some of her own medicine." Teoru went over to the still-motionless Loeyo woman and lightly touched a succession of points all over her body. He spoke softly at intervals and fixed his face into an expression of complete focus. In a moment her eyelids fluttered.

"Who are you?" he asked gently.

"Chei Pzach ere Aogo."

"Where is the alien pilot, Fsau of Myint?"

She answered in her own speech, which Sringlë translated as, "He was sent away tonight to the Ilpa Territories."

"Where are the Terran battleships hidden?"

She was silent, though her mouth quivered. "She has strong defenses," Teoru explained. "I don't think I have time to force them." He moved on to other questions.

"Is the alien still living?"

"Yes."

"What does Cziu Tae want him for?"

Silence.

"What will Cziu Tae do with the other Galactics?"

"Send them away; they are useless to him."

"How many people in Tzuin know that Ixim Cuy is no living man?"

Silence.

"Is Cziu Tae an ally or an enemy of Viharn?"

"Both and neither as it suits him."

Teoru smiled and murmured a few more words to the princess, who appeared to lapse into deep sleep. Then he turned to the others. "This is our plan. We'll drop this young lady off in some pleasant courtyard, where she'll come to in an hour. By then we will be on our way to Shuz with Lord Pzil."

This disturbed Attanio. "What about Fsau?"

"He seems to be safe for the time being. In any case, he's no longer on this continent, so there's no point in staying here. And I think Lord Pzil can be of some help in finding him. Meanwhile he can lead us to those hidden starships."

"Aren't you worried about that Viharnese squadron?" Sringlë appeared to share Attanio's hesitation.

"They've shown no sign of being a threat."

"But Cziu Tae has, and he could signal them."

Teoru pondered that a moment. In the exhilaration lent him by the *nong khla* all obstacles seemed trifling; his goal seemed practically within reach, his dreams well on their way to fulfillment.

"What do you suggest then?"

"Let me stay in Tzuin and have one last interview with our friend. Then I'll join Yencho on the lander and we can rendezvous with you and Attanio in Shuz, or Ilpa, as the case may be. And give me Ningyo as a bodyguard."

Teoru agreed readily enough. "You do seem to do well on your own, Sringlë."

Her lips curved slightly and she flashed a bold glance at each man in succession.

3

An hour later it was full day. The airships bound for Shuz had departed safely before dawn, and Princess Chei must already have awakened in some flowerbed with a slight case of amnesia. Sringlë sat calmly in the empty suite; Ningyo was out of sight beneath a discarded robe, though his own senses were in no way impeded.

The *odop*'s arrival was sudden. An escort of ten *kzeo* crowded into the room ahead of him, faceless and menacing. He spoke without preliminaries.

"Where are the rest? You have a great deal of explaining to do, my lady of Shinjuku."

"On the contrary, Cziu Tae," she said casually. "You will do the explaining."

At this insolence two of the masked guards stepped forward to lay hands on her, but Sringlë was on her feet even quicker, needlesword drawn. Under the *odop*'s control four *kzeo* made a carefully coordinated attack. Sringlë easily held them off with a virtuoso defense, and in a moment the floor was littered with various small body parts—fingers, hands, even an ear. There was only the slightest ooze of blood.

If they had been living men Sringlë might have handled them, but their wounds did nothing to slow them down, and now the other six were circling around behind her. She barked a single Martian syllable.

From his hiding place Ningyo fired a blue bolt at Cziu Tae's control box. The *odop* dropped it with a yelp of pain, his fingers badly singed. Almost in the same movement he drew a particle gun and backed toward the door.

Deprived of direction, the *kzeo* had slumped to the floor. Sringlë bounded over their corpses with her own gun out, dodging the *odop*'s beam and cutting off his escape route. Ningyo was a silver blur as he moved around to the *odop*'s other side and extended his slender arms in warning.

Sringlë and Cziu Tae stood face to face, each one leveling a weapon at the other. The Loeyo was breathing heavily but the woman maintained a dancer's poise.

"We're too fast for you, Cziu Tae," she said. "Lower that gun and throw it far away. And not in my face either."

He considered for a moment and then did as he was told.

"Good. Now oblige me in a few more requests. Tell me, how long have you been bribing the commander of the Chel squadron?"

The *odop*'s angular face betrayed some surprise. "Decades. But that's an odd subject for a Martian lady to be interested in. How do you come to be so well acquainted with Viharnese fleet movements?"

"I pick up whatever information I can get. But please don't interrogate me. What do you hope to accomplish with all your intrigues?"

"Modest goals. The expulsion of Viharn from this star system. Perhaps the right to sit on the throne of Loei openly, to rule in my own name without resorting to subterfuge."

"And you want to pick the Myint's brains so his knowledge can help you build a starfleet?"

"That's right. You seem to know this already, though— why subject me to these indignities?"

"A form of revenge. You know, Lord Teoru frankly offered his assistance in your schemes. But you chose to be unpleasant."

"His price was too high. And I don't trust him or you. You at least are obviously no Martian. You look as much like a native of Viharn as anything else, without that preposterous silver hair. Perhaps you're playing a double game."

"And if I were?"

"Then perhaps you could do me a great deal of harm."

Sringlë laughed. "Remember that the next time you think of raising the land tax. Remember that the next time a famine brings you more corpses to turn into *kzeo*. Rulers do have obligations to their subjects, but you've clearly forgotten what they are. You're more intent on turning Loei into a living hell, all for some obscure notion of glory."

No one had ever spoken to Cziu Tae in this manner. For a moment he was speechless; then he managed to say, "My goals are ambitious. They demand sacrifices from every level of society. I'm no monster."

"No? Think hard, Cziu Tae." And with these words she signalled Ningyo once more. The robot levelled a stunning wave of sound at the *odop*, who gracefully joined his soldiers on the floor.

Sringlë saw no advantage in keeping him hostage; in fact it probably would have increased their danger. As it was they reached the Martian lander without further incident and were quickly airborne.

4

Two nights later an aircraft negotiated the treacherous updrafts of a high valley in the Ilpa territories. A Loeyo pilot was at the controls; his passengers included Lord Pzil of Shuz, Teoru of the Shinjuku, Yencho the clone, and Attanio Hwin. Sringlë had elected to stay behind in Shuz to keep in touch with Momozon.

They flew as low as they dared, to avoid radar detection, and now that they neared their target the shiplights had to go too. Only stars, particularly the white blaze of the Maung Cluster, gave them any inkling of their course through this wilderness of tumbled rocks and sudden cliffs. The wind tossed them around like a kite and blinded them with momentary shreds of cloud. No one could sit calmly through such a ride, not even the seasoned veterans.

And in fact, except for Attanio, they were all veterans, old hands at midnight raids and death-defying rescues. He was painfully aware of his youth and inexperience; he even felt a twinge of something like fear. But he had begged to come along. Having joined his future to Lord Teoru's schemes, he desperately wanted to prove that he was more than just decoration. Now he found himself wondering how he had ever fallen into such naive machismo. At this very moment he could be at Lord Pzil's country estate with Sringlë—or better yet, she could be here in his place, as she certainly had more skill at soldiering than he did.

Embarrassing thought, but there it was. This was all a grand gesture to show Sringlë that he too could blast his way to glory. And she had seemed so amused at his farewell. . . .

His train of thought returned abruptly to the present. They were landing.

"We'll soon know whether they tracked us or not," Pzil said. "That narrow ledge we just saw should take us right to their front door."

All except the pilot climbed out and stood for a moment on the rock-strewn plateau, assailed by fierce mountain winds that were almost cold. Pzil was dressed as a middle-ranking courtier of Tzuin. His companions were putting on the last article of their own disguises: bland identical steel masks of *kzeo*.

In single file they followed the ledge around a modest peak. To one side their path fell away into dark emptiness, but Attanio refused to look down, concentrating instead on the back of Yencho's head. The wind played with their mantles and showed signs of wanting to hurl them off into the void, but again Attanio was not inclined to cooperate.

This lonely mountain in the wilds of Ilpa was the hiding place of thirty-odd Terran battleships. Its location was theoretically secret, but many other government officials besides Pzil had managed to puzzle it out. Before Lord Teoru's arrival it had never been considered useful information. But now that the Martians had come along filling Pzil's head with ideas of glory and revenge, of planetary dominion and interstellar competition, he was intrigued enough to play along.

The ledge widened and all stopped short. "If only I knew the password," Pzil muttered. He walked over to the weather-beaten stone portal, leaving his three false *kzeo* standing in precise formation. After several shouts, almost lost in the wind, the door opened and a rectangle of light fell over his taut figure.

Two men emerged and challenged the disguised prefect of

Shuz. In response he began haranguing them with some wild tale of a crisis in Tzuin, using many expansive gestures, until at last they fell back in confusion, their hands stealing to the little boxes strapped across their chests. Plainly they were suspicious—and ready to fight.

"Now!" Teoru whispered fiercely. As one, he and his mates dropped to their knees and fired nullbeams. Both guards fell dead without a sound.

"Good work!" Pzil heaved a sigh of relief. "With my hands away from the controls they never expected anything out of you three."

Then they were running unobstructed down a long dark passage. It ended in a huge balcony overlooking the hollowed-out interior of the mountain, a cavern spacious enough to hold a city. Banks of floodlights glared down on a dream come true.

Like towers in a galactic metropolis the ships soared, block after block of them, each one almost a quarter of a kilometer high. They were streamlined for fast maneuvering in planetary space and rested on enormous flanges, like flying buttresses. They were scarred and pitted from battle but no less splendid for these noble wounds. For a moment Teoru's brain kindled with a vision of them all polished and new, flying into the heart of the dark fleet from the Pleiades.

Suddenly a bolt of green lightning struck the stone a meter above his head and brought him back to reality. A host of *kzeo* was upon them.

All four leaped for cover and answered with steady beams of annihilation, but they faced the same problem as Sringlë had in Tzuin. The *kzeo* must be completely disintegrated before they ceased to be a threat—and there were at least fifty of them. Some already presented grisly targets, writhing one-armed and legless as they kept up their deadly barrage. Both handlers stayed well to the rear.

Beginner's luck gave Attanio a clear shot at the right-hand Loeyo. He felt obscene delight as the man collapsed: at one stroke their attackers were cut in half. Then Pzil fell with a sad cry and the odds were even grimmer.

Attanio found time to wonder how much longer he would stay alive, and in the same moment realized that all powerful emotions tend to merge into one. Playing this death game, he wasn't sure whether his heart pounded with ecstasy or terror.

It was like those bright hallucinations that flicker brings.

Hallucination—or could that be reality? Could that really be Fsau of Myint there in the passageway with his strong left arm poised above the remaining corpse-handler's head?

The arm struck downward and the *kzeo* fell with it. It was Fsau indeed.

For an instant there was no sound but the crackle of ionization. Then Teoru shouted, "Fsau! It's about time you turned up!"

The Myint ran to them, hooting merrily. "So we've managed to rescue each other! I hope you've got an airship waiting."

"Oh yes," Attanio replied. Teoru was busy examining Pzil's motionless form.

"Still breathing," he announced. As he tended the burn he continued, "We guessed you'd be here, Fsau, since you're the expert on Cluj alternators and *pandiculari*. We figured that Cziu Tae wanted you to refit his fleet."

Fsau nodded. "But I'm afraid it's a hopeless task, Lord Teoru."

The Martian paused in his work and looked up with cold eyes. "Why hopeless?"

Fsau gestured at the acres of proud ships filling the cavern. "They look magnificent, but they're not much more than hulks. Not a single one has a functioning drive. And Loei lacks the necessary industrial base to produce replacement parts. I haven't told Cziu Tae yet—I've just been putting him off in hopes that you'd find me and pull me out of here. But even under the best of circumstances it would take fifty years to get these ships in space again."

"Fifty years." Teoru considered. "We'd all still be alive in that time."

The others groaned. "Consider the political situation on this planet," Attanio protested.

"That can be changed," Teoru said. "Especially with this man's help." He gestured toward the unconscious Pzil.

Attanio had a sudden insight into the perspectives of immortality, and they looked icy indeed. He remembered back to when he had thought *Samuindorogo* one of Teoru's titles. He made no further objections, nor did Fsau, and of course Yencho never objected to anything. But the idea of spending the rest of their lives on Loei was positively revolting.

Carefully they lifted Pzil and started back to the aircraft.
Fsau told them that the starship hangar was now unguarded;
the four Loeyo they had killed had been the only security
force, along with several score *kzeo*. The remoteness of the
place was its chief protection.

When they reached the ship the pilot had news. "An urgent
message from Shuz, lords; the Galactic lady must speak with
you at once."

Sringlë's clear contralto was already addressing them from
the cabin speaker. "Momozon contacted me less than an hour
ago. It seems that one of the Viharnese ships has left the
Banaen Zaoi and is on its way to Loei Station at top speed.
Estimated arrival time within thirty hours."

"What aspect does this configuration suggest to you, Sringlë?"

"Violent confrontation, I'm afraid. I'm positive that Cziu
Tae is behind all this. We can't even call it treachery because
he made no pretensions of friendship."

"Quite true," Teoru murmured. "We're on our way, Sringlë. Keep us informed." In a few moments they were airborne. Now that there was no need for stealth they flew fast
and high, for their destination was all the way around the
world.

VII. Number Thirteen Revives

Fortunately Lord Pzil's injuries were not serious. Over the next day he recuperated in the comfort of his cliffside manor house while his guests anxiously followed the progress of the lone Viharnese ship. Teoru weighed several alternatives: whether his party should stay onworld or return to *Samuindorogo*; whether Momozon should keep the ship docked or pursue an independent orbit; whether he himself should discuss his latest scheme with Lord Pzil. The idea of empire-building held a perennial appeal for Teoru, who delighted in manipulating history from behind the scenes. To start over on Loei, backing the First Families of Shuz—this seemed a worthy challenge for his talent.

Sringlë, however, considered the local situation too unstable for any such ambitions. "Above all we must reckon with Viharn," she insisted. By halfnight hers was the only possible analysis.

The Viharnese ship docked and simultaneously broadcast a challenge to *Samuindorogo*. "Prepare to receive an official delegation from the Greater Maung Co-Prosperity Sphere," it read. "Your commanding officer will answer certain questions raised by the Martian presence on Loei."

Momozon relayed this message to Teoru, who directed him to stall. Accordingly he asked for a postponement of the official interview on the grounds that his mission leader had taken ill at an undisclosed location downworld. At the same time he prepared to disengage from the station and follow an evasive orbit.

But before he could act a dozen small fighter craft flew out of the battleship and swarmed around *Samuindorogo* like sharks around a whale. While they held their fire their threat was implicit; the Viharnese commander formally directed him to stay where he was until the crisis resolved itself.

"Enlightened diplomacy can still save the day," Sringlë assured them as they hurried to their own shuttlecraft. "Cziu Tae has told tales on us but now we can tell tales on him."

"But you told me that this squadron leader was receiving bribes from the Loei government," Teoru reminded her.

"Money can never guarantee loyalty," she blithely retorted. "We'll give the Viharnese evidence that Loei is on the brink of bloody revolution. If you can't invent a big enough lie I will —somehow we'll manage."

"I admire your confidence, if not your ethical stance," Teoru said in his dryest tones. "At least no one has any reason to connect Lord Pzil with our activities. I would hate to see him suffer any more harm after all his help."

With that noble sentiment in their ears the Galactics climbed helter-skelter into the lander. Attanio turned for a last look at the high valleys of Shuz, colorless and shadowy now in Kokob's decline. He couldn't summon up a single fond memory of his stay in this world of troglodytes and zombies and boiling seas. Though their departure was in haste and ignominious, though they fled to a greater danger, at least they were leaving.

In a matter of minutes they were above the atmosphere, and in a few more they were being tracked by Viharnese surveillance devices. When they identified themselves on demand the Viharnese commander ordered them to proceed directly to his own battleship, rather than couple with *Samuindorogo* as they intended. Lord Teoru objected in his most polysyllabic legalese, quoting all manner of diplomatic precedent and protocol, and finally managed a compromise. They would be allowed to dock at the general Loeyo shuttle bay.

Immediately Teoru sent a coded message to his own ship. "Send an honor guard to meet us, Momozon, and prepare for the worst."

They presented an oddly disconnected tableau in those last moments before docking. Each one of the five seemed to inhabit a separate universe. As pilot Fsau was all business, hunched over his console in direct interface with onboard comp, more machine than flesh-and-blood entity. Teoru likewise seemed something other than human: he knelt, immobile, deep in Za trance, centering his energies for the approaching test. Sringlë, however, exhibited all the typical mortal frailties. Her face was a portrait of wildly mixed emotions, the antithesis of the serene confidence she usually displayed. Yencho, the archetypal warrior, methodically checked over his small arsenal and made fine adjustments to his body-armor. Attanio was simply embarrassed. At Teoru's insistence he had dressed in Martian scaleplate, the same as Yencho, and he felt like an actor, a sham—more poet than warrior—waiting awkwardly in full battle regalia.

The video tank now showed them a close view of the great spinning doughnut that was Loei Station. On its shadowed side hovered the ghostly skeleton of *Samuindorogo* with its unwelcome retinue of fsherships. Counterbalancing it to sunward lay the Maung mothership—solid-bodied and deadly, finned and streamlined like some denizen of the world-ocean of Viharn.

Fsau guided them into the shuttle bay at the same side as their own vessel. The coupling valve closed, the airlock cycled, and all six• disembarked: four humans, one alien, and Ningyo. Teoru led them forth with the majesty of a prophet.

Directly before them were a few familiar faces—all too few, unfortunately. Momozon, Tutunchi, Yaaish, and four robots had come as a welcoming party, armed to the teeth. Just beyond them was a taut lineup of the warriors of Maung, wasp-waisted in segmented armor that recalled the bodies of insects or crustaceans, resplendent in polished casques with towering crests and drooping antennae. The party from *Samuindorogo* was outnumbered two to one.

But Teoru stood like a pillar of force. His silver-grey robe with its lavender Shinjuku crests swirled grandly, his luminous white hair stood out like a nimbus. He raised both arms in the sorcerer's classic pose.

"We have come in peace with goodwill for all beings of this realm." His actual words were less important than the aura of benevolent authority he radiated in wave after potent wave. "We are emissaries of the Lords of the White Bear, who renew a contact too long neglected. Our message concerns the destiny of the whole galaxy. The shadow of an alien war dims the light of the Home Stars, whereof we carry momentous intelligence to the peace-loving citizens of this Reach. Having consulted with the monarch of Loei we now require a brief respite from our task. We will gladly receive the Maung delegation in two hours time."

As he uttered these hypnotic cadences the Maung warriors

stood like waxworks, making no sound or gesture at all.
Teoru's Za-enhanced powers of persuasion held them completely entranced: they simply watched as the Martian party
advanced toward *Samuindorogo*'s entry shaft. Attanio almost
allowed himself a sigh of relief.

In the very instant that they came within reach of the
threshold a cascade of chimes rang from the Maung squad-
leader's helmet radio, followed by a string of urgent commands. The spell was broken.

There was a shouted request to halt, a warning crackle of
particle beams fired overhead. The clone warriors turned and
formed a practiced battle line while Teoru, Sringlë, and the
two Myinti leaped up the shaft toward safety. Seized by a mad
whim Attanio lingered a moment to watch Ningyo and his
four mates advance toward the Maung and vanish in a violet
blaze. Their annihilators had weapons that made the ones he
faced in Ilpa seem like reading lamps.

Along with his fear Attanio felt ridiculous: here he was
armed as a warrior and yet he had no idea what to do. At least
he could compose an elegy for Ningyo. . . .

"Attanio, you fool, come on! This isn't your fight!" Sringlë's voice shrilled down at him with persuasive logic.

She's right, he decided very quickly. I'm no hero.

And he leaped into an upward fall toward the ship, with the
three Martian warriors close behind.

Then the shockwave of a sonic-pulse bomb hit. Knocked
almost senseless, he still heard the shriek of rapid depressuri-
zation: the access tube had been torn open by the blast and
now a wild current of escaping air was forcing him back,
down, out. The Viharnese weren't going to let them off easily.

Ten meters behind him two limp scaleplated figures flew
into vacuum.

They're dead, he thought numbly. Two of my friends are
dead.

A strong arm caught him around the waist—was it Momozon or Yencho? "Use your jets!" the surviving Martian called
thinly, his words almost carried off by the screaming wind.
Attitude control—yes; these suits were equipped with all
kinds of safety features. Attanio fumbled, found the right
switch, and then arm-in-arm they flitted into *Samuindorogo*'s
airlock. It spiralled shut behind them with a hiss of finality.

Still there could be no pause for breath. Far ahead of them

Fsau yelled, "Get into your stasis pods immediately! We're lifting and the fight has only just. . . ." The end of his message was swallowed by distance as he flew to the bridge.

Stasis pod: Attanio somehow remembered that his was number three, the one with the hibernating warrior. He looked around for his companion, but he was already gone, undoubtedly seeking his own pod. Attanio followed suit.

He was about to climb into his tank when the universe went out of phase. He shuddered; so did the walls. The hairs on his arms stood on end and his stomach churned with nausea. He was experiencing the unpleasant sensation of fluctuating gravitational fields. This could be fatal, he thought sagely, and jumped in the tank. The local mind did the rest.

2

It is extremely dangerous to activate a closed Darabundit field when there is any appreciable mass closer than the length of the field's radius. But since he had no other choice that is exactly what Fsau did, and Attanio briefly suffered the consequences before his sensible hop into stasis. *Samuindorogo*, however, moaned in outrage; Loei Station rocked and rolled. The Maung fighterships scattered like frightened birds, flying back into the mothership's protective bulk. *Samuindorogo* set off at extreme acceleration on a course diametrically opposite the remaining Maung vessels in the Banaen Zaoi.

Nevertheless the pursuit began, fast and relentless. For now only the battleship in Loei orbit was after them, but it was just a matter of time before the others followed.

In the control sphere Teoru, Sringlë, and the four Myinti thrashed it out. They were in direct neural link with the guidance computers, tossing around ideas in rapid-phase machine-speech.

"They're firing on us, Lord Teoru." This came from Hsseu. "The screens won't hold forever. Do we retaliate?"

"It's best not to," Sringlë cautioned. "This squadron is in Cziu Tae's pay but it's still part of the Viharnese fleet. If we cause any casualties we'll never be able to make it up with the Maung government."

"Do we even want to?" Teoru asked. "This Polity of

Maung doesn't seem too friendly. Look at the casualties we've suffered already."

"It's as I said before. Either you come to terms with Viharn or there's no point in staying in this sector of space at all.

Fsau hooted—a peculiar phenomenon in the context of neural interface. "The only terms they want from us are unconditional surrender. Or total annihilation. Meanwhile the screens are near critical."

"Fsau, have you ever pierced the Veil this deep within a star system?" It was Teoru's question.

A split second passed before he replied. "Of course not. But there was never so little to lose."

"Then why don't you and Yaaish prepare yourselves for trance. And Hsseu, maintain the screens at any cost. Put ordinary ship functions on minimum, use all emergency power."

"What destination?" asked Kkrih.

"Let's have Sringlë's opinion."

"Then I vote for Viharn," she said. "Our pursuers will never think of that one, and if we can communicate with the authorities before Chel squadron does, we can denounce their double dealing and present our own case. It's our only chance."

"Viharn it is then, the pearl in the field of diamonds." And with that the humans dropped out of link, leaving the crisis in capable Myint hands—though Teoru still had his doubts about their course.

Normally a pair of Adepts at *pandiculari* spent a whole day meditating before it attempted Puncture. But Fsau and Yaaish were already legendary among their order for perfect compatibility and fiery élan.

Within one standard hour Fsau sounded the deep gongs of transfiguration. The serpent coiled, swayed hypnotically on an infinite spiral, and struck. Shock waves spread through Pacal's deep well and rocked the worlds. There was an earthquake here, a tidal wave there, a long streamer of fire torn out from the sun's disk. The four furthest Viharnese ships had enough warning to put up shields and so escaped with only minor damage, but the one closest in pursuit was completely disabled. Most of its crew survived long enough to be rescued by the other ships.

Even in the translight realm they might still be followed by skilled navigators. This was only a remote possibility, however, since a pursuit of this nature was as dangerous for the hunter as for the prey. Besides that Kkrih and Hsseu had a rare talent for threading the schizoid labyrinth beyond the Veil, leaving only the subtlest traces for any tracker to find.

But Sringlë had forgotten to warn them about the Viharnese Adepts.

From the bridge of the Maung ships, four powerful minds hurled a bitter psionic assault at Hsseu and Kkrih. At first the Myint pair was alone in its defense, for Yaaish and Fsau were in regenerative trance, recovering from their first Puncture and gathering strength for the second. But quickly enough they roused and rallied to the cause.

Feeling the opposition stiffen, the Viharnese called for their own reinforcements. All four undamaged ships had followed *Samuindorogo* beyond the Veil, and now they grouped themselves at the points of a tetrahedron with the Martian ship caught within.

The Myinti tried desperately to preserve their rapport but they were outnumbered. It became more and more difficult to maintain the impossible. Coherence shattered. If they would escape the fate they had planned for their enemies they must drop out of Veilspace immediately and fall like a rock through spiderweb onto reality's hard ground.

They fell. And still they were followed.

Reentry was an agony that dissolved all will and reason. Lesser beings would be dead; the Myinti survived, but were powerless to do more. Green rays sliced through the vacuum and broke *Samuindorogo* into fragments, and the Maung ships swooped down to catch what remained.

3

Attanio emerged from stasis without any sense of disjunction. One moment he had been in the nauseating grip of a variable magnetic field and now he was in absolute repose. The lights still shone, machinery still hummed somewhere, but he felt perfectly detached, as if he were floating unsupported. Then he realized that he was. He was hovering in free fall a few centimeters above his tank: and that could only mean that *Samuindorogo*'s Cluj-pulse had malfunctioned.

He propelled himself toward the pod's exit, thinking to join the rest of the crew, but the sphincter remained firmly closed no matter what he did. An ominous note impinged. He keyed in some questions on the nearest terminal and was dismayed when the reply came on video rather than audio, a clear indication that overall comp functions were impaired.

Line after line of glowing letters told him the bad news: *Samuindorogo* forced out of Veilspace and then disabled by Chel squadron's bolts—automatic breakdown into component modules, each pod flying off with reentry velocity—his own number three pod now within realspace reach of the triple suns of the Ynenga system—no other spacecraft within scan.

He was alone.

He felt a moment of despair. His sudden isolation cut into him like a needlesword. For he was utterly and unimaginably apart from everything he had ever known, with no training to help him face the consequences. His mind raced back over those short steps that had brought him here. A night on the Flicker Circuit, just like a thousand others...a beautiful woman...a leap into the void...a world of conspirators... a battle...and finally a shipwreck that left him drifting in emptiness, far from any hope of rescue. The tight confines of the lifepod were, for the present, his entire universe.

His fingers flew over the keyboard again as he reminded himself of a few significant points. Comp said he was within reach of a planetary system; this could be regarded as incredible luck. He called up the particulars on his modest 2-D screen. The Ynenga trinary: Aab, spectral type F9; Oort, type K1; and Yif, type M3. Oort had a retinue of seven planets, and the second one, Ynenga, was at least marginally habitable. No human colony, but there was an indigenous race of bipeds, precivilized nomads called the Tu'u. It was occasionally visited by ships trading with the nearby Maung worlds.

Attanio quickly directed comp to put them on course for Ynenga and asked for an estimated arrival time. Thirty-two days, the screen flashed back at him. Not the best of news, but what could a castaway expect? There was always stasis.

And of course he was not really alone. He glanced over at the tank containing the sleeping Martian warrior he and Srin-glë had discussed a few days earlier. He asked auxiliary storage for a little data on him—and was rewarded by a bewilderingly long pedigree. None of it made sense, but at least it gave a name, Yuzen, and the date when he had been put on ice. With some prodding his friendly program translated the Martian referents into a time corresponding to *Samuindorogo*'s flight from Mars in the wake of the Xillian invasion. So this fellow knew nothing about Lord Teoru's misadventures in the Antares Reach, and had never even dreamed of such people as Sringlë of Phayao and Attanio of Ashbeck. An odd companion he'd make.

Attanio was tempted to awaken him then and there, just to have someone to talk to, but immediately thought better of the idea. He wondered briefly why the monitors had brought him out of stasis, but not Yuzen of the Shinjuku. After some questioning comp revealed that there was a secret codeword involved. A problem: but one he'd deal with in due time, since for now the only logical thing to do was go back into stasis himself. He instructed the monitors to waken him in any emergency, and otherwise bring him around when the pod approached Ynenga's orbit. Climbing into his tank he flicked out . . .

. . . and flicked back in a subjective instant later. Except now his digital calender told him that the universe was thirty-one standard days older. Upon request comp showed him a picture of his surroundings.

Ynenga revealed a half-phase—a huge lemon wedge cut by long irregular gashes. From a distance of 150,000 kilometers it seemed a vast island glowing in the vacuum. Those broad yellow fields were in fact deserts, and the scarlike fissures were open bodies of water, rare enough to make most of the planet a barren wasteland. Nevertheless there was an oxygen-rich atmosphere, fueled by legions of active volcanoes and sustained by algae growing in the scattered finger-seas. At the summer pole there were even sizable patches of blue-green vegetation, the most fertile fields in the whole world.

All radio bands were silent. Since the local culture was pre-industrial that came as no surprise, but it also left Attanio in the dark about where he should land. And by the way, he wondered, just how *do* you land one of these pods? It was time for some human advice.

Convincing the stasis monitors that Yuzen was ripe for recall took a frustrating hour of tail-chasing argument. Attanio had time to feel hungry, so he broke out the emergency stores of food-concentrate. This was his first experience with that particular mode of nutrition; he prayed that it would be his last, but had uneasy feelings to the contrary.

In the end his own efforts had nothing to do with Yuzen's awakening. Just as their lifepod passed the point of no return in Ynenga's gravity well a notice flashed across the video screen: *Planetfall inevitable. Emergency program in effect. All stasis subjects released.* And Attanio turned to see a silver-haired young man staring at him in mingled suspicion and surprise.

4

His next-to-last memory was the hasty conference in the central garden with Lord Teoru, a pale ghost of his usual vital self. None of the company was unwounded. All were still dazed by the horror they had just escaped, and Yaro for one was advocating ritual suicide. They had failed to protect their liege lord. By the strictest interpretation of Martian ethics this was a burden too shameful to carry.

"No suicide pact!" Teoru commanded in cold fury. "We will recover our honor through vengeance." And he told them how he planned to seek help in Lumiphat. "We are about to pierce the Veil, so all thirteen of you will enter stasis. I will awaken you one by one, from the most senior to the most junior, and send each of you forth to do my bidding for the glory of the Shinjuku."

Yuzen's heart sank at this, for he was the last of the thirteen. Certainly their vengeance would be done before his own turn came; otherwise perhaps the whole mission would be lost, and he would never awaken at all, but pass unknowing from stasis to death. With such chilly thoughts he entered the number-three pod. At the last moment he recalled some words of his kinswoman, the excellent Lady Azunomu. "When we solve the mystery of death, then shall we be wise indeed," she had once said. "And since there is no greater wisdom than to laugh at the absurdity of life, shall we not laugh all the harder at the final absurdity of death?"

These were heartening words to carry with him into oblivion.

And now he woke. Lord Teoru was nowhere to be seen, which meant that their plans had miscarried. Instead there was a very peculiar-looking fellow in Shinjuku scaleplate waiting for him, who by his appearance had never been within light years of Mars. His features were sharp and outlandish, his pallor almost supernatural, his hair a wild thatch of black and white stripes with incipient auburn roots. He reminded Yuzen of the magical white fox in a Kabuki play he had seen as a child: a shape-changer full of tricks.

"Who are you?" was his natural first question.

"Good day, sir," the fox-boy replied in oddly accented Martian. It was quickly apparent that he knew no more than a few stock phrases in the language.

They adjourned to the terminal; since comp could handle all the major interstellar languages it functioned as an interpreter, albeit a slow and clumsy one. Then with a mounting sense of dread Yuzen learned the succession of disasters that had befallen Lord Teoru's mission. It was hard to tell which was the more powerful shock—the loss of *Samuindorogo* or the deaths of all but one of his brothers. For the second time within a few subjective hours he entertained thoughts of suicide.

But the fox-boy seemed acutely embarrassed by his grief, which of course embarrassed Yuzen even more. He struggled to master himself, to hide his feelings behind a Martian mask of courtesy. His breeding came through: in a moment he could politely type, "It seems Lord Teoru has made some poor decisions."

"Lord Teoru is not himself," Attanio replied. "Maybe *nong khla* has impaired his judgment."

"It is our duty to rescue him."

Attanio almost laughed at that one, particularly the "our." Instead he typed, "First we need to be rescued ourselves. We also need to pick a good landing site on this planet down below. I assume you have wide experience of alien worlds?"

"Not at all. This is the first time I've been away from the Solar System."

Incredible, Attanio thought. I've seen more interstellar action than he has! It added nothing to his confidence.

At their request comp made various scans of the approaching surface. Most useful was the water distribution map it displayed, warning them that large areas of Ynenga were bone-dry, and therefore uninhabitable. Only the immediate neighborhood of the finger-seas offered any hope of survival. Even more helpful would have been a guide to native settlement patterns, but the lifepod's sensors were too limited for that.

As it turned out they had little control over where they touched down. The pod was equipped only with some modest retro-rockets and a series of parachutes—primitive technology indeed for a civilization that could tamper with gravity. Apparently it had not originally been designed for actual landing; these systems were no more than a hastily improvised afterthought. And though Yuzen was an experienced pilot the controls were entirely automatic. All they could do was key-in their preferred landing zone, strap themselves back into the tanks, which now functioned as deceleration couches, and hope.

The scream of atmospheric friction mounted the scale along with the pod's temperature. The parachutes engaged with a bone-wrenching shock, slowing their descent only a fraction. They fell rather than floated down, and when they hit, both men were knocked out cold.

5

"Yuzen! Are you alive?" Attanio scrambled awkwardly out of his tank, once more in gravity's thrall, and peered down at the Martian's slack features. A moment passed—then the snow-white lashes fluttered and Yuzen was awake. He murmured a few choice obscenities and painfully stood up.

Their injuries amounted to nothing more than a few bruises. The lifepod would never fly again, but its interior had suffered only minor damage. Comp and its sensors survived and would continue to function on battery power for at least a week more. They took advantage of this respite to find out all they could about their surroundings.

They had crashlanded near sunset of a local day that lasted twenty-seven standard hours. They were in the subtropics of the southern hemisphere; the autumnal equinox was two weeks away. They stood in the midst of a glaring yellow desert full of rounded boulders, with, here and there, a tuft of brown grass. What appeared to be gnarled grey thorn trees punctuated the desolation at wide intervals.

"I wonder?" Attanio typed. "Is this wasteland, or is it the Ynengan version of a garden?"

Yuzen ignored the question. "We must find the indigenes," he typed. "They will know if and when any alien veilships visit this world. Such is our only hope of rescue."

"You think it likely that they live by the sea?"

"It is only logical. Life requires water."

Attanio smiled, turning his head aside so the Martian wouldn't see. Yuzen was so serious, so reasonable, so like his brother Momozon. Yet already he saw signs of greater liveliness and humor. If he had to be stranded on a desert planet with someone it may as well be this last son of the Shinjuku.

They spent some time taking stock of their resources. Emergency vehicles like number three pod were equipped with excellent survival gear—the gravity sled, an all-weather tent, several sleeping bags, concentrated food, water, a heater, an inflatable raft, knives, a few particle weapons, oxygen, weatherproof clothing, basic remedies, a rope, and a flashlight. During the last hour of daylight they made up backpacks and bundles for the next morning. Then they supped, lightly because the food was so unappealing.

Eating together naturally turned into a language lesson. They would be traveling companions for a long time, without any handy comp translations, so it was imperative that they learn to talk to each other.

"How shall we do it?" Attanio asked. "Do I learn Martian, or do you learn Ptok?"

"Martian would be much too difficult for you," Yuzen typed out before he caught himself. Then of course he rushed to apologize. "Forgive me. Most Martians have a despicable tendency to assume that offworlders are stupid."

"Oh—you've noticed too," Attanio replied, and they both laughed.

"In any case," typed Yuzen, "it makes more sense for me to learn Ptok. It's an artificial language, designed for rapid acquisition. And it's widely understood here in the Antares Reach, as Martian is not."

So they passed the remaining hour or two before sleep sitting diligently at the console. Attanio tutored and Yuzen played pupil; he proved a quick study.

His dreams that night were of infixes, phrase structure rules, and the hierarchy of expressives: linguistic abstracts through which a pack of white foxes romped.

VIII. Ophiz

Next morning they set out just after dawn, when the temperature was still a pleasant 20° C. Attanio was surprised to see signs of dew, but Yuzen made him understand that this was normal, even in the desert. "Ynenga very much like Mars," he said in halting Ptok. The sand slopes, the scattering of rocks and gravel, the low hills in the distance casting long indigo shadows—all this recalled his lost homeworld. But instead of familiar Sol they had two suns to light the day: white Aab and orange Oort, who rose and set together in this season. The sky they shared was deep blue and so clear that a few stars could be seen in the west.

As they were climbing into the gravity sled Yuzen laid a hand on Attanio's arm. They both became statues; a vision of fantasy was materializing out of the yellow dunes.

Like ghosts, quietly and with bodiless grace, a troop of tall angular indigenes melted into view. Apparently they had been hiding behind some rocks in the middle distance, waiting for the intruders to stir from their crumpled pod. Once they showed themselves they did nothing more, standing as calmly as the hills.

Lifepod comp had named them Tu'u and offered a 2-D sketch, so the humans weren't completely unprepared, but the reality of them on this bright desert morning was something else again.

They were tawny, like the desert, with attenuated limbs and torsoes, and magnificent plumed crests waving over their heads. The tallest among them were over two-and-a-half meters high. Four arms projected from a large thorax, each one tipped with three claws. Their faces were beautiful in an inhuman way—long and narrow with beaklike muzzles and great eyes set well to the sides of the head. The crests seemed to be natural, not decoration; from a distance they appeared

somewhere between horsehair and feathers, colored in lumi-
nescent shades of yellow-orange and sienna.

Attanio counted eight of them. Two were considerably
taller than the rest, suggesting possibly that they were of one
sex, and the rest of the other, though there were no other signs
of dimorphism. Each one leaned on a spear more than crest-
high, and each spear had a stone tip with feathery streamers.

"They make easy for us," Yuzen murmured. "*They* find
us."

"Maybe they're used to having aliens fall out of the sky,"
Attanio said. "At any rate they don't seem hostile." With that
he started walking toward the clustered Tu'u, Yuzen close
behind.

Their welcoming party reacted by shifting positions
slightly; the movement rippled down the line with a complex
subtlety quite beautiful to watch. One of the tall ones then
stepped forward alone. As it approached they noticed that its
torso was strung with tiny mirrors, flashing in the sun; a little
closer and they saw that one of those mirrors was actually a
nullbeam.

The Tu'u halted less than three meters away and began
whistling. Slowly Attanio realized that it was speaking a bizarre variant of Ptok Prime—obviously not its native tongue.
These indigenes were rather sophisticated after all; he wasn't
sure how to reply.

But the alien saved him the trouble. Reaching into its har-
ness it pulled out something small, which it then presented at
arm's length while whistling, "Gift! Gift!"

Attanio accepted the offering. "Thank you," he repeated
several times, which the Tu'u promptly mimicked. His prize
was a smooth green stone, pierced for stringing, possibly a
valuable gem on Ynenga—or possibly not. He offered his
torch in exchange, to more effusive thanks. The Tu'u switched
it on immediately. Clearly it was no stranger to humanoid
gadgets. Then it presented a finely worked stone blade, this
time to Yuzen, who replied with his own pocketknife.

The Tu'u warbled like a canary and removed one of its
mirrors, giving it to Attanio. He pondered a moment and then
remembered his tiny gold earring, which quickly found its
way into the alien's claw. Still the ritual continued. The Tu'u
surprised them now by giving the flashlight it had just ac-

quired to Yuzen. Both humans laughed aloud at the incongruity. The alien was in no way offended by their noise; it joined in with a few chirps of its own. Meanwhile Yuzen took off his belt and offered that in return.

Now the Tu'u gave Attanio Yuzen's pocketknife, and the Parmenite finally understood. He gave Yuzen the green bead and directed him to give the alien back his flashlight. It accepted eagerly and tossed its plumes in evident relief, whistling, "Thank you! All same! Thank you! Yes!" Then it squatted down in the sand and drove its spear into the ground, point first, with an air of satisfaction.

2

"Alien psychology," Yuzen pronounced as they both joined their host in the sand. "Interesting." He moved his hand in a circle, joining the three of them with a gesture, and the Tu'u warbled an affirmative. "Friends, friends!" it agreed.

They parleyed. Gestures and onomatopoeia proved as useful as words, so Yuzen was able to participate as much as Attanio. Before the double suns' heat had become too unbearable they managed to convey that their landing vehicle was ruined and that they needed to find a working veilship to take them away from Ynenga. The Tu'u said that its own party was traveling to some kind of clan gathering at a distance of fifteen days' journey, and that in this place humans appeared sometimes with ships.

"Tu'u gift," it said. "Humans travel, Tu'u travel, one party."

Yuzen and Attanio conferred; this was a hospitable suggestion, exactly what they needed. And as a gift it required a suitable countergift.

"Yes, yes," Attanio replied, "humans, Tu'u, one party. Human gift, one lifepod." And he pointed to the proud wreckage of their craft.

Their negotiator was quite pleased with this proposal, though realistically it was within the nomads' power to salvage the hulk whether the humans said so or not. Now at least everything was on a friendly basis.

The Tu'u whistled to its followers at some length, where-

upon they began swarming over the lifepod. Attanio was reminded of the mutant pigeons of Ashbeck going after crusts of
bread.

It seemed there would be no traveling for several hours yet,
so Attanio and Yuzen pitched their tent against heaven's glare
and waited for the Tu'u to finish scavenging. From time to
time the negotiator visited them and trilled a phrase or two. Its
personal name, they now learned, was a snatch of song devoid
of consonants; out of convenience they decided to call it the
Whistler, which in Ptok became Ophiz. The tribal name of
Ophiz' band was a little easier for the human tongue, consist-
ing of two abrupt syllables which could be rendered as Wiwa
—without too much violence to the original.

Sometime after noon the Wiwa were ready to continue
their northbound trek. At this hour the sky was like polished
steel and the landscape was one colorless blaze. The air itself
burned; Attanio was grateful there was no wind, for it probably would have scorched them. As it was they muffled their
heads carefully in loose hoods and wore polarized goggles.

The Wiwa were delighted by the gravity sled. Some of
them walked along holding onto its sides, or darted underneath with mad peals of song. All of them carried bundles of
scrap rescued from the pod; Yuzen wondered where their actual provisions were stashed. The answer came when they
passed a jumble of rocks about 200 meters north.

Crouching patiently in the sand were twenty or thirty creatures with an eerie resemblance to the Tu'u. They were sturdier, to be sure, and when the Wiwa whistled them to a
standing position they kept all six feet on the ground. Moreover they lacked the flamboyant plumes, bearing instead a
kind of cockscomb. Otherwise they showed every sign of
being close genetic kin to their masters, at least as close as
men and chimpanzees. And yet they were clearly beasts of
burden.

Ophiz named them *ihya'at*. They already carried saddle-
bags, and now the Wiwa added their new treasures, warbling
affectionately all the while. To Attanio's amazement the
ihya'at warbled back.

Within a short time the band was mounted and the caravan
underway. They traveled without stopping for the rest of the
merciless day, covering stony ground that tended gently but
steadily downward. For Attanio it was an ordeal. He had

never before experienced such heat or glare and it was no pleasure to do so now. As afternoon drew on the wind he had feared sprang up, every bit as sickening as he imagined. It carried a fine dust that chafed his face, forcing him to veil himself further and thus practically suffocate. Watching the countryside glide by was no distraction, since it was monotonous in the extreme.

Finally a double sunset kindled the western horizon, signaling night's welcome coolness and shadow. The tribe halted, sipped water, and lit cooking fires. Ophiz generously offered the humans morsels of food out of his own bowl; they tasted with caution.

"This is leather or plastic?" Yuzen finally asked.

"It tastes like an old pair of shoes but I think it's a vegetable," Attanio said. "Frankly I'm afraid it will poison us." He ate no more than a few bites.

But neither of them got sick, so it appeared that they could stomach the local food in an emergency. Their own rations would last two weeks more.

"Two weeks isn't much time," Attanio considered.

"And we have not reason to think starships visit Ynenga much often," Yuzen managed to say. "I think we stay here more long than two weeks."

"I'm not sure if I can stand it," Attanio replied, with no trace of pathos. "These are harsh conditions for someone raised on a world like Parmenio. I suppose it's easier for you."

"Yes, I'm used to desert. But Mars is garden compared to this."

After resting two hours the caravan set out again just as Yif, the third sun, was rising. It seemed more like an unusually bright star than a true sun, however, since it showed no disk and gave little more light than the ten thousand other stars which spangled the sky. Attanio blessed it because it offered no heat at all. After achieving a comfortable position on the sled he even managed to sleep.

"You don't mind, do you?" he asked just before nodding off.

"I take the first watch," Yuzen agreed, "but I warn you—I wake you later on."

He was as good as his word. After a moderately refreshing nap Attanio roused to guide the sled through the rest of the night. For a while he amused himself trying to identify the

Ynengan constellations with the ones he had known in Ashbeck. Most patterns were altered beyond recognition but he
thought he could pick out the Sorceress and the Tree. In fact
the Sorceress was easy, because she contained the brilliant red
star Antares, though in Ynenga's sky that luminary had moved
from her tiara to her heart. Attanio found he preferred the
change.

Dawn came with a flush of rose and lavender. The edge of
the first sun, Oort, appeared above the horizon, the precise
color of flame. At that moment the tribe halted and, as one,
began singing.

It was a hymn to the sun, Attanio guessed, a greeting to an
old friend, a swelling anthem that touched his soul. Since the
Tu'u's very language was song, their music approached the
sublime. Textures and countermelodies piled on top of each
other like the stones of a cathedral. The Parmenite suspected
that their vocal register contained more notes than he could
hear, and had an inkling of its paramusical effects in the way
his skin prickled and his heartbeat quickened. They were wiz-
ards of sound every bit as potent as the Magepipers of Tzuin.
What a planet to be stranded on without a digital recorder or
even a guitar. . . .

The caravan rested in the shade of some huge boulders till
afternoon, then resumed the march and pressed on till sunset.
For the humans it was more or less a duplicate of the previous
day's discomfort. Except now the terrain altered for the worse,
descending sharply through a series of clefts flanked by broken hills and piles of gravel. It was a fantasy of desolation.

As on the day before, the caravan halted between sunset
and Yif-rise; the Wiwa shared food and socialized like pic-
nickers. Then with a cheerful song they all set out again.

Attanio, however, felt anything but cheerful as they joined
the march. Thirty-five hours of trekking, even in the relative
comfort of the gravity sled, had already taken its toll.

"This is nothing for them," he said in amazement. "Just a
normal day's work—maybe even a holiday! Meanwhile I feel
like a corpse."

"Well, it's *their* world," Yuzen replied logically.

3

As before the Wiwa band traveled through the night. A few
times some of the *ihya'at* stumbled and fell, but there were no
serious injuries. At dawn they paused to greet the suns; on this
day, however, they did not set up camp but kept going into the
blaze of day. Ophiz explained. "Very close now—the sea,
mother of water. Very close now—excellent caves. Wiwa
march till noon." The Tu'u indicated time of day by pointing
first to the twin suns and then to the zenith; Attanio understood all too well and stifled a groan.

But he endured, though the air itself writhed and shimmered in the mounting heat. Yuzen, whose skill at Ptok had
increased phenomenally, encouraged him. "Soon the worst
will be over. Just imagine spending the rest of the day in a
cave!" On Ynenga the prospect of burial in cold darkness
seemed heavenly.

Aab and Oort toiled toward the zenith as tortuously as the
Wiwa plodded over the broken ground. In this region the
rocks were encrusted with salt, the residue, no doubt, of some
defunct ocean. It sparkled as whitely as snow.

Then they mounted a rise and the true sea lay before them,
a long channel of rolling amethyst that threw back the double
sunlight like a puddle of jewels. The Wiwa began singing the
most moving chorus Attanio had yet heard; even the *ihya'at*
joined in with their lowing calls. From here to the water's
edge the trail was clear and unobstructed, if a little steep, so
their pace quickened and their spirits lifted to the stratosphere.

"I wonder if we can go swimming," Attanio said hopefully.

"I'm afraid the water would be corrosive," Yuzen replied,
with bone-dry logic. "Too many dissolved mineral salts."

"But look! At least there are caves!" In the crumbling hills
all around the narrow sea they now could see shadowy open-
ings, obviously the cavemouths Ophiz had promised. They
looked as inviting as palace portals in the noonday glare.

With Ophiz in the van, the nomads set out for a particularly
large aperture about two kilometers away. Their course led
them over a ledge running parallel to the water, whose sharp
smell now reached them, along with the slap and hiss of the
waves.

"This is odd," Yuzen said abruptly. "I don't see any signs of life except for ourselves. We were expecting settlements next to these waters."

Attanio nodded. "It seems as barren here as anywhere else. We've traveled—what? Seventy-five kilometers? And all we've seen are eight Tu'u and twenty-three *ihya'at*, a few gnarly trees and a few more clumps of weed. This planet is practically empty."

"Which means we've had phenomenal luck in finding this tribe after exactly one day."

"Scary, isn't it."

"Yes."

"Maybe destiny is just making up for all the bad luck you've already suffered."

Yuzen shrugged. "We're still stranded here with no rescue in sight. But we may as well count our blessings."

The cave was enormous and showed signs of previous use. Ophiz told them that the Wiwa sheltered in it whenever they passed this way, and stored supplies there for convenience. In fact they were now busy unearthing some imperishable food-stuffs. Before the day was much older they had prepared a feast which the humans, out of politeness, simply had to share.

For Attanio it was his most bizarre experience yet, squatting in a circle of four-armed aliens, sampling their all-but-unpalatable fare. Some of them had caught a kind of shellfish, and this they attacked with particular relish. Unfortunately that meant eating it raw—and still quivering. The humans were forced to abstain. They did little better with the winelike beverage that the Wiwa offered in pottery bowls. Though a liquid it tasted as dry as the desert, and just as hot, and far more bitter.

"We'll never adjust to this place," Attanio said glumly.

But their hosts were unremittingly cheerful, and even across the barriers of species and culture their goodwill was plain.

They rested through the afternoon and night. This was their longest halt so far, so the humans used the opportunity to catch up on sleep.

Sometime in the middle of the night, well after Yif-rise, Attanio woke to see a flurry of activity all around him. The cavern had become a factory: or more precisely, a shipyard. The Wiwa were busily weaving reeds into round vessels and then daubing them with some kind of resin, apparent by its pungent odor. The combination of multiple limbs and perfect teamwork allowed them to do enormous amounts of work in very little time. Already three boats stood finished at the cavemouth, and four more were in progress. Attanio wondered at the number, and then realized that they must intend to transport their *ihya'at* as well as themselves. "A sailing voyage," he murmured. "I wonder if Yuzen gets seasick." And he turned over and fell back to sleep.

Just before dawn they awoke to the now-familiar sound of a Tu'u anthem. They ate quickly and joined the aliens by the shore, where they were in the midst of launching a total of eight round boats. Each one sported a short mast and patchwork sails. Attanio wondered where on this barren world the Tu'u could find trees tall and straight enough to furnish even such modest masts as he now saw; conceivably they had been brought from offworld. Both masts and sails showed evidence of great age, and had certainly been retrieved from storage in the cave where they had just slept.

They embarked without ceremony. Attanio and Yuzen sailed in one vessel along with Ophiz, carrying their gravity sled and other provisions as cargo. The remaining craft held one Tu'u and three or four *ihya'at* each. The winds were favorable, and according to Ophiz very reliable at this season, so they made steady progress all through the blaze of day. Since the waterway was so narrow they never lost sight of shore; the impression was of a river journey rather than a venture across the sea.

Monotony soon set in. They tried to dispel it with conversation. Yuzen repeatedly questioned Attanio about his experiences with Lord Teoru, especially where Sringlë figured in the story. He clearly found her an enigma.

"Yes, that's how she liked it," Attanio assured him. "The lady with secrets, the woman with a past, the *femme fatale*."

"She seemed to have many talents. From what you've told me she was a linguist, an adept at martial arts, and a computer genius."

"Also a musician."

"Right—her origin on Phayao, the music paradise. All I

can say is that it doesn't make sense."

"It doesn't?" In spite of the heat Attanio had enough energy to be surprised.

Yuzen shook his head firmly, his silver hair flying around in the sea breeze. "Not at all. She told you she grew up on one backward planet and then, after some crime or other, took refuge on another backward planet, where she studied philosophy. And yet she showed every sign of being a cool strategist and a seasoned warrior, someone whose counsel Teoru valued next to his own. No, it doesn't make sense."

Attanio found himself convinced. Examining his memories of Sringlë, he saw clearly how she had manipulated him from the very start. It was as if he had been under a spell, impossible to perceive at the time but all too obvious in retrospect. He realized all this and yet felt not the slightest trace of resentment.

"She lied," he concluded. "She probably lied about everything, but I find that it doesn't bother me a bit."

"You still feel some vestige of her enchantment, then." The Martian's narrow eyes crinkled in amusement. "But I never fell prey to her glamour, and I find good cause for uneasiness in the tale you've told."

"Well of course! *Samuindorogo* met disaster. Are you saying that it was Sringlë's fault?" Attanio frowned. "Listen to me . . . I'm still defensive about her. But I don't see how she could have betrayed us."

"No, I'm not suggesting that. But I'm not sure how well she served you by keeping her own motives a secret."

"A good point. . . ." His voice trailed off as he thought back to one of his last images of her, the way she sat in unexpected confusion aboard the Martian shuttlecraft while they approached Loei Station. It was as if she suddenly realized she had made a mistake and wasn't sure how to fix things. Fallibility at last. "You're right, Yuzen," he said softly. "She pretended to be serving Teoru, but in reality it was herself she was looking out for. But what was her purpose? What did she really represent?"

"There's no way of knowing now." Yuzen shifted position, trying to find a more comfortable posture. "Our goal must be to find Teoru. If he lives he's probably a prisoner on Viharn, so that's where we must go. Maybe then we'll find some answers."

It was noon on the mirror-bright sea. Ophiz basked in the double sunlight, idly tending the sail and chirping from time to time at the other boats scattered around them. The two humans tried for a siesta, having rigged a crude awning, but sleep proved as elusive as comfort.

So the day wore on, finally guttering into night. In darkness the Wiwa guided their flotilla close to shore and moored on some upthrusting rocks. Beyond lay a narrow beach, fine sand as soft as a foam bed, and all settled down here for the evening meal and a long, dreamless sleep.

4

They spent six days on the Sea of Amethyst. The days themselves were miserable, even for sturdy Yuzen, but the nights at least brought oblivion. And the Wiwa were unfailingly courteous. To the humans' amazement, Ophiz became steadily more proficient at Ptok as he listened in on their conversations, while Attanio, although his laryngeal modifications let him produce a wide range of sounds, never mastered more than a few phrases in the trilling Wiwa dialect.

Nevertheless the humans learned a great deal about Ynenga and her inhabitants from Ophiz. In their own estimation the Tu'u were an ancient and highly civilized race: each kin-group preserved genealogical records stretching back thousands of years, making even the humblest tribesman a pedigreed aristocrat. Moreover they possessed an extensive oral literature, including mythology, desert lore, proverbs, and poetry. They had a calendar, a cosmogony, and a huge body of ritual—not to mention the incredible richness of their music. All this was a far cry from the savagery most humans would have diagnosed.

Biologically they were no less fascinating. Like all higher animals on Ynenga they were marsupials, bearing their infrequent offspring one at a time and carrying them in the belly-pouch for a local year, after which the youngsters were ready to move about on their own.

Attanio asked one day why there were no mothers with infants in the Wiwa band.

"We leave them home," Ophiz answered. "This is only small part of Wiwa tribe; most stay in homeland in south country. Trip too dangerous for infants."

"Why do you travel to Shiie then?"

"Great festival. Make marriages."

This took some explaining. It turned out, much to the humans' surprise, that each Tu'u was a serial hermaphrodite. An individual was born without sexual differentiation; then at the equivalent of puberty, which came around twenty, these neuters assumed female characteristics. By then they had attained most of their growth and were already functioning members of the tribe.

In the present band six out of eight were neuters on the verge of sexual maturity. Their coming of age would be celebrated with great ceremony at Shiie, where marriage contracts would also be arranged. Each tribal unit had strict rules of exogamy that served to prevent inbreeding, which would otherwise be a natural alternative, considering the wide separation of the tribes. The Wiwa, for example, traded females with several different bands, all dwelling more than 200 kilometers apart. At Shiie the Wiwa virgins would be settled with new tribes, and Ophiz would take on six replacements to distribute within his own family.

The female, childbearing phase lasted for some forty years, although a given female might only have three or four children in that whole time. Then the second change occurred, and female became male. When this happened the males returned to their ancestral tribes, each one traveling alone or with one other in a test of fitness. After this final culling the survivors remained with the natal tribe for the rest of their lives.

Ophiz and his kinsman Hwa were the only males in the present band. They had been chosen to guide the youngsters not because of any outstanding wilderness experience but because they were excellent singers.

All this information came slowly, over the course of several conversations. Time and again humans and Tu'u would come to an impasse, with neither side able to make sense of the other. But eventually they would bridge the gap, and what at first had seemed unthinkable would become logical and ordinary. Usually it was Ophiz who made the breakthrough: Attanio and Yuzen soon recognized in him a wisdom as stark and essential as the planet itself.

5

They stood on the rocky northern shore of the sea just after dawn. The tribe had finished its sun-greeting and was preparing to begin the next leg of the journey. A wide flatland lay before them, saffron in this light, covered with dunes on which every gust of wind left its trace in solid waves. Occasional boulders reared up from the sand like islands.

"Not far now," Ophiz fluted. "Five, six days. Traveling hard for you, this planet no home for you. But you rest well at Shiie."

"At Shiie," Yuzen began, "you say that sometimes there are offworld ships."

Ophiz winked gravely; this was the Tu'u gesture of affirmation.

"When was the last time a ship came down?"

The Tu'u's answer was hard to follow, since on Ynenga long periods of time were computed with reference to all three suns; but he seemed to be saying about two standard years ago.

"What world did that ship come from?" Yuzen persisted.

"Phayao. Small ship, crew from different worlds, but captain from Phayao. We sell them songs."

This was news. Both Galactics had been wondering what such a barren world as this could possibly export.

"Ship comes soon," Ophiz assured them. With two of his arms he indicated the suns, Oort slightly in advance of Aab. "Two suns rise as one—great holiday, much singing. Younglings turn female, make nymph-songs. Offworlders buy holiday music." His gestures clearly indicated that Oort would eclipse Aab, which would then occasion the principal feastday in the Tu'u calendar. It seemed to celebrate the eclipse itself as much as the neuters' coming of age.

Gazing steadily into the risen suns Ophiz made one more pronouncement. "You are two offworlders, born on different planets, each one strange to the other. Now you travel as siblings from one pouch, for a long time now, keeping memories of home. But you don't see home again. You wander many worlds, many years together through death and death, never home, always one pouch." His ramblings metamorphosed into a little melody and he ambled off to find his *ihya'at*, without waiting to see what effect this strange prophesy had on its subjects.

The humans looked at each other in mild embarrassment. Ophiz was revealing a new side of his character, that of the prophet, the divinely inspired singer of songs, and they weren't sure what it meant. Was he simply joking with them? Or did the double suns really grant him clairvoyance, and now that he trusted them better he was giving them a glimpse of true vision. . . .

Never to see home again: that didn't seem hard to bear. The Mars that Yuzen had known was already gone; he had already accepted its loss. And Attanio had burned all his bridges behind him with no regrets. No, it was the rest of the prophesy that sounded odd. Brothers out of one pouch over years and death: lifelong attachment, in other words, which was not at all what either of them expected.

Attanio looked up into the Martian's jet black eyes and saw puzzled curiosity. He showed his teeth in a fox-grin and touched the long angular face, callused fingers on skin like silk. "Yuzen," he whispered: the word surprised him.

But Yuzen shrugged off the moment. He slung his arm around Attanio's shoulders, not without irony, and said, "Let's move, pouch brother. Our friends are waiting." And they set off for their sled amid the hiss of waves, in a wind that felt like flames.

They traveled till noon, making excellent progress over easy ground. As before in the southern wasteland, the whole tribe rested through the worst heat of the day in a rocky outcrop. They marched again from afternoon till dusk, whereupon they took the main meal and dozed until Yif's red eye once more surveyed the heavens. Then it was a forced march through the remaining hours of night.

Near dawn Yuzen woke on the sled's narrow deck to hear Attanio singing very softly. It was a song without words, more than a little like the Tu'u water music. This was the first he had sung since Loei, the first time Yuzen had ever heard him. He was strangely moved. Silently he watched and listened.

The Parmenite had lifted his head to the sky with half-closed eyes; his spiky hair fell unheeded over his forehead. With his lips parted and his long throat exposed he looked supremely vulnerable. His voice swelled with liquid notes, only to catch on plangent quartertones, like rocks hidden undersea. His melody glided and swooped from the bright bird trills in his head to sobbing bass notes deep in his viscera, tumbling out like a confession. At a certain point he noticed Yuzen's attention and abruptly ended his musings on a sustained quaver.

"Ynenga has been seeping into me," he said offhandedly. "I may even miss this place."

"That was beautiful." There was no trace of banter in Yuzen's tone.

"Good. It was about you."

Yuzen sat up slowly. "But it was so sad, so full of yearning."

"Was it? I guess it's just how I feel." Attanio shrugged but didn't look away.

"On Mars," Yuzen said carefully, "among the warriors of the noble houses, two men might swear brotherhood. We called it *sawaru*, touching. Thereafter we would be all things to each other—friends, companions, comrades in arms, lovers. Especially lovers. We might also know the love of women, and even marry, but *sawaru* could end only in death."

"In Ashbeck it was a little different." Attanio rolled his eyes as he thought of the contrast: Martian formality versus Parmenite trashiness. "Men could love but there was no commitment. I've always tended toward women myself, but . . ."

Yuzen's eyes teased him. "But?"

Attanio actually blushed. "But you—did you have such a friend in Tharsis?"

"Yes. He died in the invasion."

"Oh—it must be terrible for you."

Yuzen shook his head. "It was, it is, but—I'm afraid I'm spoiling this. And I don't want to."

Finally Attanio could smile. "This isn't Mars, or Parmenio, or any other world of men. So we can forget the formalities, all right?"

"All right."

Dawn broke. The Wiwa began their anthem, sound metamorphosing into light, heartbeats into sensation. The caravan halted and all were soon asleep in the sand, some closer than they had been before.

IX. The Ahrit

When afternoon arrived, they lingered much longer than usual. Attanio felt like an explorer in a whole new dimension: but everyday reality soon made its demands and they had to abandon the horizontal mode, however unwillingly.

Oddly enough the *ihya'at* shared their sentiments. Only after a great deal of urging and scolding were they persuaded to rise and take their burdens again; even then they remained sluggish, and an indefinable air of worry spread over the Wiwa.

Soon a brisk wind sprang up—not the usual furnace blast but an almost chilly gale. A patch of darkness appeared on the northern horizon and grew steadily. The sky took on a yellow-ish cast like a bruise.

Ophiz rode among his companions with lengths of rope, tethering each beast and rider to the ones ahead and behind. "Sandstorm," he told Yuzen and Attanio. "Comes in one hour, lasts maybe one day, maybe ten days. Find shelter in rocks." And he indicated their new destination, a jumble of boulders some way off to the west.

"Is that a good shelter for such a long stretch of time?" Yuzen asked.

"Not good, not bad," was the terse reply.

The Martian outlined a hastily improvised plan. For obvious reasons he was no stranger to sandstorms himself. His idea was to find a sturdier windbreak, if possible one with a water supply; his means of finding it was the gravity sled. At its maximum setting it was capable of much higher speeds than any *ihya'at* caravan.

Unfortunately time was very short, so the two humans set out at once. They levitated to their maximum altitude—a mere twenty meters—and surveyed the landscape hopefully. To the north was a forbidding wall of churning yellow dust,

the oncoming front of the sandstorm, laced with bolts of lightning and stretching hundreds of meters into the sky. Nothing
likely up that way. But out past the nearest rockpile on their
western flank, almost invisible behind a line of dunes, there
lay a cluster of three small mesas, looking like petrified tree-
stumps. As they headed toward them at top speed, it became
apparent that at least the closest one supported a few thorn
trees. And that of course meant water.

In under ten minutes they were reunited with Ophiz, telling
him the good news. Now the race with time intensified.

"If only the sled wasn't so small," Attanio complained.
"But couldn't we ferry things over—some supplies, maybe
some of the Tu'u? It would make everything move faster."

Yuzen considered. It meant dividing the party up, at least
temporarily, and that was dangerous. But in human terms it
did make sense. And since Ophiz agreed to the plan as soon as
they suggested it, it must also have made sense in Wiwa
terms.

Yuzen piloted the sled alone; that was only logical. On
each trip he took three or four Tu'u with their personal supplies, leaving the herd of *ihya'at* to gallop along unburdened,
with one tribesman guiding them. On his last hop his only
passenger was Attanio; they kept pace with the *ihya'at* to be
ready for a last minute rescue, if necessary.

By now the sky was very low, deeply overcast with red
haze. The winds had started howling as loudly as the thunder.
Intermittent lightning flickered in strobe, blue and nightmar-
ish. The *ihya'at* were practically stampeding.

Then a blast of wind almost knocked the sled out of the air.
Before Yuzen could recover the avalanche of sand was upon
them.

It was a solid physical assault. There wasn't a chance of
flying through, so they were forced down—within a hundred
meters of the mesa and yet stone-blind. Mouth to ear they
shouted back and forth—what to do? Huddle under the sled or
try finding shelter? Moment by moment the storm's power
grew, falling on them like blows from an angry mob; before
long it would be shredding their clothing and scouring their
bare skin.

Yuzen was confident of his sense of direction, even under
the present circumstances. Without argument they set out for

the rocks—bent double against the gale, arms locked together so they couldn't wander apart, packs strapped underneath them so they couldn't be snatched away.

Time faded into an eternity of discomfort and fear. For Attanio it was simply a question of one miserable step after another, but for Yuzen it was a matter of working miracles. From one instant to the next he plunged deep into Za trance. In his mind pulsed visions of the complex matrix holding them: gravitational force, planetary rotation, magnetic field, wind direction. It became an equation he knew how to solve.

In ten minutes they were in the lee of the mesa, a paradise of near-calm. Visibility was still close to zero but at least they could grope along the rocks for some kind of opening without the risk of having their flesh sanded down to the bone. Eventually they found what they needed: a fissure leading inward, a passageway ending in a narrow cave.

"You saved us!" Attanio exulted, as his torch played over the chamber's rough walls.

But Yuzen made no answer. His eyes were glazed, his face an empty mask. Like a puppet bereft of guidance he slumped to the ground and was still for a long time.

The cave was long and narrow, more a corridor than a chamber, ending in a cul-de-sac as the folded walls came together. It was also bone-dry, which made for comfort but offered no hope of an emergency water supply. They had just enough for three days of normal use.

When Yuzen had rested they took a few sips and ate lightly. They discussed the Tu'u and the *ihya'at*, concluding that the aliens were almost certainly safe and in an excellent position to last out the storm.

"But we're the ones who have to worry," Yuzen said. "The Wiwa know this world, they know how to exploit every centimeter of it, and they're used to these storms. We're not. What if it lasts for five days, seven days?"

"Too bad we don't have a couple of stasis pods."

"Isn't it. But you've got the right idea, Attanio. It's time for your first lesson in Za."

Za: the ancient Martian discipline of mind and body, with roots reaching back eight thousand years to the yoga of classical India. Adepts could control all bodily functions, whether voluntary or involuntary, enjoyed both total recall and selective oblivion, and through self-hypnosis could heighten the five ordinary senses to superhuman levels of awareness. Decades of study under a strict master were required to reach the highest grades of proficiency, but even someone of Yuzen's relative youth could perform impressive feats. After all, his own teacher had been Teoru himself.

"We don't have to worry about fine points, about correct attitudes of humility and mystification. A real master will make you learn most of it for yourself—and probably give you regular beatings for good measure. But I'm giving you the crash course. All you need to know right now is how to reach a Level Two trance. So sit the way I'm sitting—yes, that's good—and don't take your eyes off mine." And the lesson began.

They worked until Attanio could stand no more. His brain felt like someone had tied it in knots, his skull throbbed, his eyelids flashed white whenever he closed them: exactly the reverse of the state he was seeking. He was exhausted without having moved at all. But Yuzen encouraged him, saying he had strong natural aptitude and was doing well.

They slept the night through. When they woke it was to the same darkness, the same muffled howling penetrating the walls. They were buried beyond time. After a meager breakfast Yuzen guided his pupil through the elementary forms of body Za, a series of stretching, strengthening, and centering exercises. They avoided any serious exertion, however: they had no intention of working up a sweat. Then the mental gymnastics began. Before two hours passed Attanio had made his breakthrough.

Level Two is simply the condition in which a human metabolism functions at half its normal rate. The passage of time is therefore subjectively quickened. Once he had discovered how to let go and reach down that far, Attanio progressed easily to the third and fourth levels. Day and night flew by them like the razor winds outside.

Thought still continued, even with the body operating on a glacial time scale. Memories and idle daydreams tumbled across Attanio's awareness, fragments of his life in Ashbeck. Sometimes he saw images of Sringlë in situations where she never had been. Gradually, he realized that his viewpoint was receding from the images before him, covering a wider and wider angle of vision and an ever greater depth of field: he was seeing his memories through a telescope, from a ship drifting slowly away from the shores of his past.

At a certain point all he saw was a clear night sky over an empty plain. Stars flickered messages to him, slow and ancient, inevitable and mysterious. He felt very old. Ever more slowly he became aware that all he perceived was contained in something larger, whose outlines gradually revealed themselves. It was a face. The face of God? No, a very human face—narrow and fine, eyes like water in sunlight, brow clear and rising to a silver fringe, lips parted as if to speak. Yuzen's face. He was contained within Yuzen's skull, and the bones echoed with the sound of his own name called out in a long, long chant.

He woke. He was in the shadowy cave, Yuzen before him looking anxious.

"An Adept already! And only three days of training. I must be a better teacher than Teoru himself." Yuzen spoke lightly but his arm supported Attanio's shoulders and he held a canteen to his lips.

A sip; two sips. "Why did you say three days?"

"Because, my friend, that's how long you've been entranced. I was with you for most of it, but then my body started giving me warning signals and I came back up. I can't even count how many levels down we were."

Attanio managed a weak grin. "I guess I have an affinity for the lower depths. Will I survive?"

"At least a few decades more."

"That sounds reasonable." Then a little later, "How's the weather?"

"No change."

2

Two more days passed. As before they ate sparingly and spent hours in deep meditation, though not as deep as on their first plunge. Attanio couldn't escape the thought that they had become two anchorites immured in a desert hermitage, wrestling with the angels. He never felt even a hint of fear. Past and future had become unreal, his own body insubstantial.

On the afternoon of the seventh day Yuzen emerged from trance to a ringing silence. Curious and hopeful, he picked up a torch and negotiated the passage leading outside; with each step it became more choked with sand, so that he finally had to dig his way out.

He made a hole just big enough to stick his head through. Nothing was visible besides windblown sand but the storm's intensity had definitely faded. The overall lighting was brighter than it had been when they first entered the cave, and the wind's shrieks had softened into moans. "One more day, if we're lucky," he said to himself, and then turned back to rouse Attanio and tell him the good news.

They shared a little water and talked idly. Would they ever find the Wiwa again? Would the festival at Shiie already have begun? Would they miss the outsystem vessel they dreamed would meet them? They could summon up little emotion over these speculations; they were drained of vital energy, emptied by their spiritual acrobatics. Now that the end of their imprisonment was in sight they were too tired to care.

Attanio dozed off into a real-time nap, a luxury they had rationed as carefully as water these past seven days. Yuzen was on the verge of joining him when an inner alarm went off with shattering force. From the passageway he had just cleared came the sound of heavy breathing.

They had a visitor.

Slowly he extended an arm to relight one of the torches. The breathing quickened as if in response. Then several things happened at once. The light flared; Yuzen grabbed his needle-sword; Attanio woke and cried out; and a grotesque figure stood framed in the entranceway, rearing up to strike. In that first agitated moment the humans thought it was a Tu'u. The creature was bipedal, four-armed, covered with yellowish down, possessing the same general facial structure. But then it let out a gurgling howl like no sound they had ever heard among the Wiwa, a bestial cry designed only to inspire fear and give challenge. In that same instant it leaped for Yuzen.

Attanio scrambled frantically for a particle gun as man and not-man struggled, claws against blade. Unfortunately the intruder had four sets of claws against only one sword and fought with the ferocity of a demon. Black blood splattered everywhere, revolting them with its stench, heightening the sense of horror they felt. Yuzen cut the beast several times without any damage to himself but still the creature pressed on, unflagging, driven by a pain and rage the humans could scarcely believe. It had already received mortal wounds—but would it die before it succeeded in taking Yuzen along too?

Attanio's trembling hand closed on the butt of his pistol. At point blank range there was no hesitation: the beam flashed and the creature screamed and died, half its torso burned away. They stared at each other over the corpse, Yuzen holding his bloody sword, Attanio the fatal gun. But only for a split second: then the weapons fell and they were in each others' arms making strange noises somewhere between sobs and laughter.

"You're not hurt, are you?"

"No. Are you?"

"No."

"So what was it?"

"A demon, I think. The *ahrit*, remember: the demon of the open sands. Ophiz mentioned it."

"It must have been starving to death."

"What a smell."

"What a climax to all these days of meditation. I feel like a shadow, a broken balloon, a ghost."

Together they dragged the corpse outside. They considered eating it but then decided they weren't that desperate. They left its remains a little distance from the cave mouth, to be covered by windborne sand. Since Yuzen's earlier reconnaissance the storm had abated even more, renewing their hopes, but it still prevented visibility beyond five or six meters.

They were exhausted, but before they slept they felt compelled to share more thoughts about the monster.

"That thing, the *ahrit*, looked so much like one of the Tu'u. It disturbs me." Attanio's face was deeply shadowed by the feeble torchlight, creased with privation and fatigue.

"The *ihya'at* also resemble the Tu'u. I wouldn't be surprised if all three species have a very recent common ancestor. This world is poor in lifeforms; the few species there are must fill all available niches in the planetary ecosystem."

"Imagine that happening on a human world—yes, that's the thought that bothers me. That sapients can still be only a few steps away from cattle, and even closer to man-eating devils."

"Hunger and exhaustion have turned you into a grim pessi-

mist, Attanio. It will pass. Meanwhile I find the setup
strangely satisfying. The *ihya'at* are the herd animals, the ru-
minants. The Tu'u are the shepherds. And the *ahrit* are preda-
tors, thrown in to spice up the soup, to cull the feeble and the
aged, to make life a little dearer, a little more exciting."

Attanio protested. "You were excited?"

The Martian shrugged. "Facing death with a weapon in my
hand is the game I was taught to play. I must confess to a
certain thrill when my turn comes up."

"Where do your breeding and training end, and where do
you begin?" Attanio was a little exasperated.

"You'll have to ask Lord Teoru—he's the philosopher."

"Now that's a Martian kind of answer if I ever heard one."
He thought for a moment and ventured his own hypothesis.
"You belong to a type that needs male companionship, especially a comrade in arms. Very useful to the Martian state, I
might add. Then there's Lord Teoru, who can't survive without his underlings and his schemes. It's a little like the *ahrit*
and the *ihya'at*, don't you think?"

"Which type would you be?"

"Oh, I don't fit in. All I ever wanted was to play music."

"Then how did you end up here?"

"A woman."

Yuzen gave a short bark of amusement. "There's the *ahrit*
in your biosphere—Sringlë herself."

Yes, it all turned on Sringlë, wherever she came from,
wherever she might be. Remembering her Attanio fell silent.
Moments later they lay down to sleep.

3

As on so many mornings in this world of Ynenga they woke to
the song of the Wiwa. Grogginess didn't blind them to the
paradox; they sprang up to investigate.

Halfway out of the passage they met two or three members
of the band busily digging their way in, trilling and tooting as
they worked. Their song became a paean of joy when they
saw the two humans safe and sound. Beyond them, in the
open air, the day was dawning—clear and mercilessly hot.
The storm was over.

It was cause for rejoicing, even in that infernal heat. Still Yuzen shook his head ruefully. "What helpless fools we are!"

"What?"

"It's just that the Tu'u always find us, and never we them. They're always coming to our rescue."

They found breath enough to laugh. Moments later a small commotion caught their attention. More of the Wiwa were arriving, and the newcomers had found the half-buried carcass of the *ahrit*, occasioning great hoots and arpeggios. But the first group already knew about it: it was that carcass which had led them to the cave.

Ophiz was on hand to make sense of the chaos. "You killed the *ahrit*, not so? Among us this is a rare thing, very rare. Please explain how it was done."

They did, Ophiz winking sagely all the while. Once he interrupted the tale to clarify a few points. There was a strong impression that in some way he was passing judgment on their deed.

When they had finished the Tu'u chieftain spoke at length, in a peculiar echo of Yuzen's sociobiology. "*Ahrit, ihya'at,* Tu'u—all brothers of one pouch. Tu'u are namers of names, dreamers of dreams, singers of the Great Song. *Ihya'at* are bearers of burdens, and in famine-time, food for hungry bellies. Yes, it is so: to save our own lives our dear servants give us theirs. Very beautiful, very sad.

"*Ahrit,* now: as *ihya'at* give, *ahrit* take. As Tu'u judge, *ahrit* stand outside judgment. As Tu'u dream, *ahrit* lurk at the edge of dreams. For life to continue, death must cull. *Ahrit* are death's own claws.

"If we are strong, clever, and fast, death will not catch us. This is good. But to kill death—this is not done lightly. Each clan has rituals. Very serious thing. You are offworlders, you don't know. I judge you innocent of crime. But Wiwa clan is responsible for you; now we must make proper songs."

Thus the rest of the day was occupied by an elaborate series of chants and posturings. Yuzen and Attanio played no part in any of it; they merely observed and kept out of the way, passing back and forth a canteen the Tu'u had filled for them, and eating local food.

The ceremony concluded at sunset, which now fell much earlier. While the humans had been buried away the equinox had come and gone. The tribe assembled their *ihya'at* and prepared to set off; now that the rituals were done they returned to their everyday selves, all solemnity discarded.

There was one problem. When the storm had first assaulted the two humans they had abandoned their sole means of transportation, the gravity sled. Eight days of wildly driven sand had buried it beyond hope of recovery. Though Yuzen summoned up his Za-derived abilities and located the spot where they had left it, no amount of digging brought it to light.

First they had violated a Wiwa taboo: now they must ask their offended hosts for more favors. It was embarrassing, but there was no other way.

As it turned out the Wiwa seemed quite pleased to offer the humans two *ihya'at* to ride. "It is just," Ophiz said. "Your flying boat helped save the tribe. Now we offer you *ihya'at* in return, since the desert has taken your boat instead of our lives." His long snout quivered in an unreadable gesture. "The desert takes all offworld machines, sooner or later. Only things of Ynenga survive Ynenga's demands."

Attanio caught himself thinking that this looked like yet another form of Ynengan exchange: one dead *ahrit* for one gravity sled. He said nothing, though, and the Tu'u remained inscrutable.

They traveled for three days over a sandy plain broken by scattered mountain peaks. Compared with the southern desert, this new landscape was almost picturesque, and the going was easier than it had been. Even the *ihya'at* proved docile mounts. To his amazement Attanio found that he was adjusting to Ynenga's cruelties. Their afternoon treks were still an ordeal, but the night journeys beneath Yif's ruby glow were actually pleasant. His newly acquired Za discipline helped a great deal. The desert's fine air became inspiriting: his lungs rejoiced in its purity and his thoughts became as clear and luminous as the night sky. The future was there to be lived. He would know new worlds, he would journey onwards to new delights.

The northern plain was a more fertile country than the lands to the south. Twice they glimpsed herds of wild *ihya'at* foraging away in the distance, and once they saw a pair of creatures that could only be *ahrit*. These ran with supple grace on six legs, well out of weapons range, pausing from time to time to rear up on their hind feet to scan the horizon. Then they looked eerily like mad Tu'u.

In the Wiwa caravan there were no young or infirm *ihya' at*; otherwise the *ahrit* might have trailed them for days. As it was they vanished quickly and were seen no more.

X. The Great Cube

On the twentieth evening of the march, while the band was halted for its main meal, Ophiz came to visit the two humans where they sat apart preparing their own food. For a long time he merely squatted down watching them, saying nothing. They were used to his unpredictable moods and paid no heed.

Eventually he made what seemed an irrelevant observation. "You survive well. Ynenga still cannot kill you. Surviving, you begin to resemble one another." The humans laughed and kept eating.

Ophiz said no more until they were done. Then he rose and uttered a brief command. "Come. I will show you something." And he set off in his rippling gait without waiting to see if they followed; they had a hard time matching his pace.

Attanio expected a short trip to some nearby spot, where Ophiz would point out an unusual rock formation, or perhaps a remarkable plant. But they passed the boundaries of the camp and kept walking on and on, picking their way around boulders, eventually climbing up into the surrounding hills. Both humans were consumed by a curiosity which Ophiz did nothing to satisfy. He kept his silence and strode tirelessly on, always a little ahead of them, always forcing them to catch up.

Around the time Yif was rising they mounted the crest of a low hill overlooking a broad expanse of dunes. And caught their breath. For there on the desert, ghostly in pale starlight, lay a relic of the dawn eras: a huge stone structure that could only be the work of Tzokol, a megalith that had endured for eight million years.

It was an enormous grey cube, featureless except for the scars inflicted by millennial sandblasting. It measured a good 200 meters along each side and rested on dozens of squat quadrangular pillars. Since the cube itself overhung these sup-

ports its perfect squareness stood out boldly in silhouette.
Underlying everything was a stone platform 300 meters
square, rising in a series of shallow steps above the desert
floor.

"You are the first offworlders ever seeing this place,"
Ophiz piped solemnly. "Until last year it lay buried in sand.
No explorer found it, no Tu'u spoke of it, except in ancient
songs which your kind never hears. Then great storms of
winter uncovered what long years concealed. News traveled in
song from band to band over all Ynenga. Now pilgrims come,
chieftains, singers of Deep Songs. Even you yourselves come,
aliens though you are.

"The Wiwa lived once in this territory. Drought forced us
south, nine generations past. So we keep the old chants,
chants telling of dawn ages, when the Lizard Kings came
down from stars and lent us wisdom. They were the first
beings ever rising above beasts, the first crossing from star to
star. They taught us to recognize our own hearts. They gave
us many gifts and took no counter-gift. This was their last gift:
we call it the Index of Tones, the Great Cube. Come and we
shall hear its song."

They climbed down, moving more slowly now that their
goal was in sight. It grew and grew with each step they took
until it blanked out half the sky.

Awed though he was, Yuzen could not refrain from asking
the question that had haunted human scholars for thousands of
years. "The Tzokol were mighty beyond the dreams of any
living culture. How then could they vanish so completely, and
where did they go?"

Ophiz said nothing for several breaths: Yuzen's words
seemed to have been swallowed by the night and forgotten.
But then, as if he were merely thinking aloud, the Tu'u began
to speak.

"The Lizard Kings loved knowledge, loved things, loved
knowledge about things. This universe of worlds and stars was
for them a puzzle to solve. See how like children they were,
yes? They learned more and more, and with their learning
came fear. For they saw this universe as a snare, as an illusion. A trap set by hungry *ahrit* for wild *ihya'at*. Their instruments let them see clearly, more clearly into the true nature of
things. What they saw was evil's face."

Ophiz continued speaking in the Ptok language, but his

words were metamorphosing into poetry, into fluent and impassioned song. "This they taught us, the Lizard Kings who came down from the sky. The world is a place of punishment, a vast dark prison. You see the cruelty of Ynenga. Is it not so everywhere? The Lizard Kings wandered long through worlds and generations, and in all worlds they found suffering. They helped where they could but there was little they could do. Everywhere sentient beings know hunger and death.

"The only answer they found was to escape from the bonds that bind us. And the only escape is by turning inward. We cannot shatter the prison holding us, so we must shrink, shrink so small that we pass through the bars. We must go back to the embryo, back to the seed, back to the spark that flashed before all things. Here is the only goodness in all existence: for here is God, the hidden, the secret. When we find that spark we will escape from the world of evil."

The Tu'u's voice returned to its ordinary tones. "So the Tzokol taught us at time's overture. We preserve always their teachings, for so many contain useful things. But in the center is this thing concerning life's evil. And this one we never properly understand." He trilled a few notes, which the humans recognized as laughter. "I try to give you what the old songs tell, but in your speech so much falls at improper intervals. My people hear sour notes there too. We realize, yes, life offers dissonance, but also we hear deep concord. Even pain has songs to sing."

"I begin to see why the Tzokol chose oblivion," said Yuzen. "But you still haven't told us how."

"Only they know, and there are none left to say. They came to us one last time. They said they had found a way to penetrate reality's fabric. They had learned how to rip through to the realm of light beyond all things. And they were eager to pass on. They left us this monument so we would never forget what they did.

"Then they departed. As far as we know, all vanished at once, with all the things they made. Some say they even smashed their homeworld. Certainly none can find it now."

"Suicide," Yuzen whispered. "*Seppuku*—but no. There was no shame. They were mad. They were revolted by the very fact of existence. They destroyed their own civilization to escape that revulsion."

The Great Cube was now directly before them. Its earlier

glamour had dissipated, driven off no doubt by Ophiz's pessimistic sermon. Now its squareness seemed an exposition of the mundane world, squat and graceless, a monument to the horror of thing-ness. Attanio muttered, "So they crawled up their own assholes and were heard from no more."

They mounted the steps and passed between two square pillars, entering the Cube's substructure. Humans and Wiwa alike switched on electric torches.

They were in a lofty chamber about ten meters square. For a moment Attanio thought his ears were ringing; then he realized he was hearing a pure musical tone, carried down from somewhere above him. It was high and thin, at the very limit of human perception. Ophiz led them through this chamber so quickly that there was no time to examine it in any detail; they were left with an impression of visual dullness.

The next chamber was also square, but much smaller. It too housed a single ambient tone of slightly flatter pitch.

They hurried from room to room, wherever Ophiz guided them. Many of the chambers had several possible exits, so that only the Tu'u's knowledge of the overall layout saved them from wandering in aimless circles. Ophiz never hesitated; he always knew which way to turn. And slowly the humans realized that he was guiding them through a melody. Its progress was stately, its intervals unfamiliar, but it definitely struck them as melody and not just random tones. It proceeded with a clearly perceptible structure—exposition, repetition, abbreviation, recombination, and reiteration. And yet this progress, this structure, was entirely determined by the action of their own feet, and by Ophiz' choice of itinerary. Audience participation with a vengeance, Attanio thought wryly. He wondered if they would eventually retrace their steps and hear the whole thing in reverse.

After a good hour of vigorous musical hiking Ophiz called a halt, in a chamber reverberating in *basso profundissimo*. "We have crossed only a few of the chambers this Cube contains, heard only one of the thousands of possible songs." The alien's spindly shadow loomed over them on the grooved walls; it was a scene from a nightmare. "This was one of the outer paths. Now I will show you an inner path."

They set off through another, much smaller maze of rooms. Now the chambers were hexagonal, recalling the cells of a beehive, and their ambient tones were frequently outside the range of human hearing. Nevertheless the humans experienced paramusical effects: chills, goosebumps, nausea, occasional stabs of headache. None of it was pleasant. Attanio asked Ophiz if he were similarly discomforted; the Tu'u, however, said he only experienced a mood of bittersweet sorrow.

This sequence climaxed in a large chamber quite unlike any other they had seen. Its pitch was mid-range, soothing, and it contained a variety of objects cast in polymerized stone. They were sculptures of a sort, a collection of solid geometric figures: cubes, cones, cylinders, spheres, pyramids, icosahedra, and so forth, ranging in size from toys that would fit in the palm of the hand to colossi ten meters high. All were the dull grey of the Cube's interior walls.

Here as nowhere else the ambient pitch was in the process of modulation. What at first seemed gentle and unstressed slowly became tense, abrasive, threatening. Even Ophiz was affected. They did not linger. As they exited, however, they heard the tone relaxing toward its original level: was the effect based merely on the listener's position?

The third and last melody they heard within the Great Cube was a sort of recessional: uplifting, unthreatening, somehow familiar. It was of briefer duration than the other two. As it ended they emerged from the Cube into the silver light of just-before-dawn, with the stars paling and a hint of radiance on the eastern horizon. They felt a powerful relief.

For a time they just squatted on the broad steps of the Cube, their backs to the frowning megalith. Ophiz was standing well apart from them in perfect stillness.

"What do you suppose was the point of all that?" asked Yuzen.

"Maybe this." Attanio held out his hand. In it was a tiny grey tetrahedron.

"You stole it!"

The Parmenite laughed. "It's not the first thing I've ever stolen."

"But—aren't you afraid?"

"Of what? The wrath of the Tzokol? The disapproval of the Wiwa?"

"I was thinking more of the little object itself. We have no idea what it is. It might have—unpleasant properties."

Attanio presented a profile, chin on fist. "You're right, of course. I've no defense. I really have no idea why I even took it. It just seemed to make sense."

"Maybe it's a good luck charm." But Yuzen's tone was dubious.

"That's what I was thinking. Look, when we get off this dried-up mummy of a world maybe my little souvenir will prove valuable. Maybe we could sell it for a small fortune. Anyway, I'm keeping it for now." With that he dropped the tetrahedron into his belt pouch, next to the two Suutish gems Sringlë had given him so many light years back.

By now it was daybreak. Ophiz had begun his hymn of greeting, and as if in echo a great chorus of voices floated down from the nearby hills. It was the rest of the Wiwa, *ihya'at* and all. They had arrived all unnoticed while the humans conversed, moving with their usual ghostly silence.

In the east only one sun was rising. "This is the day!" Yuzen exclaimed. "Their holy day, the eclipse!"

And all around the valley of the Cube, as if melting out of the rocks, parties of Tu'u were arriving—the first non-Wiwa the Galactics had ever seen or heard. They came in groups of ten or twenty, singing all the while. But no two groups sang the same song, or even the same language. Some had liquid fluting voices, much like the Wiwa, but others cawed harshly or gurgled darkly or screamed shrilly, or produced sounds like sandpaper rasping on wood, or wind sighing. These were human reactions, of course: for the Tu'u it was all music. And even for human ears these hundreds of singers somehow did not add up to a cacaphonous din, but rather produced a weird shifting chord like the sound of waves breaking, or a jungle nocturne, a steady process of nature rather than any device of sentient beings.

Attanio and Yuzen sought the shade of the Cube's overhang and settled in for an hour or so of serious listening. The disparate voices blended more and more as the different bands felt each other out, and periodically the chorus would fade, so that a single individual was heard clearly. A sort of call-and-response pattern emerged; very often the soloist turned out to be Ophiz himself, to the humans' amazement. Their guide and mentor seemed to be a personage of global importance.

"Maybe he's their star singer, like I was in Ashbeck," Attanio whispered.

"Egotist," Yuzen replied. "Maybe he's a prophet or a saint. Which you certainly are not."

The massed chorale ended, incredibly enough, on a long unison drone. This blended imperceptibly into the normal sounds of a crowd of Tu'u—conversation, bursts of trilled laughter, lowing of *ihya'at*. There was much mingling, much renewal of old acquaintance. The human pair attracted no obvious attention; they merely stood on the fringe like the alien outsiders they were.

In time a small procession came their way. It was a band of Tu'u unknown to them, carrying a bundle wrapped in hides. As they approached, some members of the band pointed at Yuzen, gesturing towards his startling mane of hair. But as they came closer still all such frivolity subsided; a hush fell over everyone as they lay the bundle down.

Strange, uncanny, to feel a chill under Ynenga's blistering suns. But from out of that furry shroud came a cascade of silvery hair. And attached to that hair was the corpse of a Martian warrior.

Attanio cried out. Yuzen made no sound at all, falling to his knees beside the shrivelled mummy of his brother. The irony was too profound, too painful. It was Yencho, or what remained of him, whom Attanio had last seen during their flight from Loei Station, whom Yuzen had last seen at the fall of Tharsis. It was immediately clear what had happened. His lifepod, number seven, must also have escaped the Viharnese attack and landed on Ynenga. But he had not been as lucky as they in surviving the planet's cruelty.

The multitudes stood well back from this spectacle of grief. Avoiding death's pollution on their holy day, Attanio thought. He recognized Ophiz in the crowd, but even he kept his distance.

An explanation eventually came their way, delivered of course through Ophiz' translation. A tribe calling itself Ahsyi had found the wreckage of a lifepod only three days' march to the north of this valley. Naturally they had explored it, uncovering Yencho's body in the process. As the Galactics could see for themselves he had suffered grave injuries. The crash must have disabled him, and there, alone, with no one to look after him, he had died. Ynenga's aridity had preserved his body from corruption until the Ahsyi stumbled upon it. They had carried the corpse along with them to Shiie, to seek the advice of the other tribes.

On Ynenga even dead aliens were objects of wonder.

Once the Ahsyi had reached the valley of the Cube, once the sun-greeting was concluded, they had learned of the presence of living offworlders among them. And so their pathetic offering.

It was mid-morning by now. The crowd was breaking up in good spirits, trickling away toward their ultimate destination: Shiie. From a discreet distance Ophiz spoke to the two humans. "These people of Ahsyi will stay with you now and help you bury your kinsman. I must go with my people into Shiie. It is very close, a matter of a few hours. The Ahsyi will guide you there when it is fitting. I will seek you out. Until then."

And he was gone. Yuzen and Attanio carried Yencho's body to the nearby hills, and with the Ahsyi's help dug a grave in the sand. Without ceremony they heaped it over with more sand and rock to make a crude cairn. Yuzen said very little; the Tu'u however seemed to expect a greater formality. When none was forthcoming they provided it themselves in the form of a deep rumbling dirge.

None of these tribesmen knew any Ptok Prime. Still they managed to communicate a few simple ideas through charades and onomatopoeia, chief among them the ritual necessity that they all stay there by the grave until sunset. Given the heat, this was an unwelcome vigil—but they had no choice.

So the hours wore on. The Ahsyi spoke idly among themselves in their booming dialect, apparently well content to rest out the day. They produced food and made a picnic, offering some to the humans with typical Ynengan hospitality. For their part Attanio and Yuzen nibbled on a few tidbits and dozed through the afternoon.

"I am the last," Yuzen said finally, breaking a long silence. They squatted in the shade of some rocks watching the conjoined suns' slow, slow descent. "I was the youngest of Prince Myobu's heirs. Now everyone but me has come to a violent end. We knew such glory in our time, never dreaming what would come. We looked forward to a proud future, building an empire with Mars as its crown and ourselves as its protectors. Now see how low we've fallen."

"The past is a dream, no?" Attanio spoke in a feeble attempt at consolation. "You still live. You've done all you can. Why, by rights you're the Prince of the Shinjuku now, aren't you? Though I suppose there are no Shinjuku left to be Prince of. But look at me. My mother died when I was a child, and she was all the family I ever had. It's not so bad being the last of your line. Forget you're a Martian."

Yuzen managed to smile. "You're miserable at comforting the bereaved. But yes, why not; from today I'll just be a Galactic bum like you."

"It's really a lot easier," Attanio said cheerfully.

Sunset came at long last and they set out for Shiie. The path was uneven, crossing broken hills and valleys heaped with rubble. But by now the humans were old hands at this kind of journey and took it in stride, moving almost as easily as the Ahsyi.

Eventually, they came to Shiie.

It turned out to be a village not too different from what might be found on any primitive human world: a great jumble of clay huts. There were squat towers with pointed thatch roofs, low walls pierced with triangular holes, and squarish houses covered with grooved designs, painted a faded ochre. In form, texture, and color, the whole village blended seamlessly with its surroundings; like everything the Tu'u did it was a perfect complement to its environment.

But this revelation of Ynengan architecture didn't hold their attention long—not when there was something else far more interesting in sight. A hundred meters away from the edge of town, squatting on the dunes, was a veilship.

Attanio suddenly found that he was crying. "Yuzen, Yuzen, it's there—we made it!" He would have started running madly if his friend hadn't held him back.

"Don't lose your caution now," Yuzen said quietly. "You've always been the suspicious one—use your head."

"I guess you're right. We'll have to cook up some story—obviously we can't tell them the truth, whoever they are." But Attanio still felt a rising exhilaration, and he could tell by looking at Yuzen's face that it was shared.

They spent a few moments taking stock. They were gaunt, dusty, filthy—like wild men. Anything they said to these starfarers would be doubted, questioned, weighed against their dubious circumstances.

"We may as well tell them we're criminals, right?" Attanio joked. "They'd have to believe that."

"I think we can come up with something a little better," Yuzen countered.

A few minutes later they were calling up to the airlock of the great ship. The Ahsyi tagged along, evidently intending to maintain custody until everything was settled. Their spindly alien figures made an appropriate entourage for the two wild-men of the desert.

Lights flickered. The ship's port slid aside with a hiss. Two human males stood framed in the doorway, and one of them swore in amazement.

"Black tits of Maria! Where in nine hells did you come from?"

Attanio did the talking. "We're exiles, mate. We come from Ashbeck on Parmenio, and we've spent close to a standard month on this dustball. We're looking for a way off."

The man who had first spoken climbed down the gangway, while his companion stayed where he was covering the scene with a particle gun. Both were copper skinned and dressed in plain baggy jumpsuits. The chief negotiator was of middling height, broad and powerfully built, his age indeterminate but well past the first bloom of youth. Curly brown hair fell down his back in a bundle of tiny braids, and his eyes were flinty and narrow.

"Name's Damashek," he allowed. "My partner's Bezoza and this is our ship. If you're looking for passage maybe we can arrange something—but first I want to hear a little more of your story."

"I'm Attanio Hwin, and this is my sworn companion Jaime Vargasz." They had deemed it prudent to conceal Yuzen's origin: to this end, his hair was bound up in a hastily improvised turban. "We used to work the Flicker Circuit in Ashbeck, doing cybercabaret. Maybe you recognize me? I was pretty famous."

Damashek looked closely into the grimy fox face. "I don't think your own mother would recognize you today, pal. But yes, we've passed through Ashbeck from time to time. Where did you play?"

"Mostly the Succubarium and the Necrotek."

Damashek glanced back at his partner. "At least he knows a thing or two about Ashbeck. Why don't you sing us a song, or something. Show us what you used to do."

So there in the soft radiance of newly risen Yif, over the millennial sands of mummified Ynenga, Attanio performed an excerpt from one of his nastiest and most popular numbers:

Why Can't Girls Be More Like Boys? In spite of themselves the starmen burst into a chorus of guffaws, and even the Ahsyi mumbled appreciation—without understanding a word.

"All right, now at least we know you're really what you claim to be." All trace of humor had passed from Damashek's face. "Next you better explain how you happen to be on Ynenga with no veilship in sight."

"Our own stupidity, really. If you know Ashbeck you must know Ypousef Makhlouf." Damashek nodded, with a trace of a scowl. "We got into trouble with him. We had a racket going with the doorman at the Succubarium to skim off the top of the nightly take. It was a pretty clever scheme, really—I used my stage synthesizer to key into the house account, and he told me how much I could safely doctor the figures every night before Makhlouf saw them. We had this whole signalling thing worked out—"

"Spare me the details. Just tell us what happened."

"Well, we got caught."

"Apparently. How come you're still breathing?"

"The doorman did get fried. But Makhlouf decided to be a little kinder to me and Jaime, for old time's sake."

"Meaning what?"

"Well, Makhlouf is my father."

Damashek whistled. "Only on Parmenio! So this was your punishment."

"That's right. He sent us out in one of his ships, and we were dropped off in the middle of the desert with just a couple of survival kits. We were lucky enough to hook up with some natives. Eventually we wound up here."

Damashek and Bezoza put their heads together for a minute. Then, for the first time, Bezoza spoke. He was tall and slightly built, with clear signs of advanced age. His face was wrinkled and weathered by a thousand suns, and what little hair remained on his head was snow white.

"Well, friends, you tell a good story," he said in well-modulated tones. "And after all, you *are* fellow humans in distress, so we're inclined to help you. But we're a small operation. We play it close to the line. If we give you passage, how will you pay us?"

Attanio was ready for that one. He held up one of the teardrop-shaped jewels of Suut so that it sparkled pink and violet in the starshine, and asked, "Will this do?"

Bezoza examined the stone with a practiced eye, nodding slowly. "I think this will do nicely. Where were you thinking of going?"

"That depends a lot on you, I guess. What's your itinerary?"

"Actually this is a special run," said Bezoza. "We would normally be heading back to home base on Phayao when we're finished here."

Attanio's heart gave a lurch at the mention of Sringlë's homeworld, though his face did nothing to betray him. These men must be her fellow citizens. "That's not too far from where we want to go, as the Veil twists. We thought we'd try our luck with the Maung, and head for Srasuri in Luo Viharn."

Damashek barked out a short laugh. "You won't get far playing cheap swindles on those guys, I'll clue you."

The Parmenite smiled. "We thought we'd play it straight for a change. Viharn is rich—I'm hoping I can sing for my supper there."

"Maybe," Bezoza said. "Obviously you can't go back to Ashbeck, and there aren't too many other places where your talents would be appreciated."

So the bargain was concluded. For the price of one Suutish gemstone, Damashek and Bezoza would carry them to Srasuri. Departure was four days away.

2

Even after all the time they had spent among the Wiwa nothing prepared the two humans for Shiie's downright alienness. Ophiz had arranged for them to stay in a tiny one-roomed house, but in spite of this unaccustomed comfort they passed the next few days in a state of bewilderment.

Everywhere there was constant activity, day and night. It was impossible to say what was ritual and what was ordinary spontaneous behavior. Most of it revolved around the younglings, who by their second day at Shiie had definitely completed the transition to femininity. They were herded by their kinsfolk along the winding alleyways of the town, presented at feasts and gatherings, harangued and extolled, made to perform an endless succession of songs and dances, all the while bedecked in the most bizarre finery imaginable. Fragile headdresses like lampshades wobbled on their heads. Flakes of mica spangled their delicate snouts, sparkling and flashing in the double sunlight. Chains of scrap metal festooned their torsoes; strings of tiny bells chimed at their feet. For the Tu'u, at least, they were the embodiment of girlish charm.

Shiie was undermined by a network of caverns and catacombs at least as extensive as the upper town itself. Here the most solemn ceremonies occurred. As outsiders, Yuzen and Attanio were not allowed to attend, even though they had eavesdropped on the gathering by the Great Cube; but they heard rumor enough of what went on. Strange powders were burned while the Tu'u sat entranced amid swirling vapors, dreaming dreams and hearing the voices of their ancestors. Sing-alongs were held from dusk till dawn, with massed choirs accompanied by percussionists pounding on huge hollow stones. The noise of these ensembles seeped up through the ground and kept the humans company all night long.

Damashek and Bezoza, meanwhile, tried to be everywhere at once with their microphones and lasers. Years earlier the Tu'u had granted them a concession to make audio recordings of selected rituals, provided they supplied Ynenga with a wide variety of trade goods. They had since turned a tidy profit marketing their cubes among the civilized worlds of the Antares Reach. Their own homeworld was particularly receptive to the subtleties of Ynengan music. Therefore Yuzen and Attanio saw very little of them during the four days they sojourned at Shiie.

Likewise Ophiz was rarely at hand, occupied as he was with ceremonial and negotiation. His absence left the two humans rather cast adrift, since only one or two among that whole multitude knew any offworld tongue. They had come to depend on his explanations, his interpretations of all the bewildering facets of Tu'u existence, and now that he was no longer their constant companion they realized how much they missed him simply for the pleasure of his company. He had always been baffling, inscrutable, unpredictable—in a word, alien—and yet somehow he inspired deep affection.

Then on the eve of their departure Ophiz came to visit. Attanio had just lit a stone lamp fueled by *ihya'at* droppings, and Yuzen was finishing up with the packing, such as it was. The Wiwa's spindly figure loomed suddenly in the doorway;

in that inimitable voice he called out a blessing on the house
as he stepped in to greet them.

"The men of Phayao tell me that tomorrow you leave us."
Ophiz arranged his long limbs in a sitting posture on the floor.
His angular frame balanced the room's alien proportions.
"You are determined to go, then?"

The humans were confused: how could there be any question about it?

"It seems we must," Attanio replied. "The Wiwa, the
Ahsyi, the Shiie have all been kind to us, but nothing can
change the fact that Ynenga will not support human life, at
least over a long period of time. We could sicken and die if we
stayed."

The great dark eyes blinked once, twice. "Perhaps. But
you have survived very well. Here at Shiie you gain flesh,
your faces shine again."

Choosing his words carefully, Yuzen said, "Ynenga is
beautiful, Ynenga holds many mysteries. Attanio and I have
grown in wisdom and strength here. You are a great and kind
teacher, a most excellent being to whom we are grateful
beyond words. But I have a duty to my sole surviving kinsman, who even now may be a prisoner on Viharn. We must go
and seek him out."

"Ah, a duty to the tribe." This Ophiz understood. "Then it
must be so." Now he seemed to change the subject. "The
other humans, the ones who buy our songs, they do not seem
to have learned of the Great Cube. Have you not told them?
Could they not see it in the desert as they came down in their
ship?"

"Not necessarily," Yuzen answered. "It blends in nicely
with the sand and rocks surrounding it, at least when seen
from above. If you weren't looking for it, it could be easy to
miss."

"And we didn't tell them anything," Attanio said, answering the Wiwa's first question. "We thought it should be your
decision whether or not they should know about it."

"Yes, yes," Ophiz agreed. "But don't you trust these
men?"

They both shrugged. "We trust them enough," Attanio
said, "but not too much. They're pretty tough characters. We
just have to be careful."

Ophiz winked in affirmation. "Certainly be careful. And as

for the Lizard Kings' monument, other humans will learn of it soon enough and come down with their instruments and machines. It doesn't matter. They will find nothing that makes any difference. Soon they will abandon it again."

He stayed awhile longer, sharing bowls of the fiery Ynengan wine and discussing the progress of the local festivities. Yuzen and Attanio savored every moment of his presence. Then, with a courtly farewell, he was gone. Neither human doubted that they had seen the last of this wise and gentle being, their only friend in an unfriendly world.

XI. Damashek and Bezoza

Just before dawn the next day they hurried out to the desert where the Phayonese veilship lay. Bezoza appeared at the portal, ushered them in, and showed them to their berths. Then he disappeared. A moment later they felt the gentle pulse of the drive as it engaged. Without any sense of acceleration they were carried up into the void, leaving Ynenga's wrinkled yellow globe behind them forever.

Cho Tzrep was the ship's name—a Ptok expression meaning roughly, "We've got nothing to lose." Since most private ships were christened something like *Lucky Flux* or *Flower of Ptanga* or *Vimnathi's Dream,* this was an eccentric choice, suggesting an equally eccentric crew. She was a tiny vessel of the Turtle class, designed for takeoff and landing from planetary surfaces, as most veilships were not. She was also something of a relic. Yuzen and Attanio guessed that her maiden voyage had occurred a good two-and-a-half standard centuries earlier.

Her appointments were a far cry from the luxuries of *Samuindorogo.* There was nothing that was not strictly functional, nothing that was not worn by generations of hard use. There was a bridge, where they were never allowed to venture; a stateroom each for Damashek and Bezoza, also off limits; a combination lounge-galley-library-gym open to all; a dormitory; and the cargo hold. The dormitory was a cramped room containing six enclosed bunks, each one large enough to accommodate two sleepers, if so desired. Toilet and washroom were in tiny closets opening onto this chamber.

A few hours into the voyage Yuzen and Attanio discovered that *Cho Tzrep* carried more than a two-man crew. They were sitting idly in the common room when two strange individuals entered from the direction of the bridge. At first glance they didn't seem human. Closer inspection revealed that they were, and female at that.

"Well you needn't stare," one said pleasantly enough. "You'll see enough of us over the next few days. You must be those crazies who walked out of the desert carrying a fortune in jewels."

"Hardly a fortune," Attanio protested. "I'm Attanio and this is Jaime."

"Pleased to meet you. My name is Ilah."

"And I'm Shihr."

The two women were of a physical type neither of them had seen before. Small and delicate, with sharply defined, almost elfin features, they seemed creatures of myth. Neither one stood taller than Attanio's breastbone, which gave them the semblance of oddly wise children; but their physical proportions and air of confidence were definitely grown-up. Their skin was an unappealing slate-grey, and its uneven texture hinted at scales. Their skulls were lofty, narrow, and practically bald. What hair they did have grew in scattered blue tufts; it was impossible to say whether this was the result of nature or artifice, and the occasion certainly precluded any intimate questions.

"Forgive our curiosity," Yuzen said, "but where in the galaxy are you from? I've never had the pleasure of meeting anyone of your race before."

"Pretty talk!" Ilah made a moue. "But oh, are we ever used to it. We come from Wajj. That's well outside the Antares Reach, toward the Core. Our people are the descendants of an unsuccessful experiment in gene-manip. We were designed to colonize an oceanic world, but things didn't work out, so the Sun Company resettled us on Wajj. Bless their hearts."

"Wajj is in an ice age," Shihr explained. Her voice was softer, shyer than strident Ilah's. "We weren't cold-adapted at all. We're still not really at home there, even after a thousand years."

"Though we did adapt well enough so that someplace like Ynenga is sheer hell," Ilah put in, with some eye-rolling. "That's why we never disembarked while we were there."

Neither woman had sat down, so it didn't seem to be the time for any long conversations. Still, Attanio wanted to learn as much about them as he could, on general principles; Damashek and Bezoza had been extremely uninformative on all particulars.

"You must be crew, right?"

"We're Adepts, trained in Luo Viharn." Ilah did the answering—and rather proudly at that.

"How long have you worked for Damashek and Bezoza?"

The women exchanged unreadable glances. "Half a standard year, I suppose. We won't be staying on past this run."

Attanio's ears pricked up. "Lousy pay?"

Both women laughed. "You guessed it," Ilah replied. "We only took the job because we were down and out, and on Phayao they send indigent foreigners to the tuba factory. That's where we met up with these characters. They're not bad guys but they do hate to part with their money."

"What sort of cargo do they usually carry?"

Ilah snickered. Shihr said quietly. "You know they can monitor any part of the ship whenever they want to."

"I never thought otherwise," Attanio retorted. "Jaime and I are from Parmenio," he added, as if that explained everything.

"Then you can probably guess," Ilah said. "What else can a ship this size carry and still turn a profit? A few luxury items, yes—this run is a good example of that. They were definitely smart to wrangle those concessions from the Tu'u. But mostly what they carry is drugs and weapons. They have an understanding of some sort with the Maung fleet." She raised her eyes to the ceiling. "There! You don't care if they know that much, do you?"

There was no reply.

Yuzen and Attanio nodded, and the former said, "If they're so cozy with the Maung, I suppose we won't be having any legal problems as long as we're aboard."

The two Wajji were already on their way to the dormitory, but Ilah turned back with a sly grin. "Were you expecting any?"

Both men just shrugged innocently and said nothing.

2

It took three days of acceleration to reach the threshold of the Veil. During that time Yuzen and Attanio relaxed and took things easy, eating and sleeping a lot to recover from the ordeal of Ynenga. While cramped and spartan, *Cho Tzrep* was comfortable enough.

They socialized with the Wajji during the women's off-shift; as Ilah had forseen, it was impossible not to. There was no bunk-hopping, however; in fact the Wajji slept together, so the men had no qualms about doing the same. To their surprise this scandalized Ilah.

After their first sleep-shift, she said in tones of mild incredulity, "You two slept in the same bed."

"That's right," Yuzen replied blandly. "Everything's soundproofed, isn't it?"

"Yes, but—"

"You and Shihr do the same thing."

"I wouldn't be too sure of that." Laughing.

"Oh?"

"Well, we're from Wajj. It's cold there. There's no such thing as sleeping alone. Whole families sleep together just to keep warm."

"But this ship is very well heated."

"Of course, but the habit is so ingrained in us that it would be unthinkable not to share a bed with someone. I know I'd never fall asleep. I'd feel—incomplete."

"I see," Attanio chimed in with mock gravity. "Are we offending your Wajji morals?"

"No, no, you just surprised me—that's all." She smiled.

"Maybe you'd be happier if we all slept together."

This brought peals of merriment and a quick babble of the Wajji dialect. "Shihr and I would love it," Ilah said. "It would be just like home."

But as it turned out their sleep-shifts didn't coincide again until after Puncture, so in the meantime they had to content themselves with video games and small talk.

One off-shift Bezoza decided to be friendly. He proceeded to get high on blood crystals in the common room, inviting his two passengers to join in. He then held forth on his checkered past shipping among the Maung worlds. His anecdotes and ironies quickly put Yuzen and Attanio at their ease.

After an hour or so the subject somehow shifted to politics, and the prevailing currents of history. "There's no standing still," Bezoza declared, his eyes bloodshot and his voice furry. "The Maung think they're maintaining the status quo but what we have here is decadence. We should be striding forward into the future, not tumbling ass-first into chaos."

"Then what program would you recommend?" Yuzen asked politely.

"Free trade, first of all—a large-scale interstellar commerce the way there was under the Fujiwaras. Of course we don't have the ships for that right now, but we could build them. The Maung play it too high and mighty out here in the Reach. They hoard their wealth and keep their technologies secret, instead of sharing everything with their fellow men. All the poorer systems need is some backing; then they could start making their own contributions to galactic civilization. We could have a commonwealth of equals here, a great glittering constellation of sovereign worlds—but instead we're just being exploited to feather the nests of a few rich Viharnese twits."

"Do I detect a certain antipathy to the Maung?" Attanio teased.

"Antipathy, resentment, and frustration. All my life I've nipped at their heels like a dog, picking up whatever scraps I could, running whenever they aimed a good kick in my direction. And I swear to you it's been the absolute best any man could do. They won't allow any better. Their policy is to keep the peasants down, to maintain a low profile, to create poverty and disorder throughout the Reach of Antares."

Yuzen had never thought about any of this before; it puzzled him. "What can they be afraid of?"

"Ah! Good question." Bezoza's voice squeaked with enthusiasm. "They're afraid of success. They're afraid of empire. Empires are synonymous with struggle and war, and after every rise there inevitably follows a collapse. Human history has demonstrated the same pattern for ten thousand years; the Maung seem determined not to fall into that particular trap. But meanwhile they've fallen into another one—the trap of hesitation, indecision, failure of leadership."

"It doesn't quite seem human, does it."

"Not by half. And here's the crux of the matter. Behind everything the Viharnese do you must look for the Xuun. I'm not saying they're in control, but they certainly do exert some profound influence, in ways that even I don't quite understand. They're not puppeteers pulling strings, no; they're more like unconscious motivations subtly guiding conscious deeds. They're a light that we only know by its shadows."

"On Parmenio we tell jokes and stories about the Xuun," Attanio said, "but neither Jaime nor I really know anything about them."

"Nor do I know much more," confessed Bezoza, sprinkling a few more cyrstals onto his rosy tongue. "Individually, they're not intelligent beings, that much I've learned. They have powerful instinctive drives that allow them to function collectively in great hives, something like the bees of Old Earth. But they're not properly insects at all. That is, they might remind you of bugs if you ever got a look at them, but they've got lungs and blood vessels and they're about a meter high—at least the ergatives are. The warriors are another story, and the imagoes. . . . Well! They interact quite successfully with human beings, which does mislead you into thinking *they* can think, but actually they just seem to be organic robots carrying out the commands of an incredibly detailed and incredibly powerful program. No one can fathom how it all came about. The best guess is that they were some sort of experiment of the Tzokol which survived its makers' downfall."

"The poor Tzokol get blamed for everything humans can't explain," Attanio protested.

Bezoza laughed. "Convenient catchall, aren't they. But of course there's the possibility of independent evolution. Who knows what nature can come up with, given enough time. Humans have only been around for three million years. Honeybees go back about seventy-five million. We can't comprehend that much time any better than we can conceptualize the real-space distance between one star system and the next. Anyhow honeybees stopped evolving a good fifty million years back—but what if they hadn't? Maybe they too would have learned how to build crystal towers a hundred meters high, and turn continents into flower gardens, and raise interplanetary rocketships in their nurseries."

"The Xuun can do all that, eh? What about the Veil—can they glide through the Translux too?"

"Absolutely not." Bezoza struck fist to palm in emphasis. "That's beyond them, physically, psychically, and intellectually."

Yuzen nodded. "Then there's no threat of great swarms of them descending on the galaxy and picking it clean."

"What a relief!" Attanio cried.

"No, no threat of that," Bezoza agreed. "But their isolation, in a sense, makes the Xuun a target. They live on a planet that any number of starfaring races might consider prime real estate. Over fifty million years—I'm just using that number for the sake of argument, you understand—they seem to have learned how to avoid conquest by any expanding interstellar empires, and we know they've come into contact with at least two."

"Meaning the Tzokol and the humans?" Attanio asked.

"That's right—assuming, of course, that the Tzokol didn't manufacture them in the first place."

"So how do they do it? How do they manipulate sophisticated aliens?"

Bezoza spread his hands. "Most of what I've been saying is sheer personal fantasy, so don't take me seriously as I go off the deep end. But I'd guess that they've got something to offer sentient beings that's more attractive than a colony on a nice habitable planet, and more advantageous to their own physical well-being in the bargain."

"Immortality?" Attanio guessed.

"Immortality!" Bezoza made a rude noise. "That old scam! Everybody's got immortality—the Lumis, the Loeyo, the Fujiwara board of directors, the pirates of Parmenio. No, I don't think so."

"Then what?"

Bezoza shrugged a pair of frail old shoulders. "Just a guess, you understand. But how about—direct personal contact with God?"

Attanio laughed nervously; Yuzen maintained his typical Martian composure. "Do you mean some kind of religion?" he asked.

"No, no," Bezoza said, a bit impatiently. "Religion is to God as pornography is to sex. I'm not talking about peep shows. I'm talking about the real thing."

"A revelation of the divine," Yuzen murmured. "A conversion, in effect. An experience of gnosis. Hypnosis, perhaps? Some sophisticated form of thought control?"

"You could call it that," Bezoza conceded, "but somehow it doesn't sound as compelling as the way I put it."

"To you, that is," Attanio said. "But no matter how it's phrased I find I like the idea. And I'm told that no outsiders are actually allowed on the surface of Viharn—Phra Viharn, I should say. That immediately gets me to guessing about what's down there. Vast temples? Cloistered gardens filled with ecstatic worshippers? Chrome-plated anthills crawling with human slaves, and Xuun hierophants subsisting on a diet of newborn babies?"

"So my foolishness is contagious." Bezoza's voice held a certain tired satisfaction. "I've had those nightmares too. All I can say is that we just don't know. Phra Viharn guards her secrets too well."

"But let's get back to what you were saying before," Yuzen urged, "about the decadence of the Antares Reach, about the way Maung policies encourage poverty and decline. How does this serve Xuun interests?"

"Camouflage," he replied. "What would-be invader would bother with a backward region of space like this one? It has nothing to offer. There's Lumiphat, of course, and the fungus of immortality, but that's a wild card. It's nothing that could be exploited on a large scale. Even Viharn isn't a rich world, judged by the standards of the Sun Company in its heyday. That leaves a dozen or so dingy backwaters like Parmenio, Phayao, and our friendly deathtrap Ynenga. The Antares Reach is the garbage dump of this whole spiral arm."

"Hey, it's still home!" Attanio protested.

"True enough," Bezoza said dryly. "I don't enjoy providing cover for a race of organic robots myself." Then his tone shifted abruptly back to its earlier lightheartedness. "But let's not worry about the affairs of the galaxy. We have our own lives to lead, and that's not necessarily such a bad thing, is it? Forgive an old man who likes to daydream about the mysteries of time and stars."

So they did, lapping up one more round of blood crystals. But like a child who can't resist picking scabs, Attanio had to ask one last question about the enigmatic Xuun.

"You theorize that the Xuun are in effect hiding from possible invaders. But where in space would they come from? As far as we know, there are no powerful starfaring races left anywhere in this region of the galaxy."

"My dear boy," Bezoza replied, "you're speaking from an extremely limited perspective. At this very instant there could be a million deathships en route to Xuun, and until they came within fifty light years, none of us could possibly know anything about them. Or such a fleet could arrive in a thousand years: you see, the Xuun are an ancient race, and in whatever fashion they do it they're used to thinking in astronomical terms. They take a very, very long view." He sipped some weak green tea, and a little smile played at the corner of his lips. "You know recently I picked up a strange rumor at Phayao station, talking to an old Maung spacer I know there. He said the Martians were coming."

Everyone had to laugh at that hoary old line, willingly or not.

"Yes," Bezoza continued, "he told me the Maung fleet had captured a Martian scout ship full of spies, running surveillance on this sector for stars know what infernal purpose. Martians! And after all these centuries! It just goes to show you that anything can happen, and therefore the wise being, whether human individual or Xuun hive, will take all appropriate precautions."

3

Cho Tzrep lacked isolation tanks. Therefore Yuzen and Attanio decided to spend their passage through the Veil on drugs, since that seemed preferable to a descent into Level Twenty trance. When they finally climbed out of the haze, it was to greet both Wajji females returning to the dormitory from their stint on the bridge. As they had just emerged from Ablative mode, the last phase of reentry into the cis-lucid universe, they were as groggy and disoriented as the men; in fact there was almost a haunted look about them.

"Rough transit?" Attanio asked sympathetically.

"You might say that." Ilah spoke very slowly, though her eyes darted furtively around the room. Shihr as usual remained withdrawn.

Attanio had small experience with Adepts; he wasn't sure how proper it was to chat with them right after Puncture. But since he had little regard for propriety in any case, he kept at it.

"So we've arrived safely in the Viharnese system, right? Were you doing *pandiculari* or *labi?*"

"*Pandiculari,* of course. That's the hardest part." Her voice retained its leaden tonelessness. "It can be almost routine. But this time it was . . . well, just *different*. Especially the reentry. As if reality didn't want us back." Now she looked Attanio steadily in the eye. Hers were bloodshot and shadowed, in a face that even at its healthiest was grey.

Unexpectedly, Shihr spoke. "You've deceived us, haven't you. At least through omission. You're carrying something you shouldn't be."

"Shouldn't be?" Attanio echoed. He suddenly found himself on the defensive. "Whoever ordained the laws of the universe neglected to tell me what they were. I just stumble along as best I can. But please, make yourself a little clearer."

"You know how delicate Veil transits are," Ilah said. Both women had sprawled on the edge of a bunk. "There are so many factors that can upset them. Imperfect resonance between the two partners, insufficient preparation for Puncture, intrusive gravitational or magnetic fields, even outright telepathic assault." She paused to consider her next words. "I can't really accuse you of anything, nor do I want to. But there was something very odd about this Puncture. Its form was a pyramid, its color was no color at all, its attraction was all but inescapable. And its flavor most definitely suggested you, Attanio Hwin." She smiled. "Please give me the recipe."

Attanio and Yuzen exchanged glances; since Ynenga they could almost exchange thoughts, at least on occasion, and this seemed to be one of them. Both wanted to oblige Ilah but both were unwilling to betray the Tu'u's confidence, especially since Damashek and Bezoza might be listening. Through a few quick gestures they managed to suggest as much.

Ilah nodded and produced a small holoprojector from one of the lockers in the wall. "This is just a precaution," she murmured. "I doubt anyone is watching now. They're too busy programming our approach to Viharn." She aimed the projector toward the inner section of the dormitory, where a scene from an old historical romance shimmered into being. Characters dressed in the style of the Yadu period gestured and spoke dramatically, bounding off into violent action at the slightest provocation.

For a few minutes they all pretended to watch the story, just to avoid looking suspicious. Then Attanio withdrew the tiny Tzokol pyramid from his pouch and showed it to the two women.

"That's it," Shihr breathed.

Neither would touch it.

"That's what I felt out there in the Translux," Ilah said after a moment. She was no less exhausted than before, but now her curiosity lent her voice some animation. "That object is what held us back from the real universe. No human hands ever made it, did they?"

"The Tu'u say it came from the Tzokol."

"And they just gave it to you?" She was a bit incredulous.

"Not exactly."

"Ah, well. Being an Adept I can perceive with more than six senses, and that little pyramid is telling me more than I can comprehend. It exists here and now, in our commonly-agreed-upon reality, but it also has—shall I call them extensions?—into quite other places. It looks perfectly inert, but it's in a continuous state of transformation, of ontological flux."

"Aren't we all?"

"Oh, no doubt, but your pyramid there is off on its own tangent entirely. It's not in step with the rest of creation."

Attanio was perplexed. "I thought it was just a piece of stone. Its peculiarities—would they be obvious to any normal scanning procedures? Does it exhibit magnetic anomalies, or anything like that?"

Ilah shook her head. "Only someone with paranormal abilities, such as an Adept, would notice anything. And even we were unaware of it till we pierced the Veil. No, the authorities at Luo Viharn won't find anything odd, if that's what you're worried about."

"What about Damashek and Bezoza?"

"True, they have Adept training, but—they're just not as sensitive as Shihr and I. For example, neither one of them has any resonance with either of us. On this transit they were handling *labi,* which went okay, so I don't think they felt the . . . weirdness."

This came as a relief to Yuzen and Attanio. They considered themselves very much in the power of the two old pirates, and while there was no particular reason not to trust them, they still weren't at ease aboard *Cho Tzrep.*

"Do you have any idea what it is?" Attanio asked hopefully.

Ilah shrugged, looking exactly like an eight-year-old child.

"Maybe it's a toy. Maybe it's a kind of telepathic weapon. Maybe it's the Tzokol equivalent of a memory cube. Alien artifacts aren't my specialty."

"Do you feel any better knowing about it?" Yuzen's deep voice asked. "You seemed frightened before."

Ilah laughed but Shihr remained perfectly serious. "Yes, I do feel better," Ilah said. "I thought it was us—I was afraid we were slipping."

"I'm just glad you two are getting off in this system," Shihr added. "I know I couldn't do another Puncture with that thing aboard."

Hardly tactful of her, but there was no doubting her sincerity. Ilah gave a lopsided grin as the silence lengthened. "I have one question," she said finally. "Just what do you plan to do with that little speck of nightmare?"

"I thought I might sell it." Attanio's answer came without hesitation, but suddenly it didn't sound like such a good idea anymore.

Shortly after, the Wajji turned in for a well-earned rest, while Yuzen and Attanio remained in the dormitory talking softly under cover of the Yadu holodrama.

"This is it," Attanio was saying. "We've almost made it to the end of the line—and I think I'm going to be terrified."

"The prospect *is* pretty formidable." But Yuzen sounded confident. "From what Bezoza has said, the first step is to get a visa. And we don't have any documents at all—we're lucky that *Cho Tzrep*'s crew is prepared to vouch for us. Then we have to sell your Suutish jewel for survival money, in a place where we have no friends and no idea how to do such things. It's going to be interesting, no doubt about it."

"And then we just settle in and find out what we can about Teoru and Sringlë? That's the part that doesn't sit right with me. Isn't there something more dynamic we could do?"

"Of course. We could go before the authorities as soon as we dock and demand to know what's become of them. But somehow I don't think that will do us much good. Do you?"

"Certainly not. I meant—"

"The problem is that we're in a state of almost total ignorance. It was such a relief to hear Bezoza drop that remark about the captured Martian spies—that's the only evidence we have that we're on the right track. We still have no idea what the Maung do with political detainees. They may have inter-rogation techniques we've never dreamed of. They may prac-tice unspeakable tortures, barbaric excruciations. Then again maybe Teoru told all at the first opportunity, and maybe he's an honored guest of the Queen at this very moment, dining off silver plate and drinking out off eggshell porcelain."

"Dream on, friend. That's too good to be true."

"It's just as possible as anything else."

"But you are worried, aren't you?"

"Yes, I'll confess to a little uneasiness." Yuzen stared darkly out at the nearest wall. "Things looked bad when there was a whole crew of us with a starship at our disposal and Teoru at our head. Now see what's become of us."

Yes, just look, Attanio thought to himself. What am I doing in this mess?

For the thousandth time he reviewed the improbable chain of events that had led to his present quandary. He had always steered clear of involvements, yet now he was putting himself in danger, and not for the first time, over another man's prin-ciples: principles he himself hadn't the slightest use for. Loy-alty to the clan, and here he was an outcast. Vengeance for an outrage, committed on a planet he'd never seen. Honor to be restored, and he wasn't sure he knew the meaning of the word.

These were abstractions. In fact they only obscured the real issue, which was Attanio's very real devotion to three flesh-and-blood human beings; Sringlë, Teoru, and Yuzen. Once he was in touch with those feelings again, everything else made sense.

"I was just thinking," he confessed. "I was trying to find an alternative to the course we're following right now. Such as, what if we abandoned all our ties, forgot our commitments, and pretended that we were two free men with the whole An-tares Reach at our fingertips. Where could we go? Lumiphat? Maybe Phayao? Neither one is attractive. They'd be little more than hiding places, because we'd only have the freedom of fugitives. I'm running from Parmenio and you're running from the Maung fleet. In fact, going to Viharn makes excel-lent sense. Its the richest system in this sector and it's the last place the Maung would expect us to turn."

"Then I'm glad you've talked yourself into it," Yuzen said,

with a touch of irony. "It would be tedious if you were constantly trying to make me reconsider something that's practically—well, programmed into my genes."

"You poor clone!" Attanio laughed. And his mind rested much easier on the subject of Luo Viharn.

XII. Doctor Lusu's Pets

Three shipdays later *Cho Tzrep* approached the orbit of the Maung homeworld. For his passengers' benefit Damashek patched through a visual scan onto the wardroom's holotank, and they eagerly gathered round for the show.

The planet swam before them like a vision of Old Earth: a blue crescent swathed in dazzling white clouds. All that was missing were the reddish-brown landmasses which would have been so obvious in any view of Earth, for Viharn's scattered islands were well-concealed by that vast expanse of ocean and cloud. Just past the limb they could see the golden circle of the primary star, called Phosphorus under the Fujiwara, but now known simply as Mnai, the common Ptok word for "sun." Further out was a brilliant yellow pinpoint, the primary of the Xuun system, actually a distant companion of Mnai at a separation of more than half a light year. Men had once called this star Hesperus, but that name too was long forgotten.

Over the period of an hour or so the veilship's orbit brought it around to the sunward hemisphere for its upcoming rendezvous with Srasuri. The sky-city's image grew steadily, crystal clear in the surrounding vacuum. It was like no L-5 habitat either young man had ever heard of.

"By my blood," Yuzen swore. "It's a great palace."

"But it looks . . . all wrong." Then a sudden insight lit Attanio's confusion. "Not only isn't it spinning, it's not built with centrifugal symmetry at all. It's all up and down—it looks like it was designed for a planetary surface, and yet there it is hanging in space."

"Amazing! That means they must have artificial gravity throughout the whole structure. What extravagance!"

Extravagance indeed. Srasuri was a vision of fairyland, rising tier on tier in pillared terraces topped by slender minarets and pointed domes. On its longest axis it measured six

157

kilometers, with an average diameter of about three. The upper levels—anomalous to use such a term in free fall, but quite correct within a Cluj/Darabundit field—had actual windows on the void: and what sights they must show. The city itself in its spidery glory— the colorful sphere of Viharn, with its shifting phases,—the glittering starfields stretching out into infinity. Veilships never had windows, only holotanks, and the view from any spinning habitat must necessarily induce nausea. Srasuri was clearly designed with the epicure in mind.

Doubts and misgivings gave way to anticipation as the sky-city loomed nearer. Its docking area, logically enough, was beneath the lowest tier, where a long vertical tube gave access to the city. Under constant radio direction from the portside dispatcher, *Cho Tzrep* maneuvered opposite one of the scores of available bays and locked in.

Attanio and Yuzen were already waiting by the airlock. They had long since packed their belongings, and on Bezoza's advice carried their weapons in locked and labelled cases, impossible to reach at short notice. Entering Srasuri under arms was simply not done. As an added precaution Yuzen had dyed his hair black their first day aboard *Cho Tzrep*, to avoid any sticky questions about his unusual pigmentation.

The port authorities, of course, had advance notice of their arrival. Thus it was no surprise to see a knot of officials awaiting them when the lock finally cycled open: but what was unexpected was the small squadron of soldiers, bristling with weapons and body armor, all aiming nullbeams into their faces.

Somehow things weren't looking good.

For once even Yuzen was at a loss. He hesitated for an instant, looking back over his shoulder toward the airlock. Both Damashek and Bezoza stood there like stalwarts, also aiming projectors at point-blank range. It seemed to be a classic case of betrayal.

"Don't try anything, Vargasz, or whoever you are." Damashek's voice was casual and soft. "We know you're fast but at least one of you is sure to go down."

"So why don't you just drop your parcels, very gently, and put your hands on your heads," Bezoza suggested.

They did.

Now an unarmed Maung stepped forward. His torso was encased in a polished carapace, his legs were covered with webwork hose, and his black hair was elaborately knotted and braided. "We are very pleased to welcome you to Srasuri," he said in the lilting accent of Vilharn. "You must be Attanio Hwin," this with a nod in the proper direction, "and you must be one of the scions of Prince Myobu of the Shinjuku."

When neither of them responded he continued unperturbed. "A show of force was necessary only to ensure your cooperation, since we had reason to believe you would conceal both your identities and your motives. As you can see that is superfluous. Please come peacefully now to your quarters: they were prepared against your arrival with every comfort in mind. As soon as you've settled in your orientation can begin."

All through this polite speech the beam projectors never wavered. Attanio felt like throwing up. Yuzen suspended judgment. This much was clear: they had lost control of the situation. There was no choice but to do exactly what the Maung gentleman directed.

Once they had indicated as much the tensions relaxed. The Maung lowered their guns, but stopped short of holstering them; two warriors picked up the Galactics' bags and the whole party began to move off along a short corridor. Attanio glanced back at *Cho Tzrep*'s airlock just before it passed out of sight. The two pirates stood there conferring with one of the Maung officials.

"They sold us down the river," he said bitterly. "They must have known who we were from the start. Damn! We thought we were so clever. And shit! We even paid them passage money!" This was the cruelest outrage of all.

"It must have been a very profitable run for them," Yuzen agreed. "I wonder if Ilah and Shihr were in on the scheme."

"Stars know. Somehow I doubt it."

By this time they were crowded into an elevator car, flying up through the myriad glittering levels of Srasuri. Their escort remained silent but offered no objection to private conversation. The elevator delivered them onto a long empty corridor, apparently a service route, which they followed to yet another lift, and thereafter another bare corridor. Thus in a series of stages they traversed most of the six kilometers of the city's vertical axis, never meeting any other human beings.

Finally they emerged in the lap of luxury. Their escort guided them down a curving passage bathed in golden light.

Carved wooden tubs held evergreen trees and flowering shrubs; marble walls sprouted moss, and in places cascades of water trickled down to collect in pools stocked with ornamental fish. This promenade ended at a pair of massive wooden doors which opened at a touch.

"I hope this will be suitable," the Maung gentleman murmured.

Within was a suite of rooms furnished with comparable taste, even to the hint of jasmine in the air. It appeared to occupy one of the lacey towers they had noticed during their approach; its tall windows afforded vistas of neighboring spires and of the starry sky. They nodded approval.

"We must ask that you surrender your weapons," their guide said apologetically. "They will be kept secure for you until you are granted clearance to reclaim them." At this a few of the warriors began picking through their belongings to confiscate all possible instruments of destruction. That done, the entire escort withdrew, leaving them at their leisure in the palatial suite.

The door, however, was securely locked from the outside.

"So this is a Viharnese prison," Attanio mused, fingering the rich hangings and antique porcelain. "No doubt our interrogation is next."

Yuzen grunted from his seat on a silk-upholstered divan. "Do you remember how strangely Ophiz behaved our last night in Shiie? How he asked us whether we really had to leave, and whether we trusted Damashek and Bezoza? He must have forseen something like this: in his obtuse manner he was warning us."

"That makes sense," Attanio agreed. "But then so does this." He chose a piece of fruit from a conveniently situated bowl. "At least we'll be finding out what happened to Teoru and the others."

"Yes, and maybe we'll spend the rest of our lives in a platinum cage."

There was no arguing with that, so Attanio strolled over to a window. Out of the thousands of unblinking stars he managed to trace the constellation of his old friend the Sorceress. Her figure was not at all what it had been on Parmenio, or for that matter Ynenga. Nor was she impossibly rearranged. Her most obvious innovation was the displacement of mighty Antares: rather than forming the jewel in the lady's crown or her heart, it now sparkled from her hand.

Turning back to tell Yuzen he noticed that the air in the room seemed cloudy and dense. Were his eyes already fatigued from stargazing? He tried to speak and found his tongue too thick to move. It was like a dream or nightmare. Could that be why Yuzen was fast asleep? Attanio's brain was unwilling to speculate; suddenly sleep seemed the most desirable thing in the world. So he did.

2

Slowly, slowly Attanio surfaced, as if floating up from the bottom of a deep well. For a few moments he simply reveled in drug-free consciousness. His body felt weightless, insubstantial, transparent as glass, and his skull felt like a vacuum chamber. *They've emptied me out*, a little voice whispered inside. He was blank, void, washed clean.

At least this time there was ordinary golden light, which was something to be grateful for, and they had left him lying comfortably in bed. His little cell was clean and adequate. Apparently squalor was unknown in Srasuri, except for one place he knew too well. He was alone now, of course. He hadn't seen Yuzen since they'd been gassed into unconsciousness in that luxury suite of Fairyland Towers. He had no idea how many days had passed since then.

Unbidden, a vision of Doctor Lusu's laboratory, the scene of his recent dismay, flooded his brain. It was as vast and shadowy as a cave. What illumination it possessed came in undersea hues, like murky green, cloudy purple and dull rose, and its moist walls were hung with bunches of phosphorescent mold. There was none of the usual apparatus of a laboratory: just those amorphous banks of fungi strung together by lengths of serpentine tubing.

And the good doctor's pets, of course. Attanio unwillingly recalled his first session. Lusu, an elderly man with a kind face, had been attended by a handful of official-looking Maung. Attanio was strapped down on a couch and ignored. He had expected an interrogation, but time passed and no questions were asked. Finally Doctor Lusu came over to him holding something in his hand, something segmented and multilegged. He crooned to it, stroked it, and then placed it carefully on Attanio's naked stomach.

It was very much like a large beetle. The Parmenite had never had any particular aversion to insects, but now that an especially large one was crawling around on him he did find it disgusting. It made ticklish progress up his torso to pause at his throat, where it clicked its mandibles a few times and then sliced open an artery. When it inserted its proboscis Attanio couldn't help screaming.

But his fears passed quickly. Horror dissolved in a wash of euphoria, a giddy, disconnected feeling of trust. And then one of the Maung gentlemen said, "Tell us all you know about the woman calling herself Sringlë of Phayao."

And he did. His voice babbled on and on without conscious direction, answering whatever they asked and then some, while the tiny speck of awareness he thought of as *himself* stood back in drugged confusion. When they had heard enough, stars only know how many hours later, he was carried back to this little cell to toss and turn feverishly till they called for him again. And when that time came it was more of the same, or worse: Doctor Lusu had many pets and not all were as benign as the truth bug. Once he was hurled into a pit of spiders; apart from the extreme revulsion they inspired, their bite induced wild hallucinations, and ultimately a gut-wrenching attack of the dry heaves. Another brand of venom caused him to evacuate his bowels, whereupon the Maung left him to lie in the mess; another made him weep uncontrollably, and still another sent him into convulsions.

In a way the ordeal reminded him of Ashbeck's diversions: but he never once felt homesick.

All the while came the questions, often the same ones repeated over and over, day after day. His interrogators were particularly interested in Sringlë, but they also asked about Teoru, about Fsau and the other Myinti, and about his experiences on Loei. They touched on Ynenga without delving deep, even when he mentioned the Great Cube. Their curiosity was confined to political and military matters.

Now, in the cold light of reason, their motivation remained perfectly obscure. What after all could they expect a Parmenite lowlife to tell them about galaxy-wide politics? It seemed insane.

But maybe reason and sanity had nothing to do with it.

Maybe this was simply the "orientation" their welcoming party had mentioned. Maybe the Maung had to make sure he was completely harmless before they'd start treating him like a human being. If so—what horrifying arrogance! And arrogance and cruelty were all he'd learned to expect from the lords of Srasuri.

With an effort of will he sat up and forced such disturbing thoughts from his head. A table nearby held fruit and cakes; suddenly he realized how hungry he was. He attacked the food with gusto.

Perhaps they were through with him. Perhaps he'd never see Doctor Lusu's shadowy lair again. Maybe Yuzen had figured out some sort of escape and would be coming to his rescue any second. Then again, maybe Yuzen was waiting for him to do the same. . . .

He was within a few bites of finishing when the door slid aside and a nondescript young man stepped in. Almost by reflex Attanio cringed back, expecting more mistreatment, his recent well-being obliterated.

"Relax," the Maung said. But his own face was taut and he spoke quickly. "This may be hard to believe but I'm here to help you escape." Attanio's jaw dropped. "Put these on while I'm talking." He offered a bundle containing baggy knee-length trousers, a long woven belt, a pair of soft slippers, and a knotted headcloth of striped silk.

Attanio wasn't sure whether he should be ecstatic or suspicious. Could this be another trick, like that palatial suite? A few days in Maung hands had already turned his mind inside out. Nevertheless he started changing.

"Our timing has to be very tight," the young man continued. "Follow me and look confident. First we'll get your friend and then we'll head for the docks."

"Who are you?" Attanio asked, winding the belt around his hips and swallowing his disbelief.

"A friend of all enemies of Luo Viharn."

Then they were out the door, walking down the deserted passage at a brisk pace. No words were spoken; Attanio was in a state of shock.

The Maung led him to an unguarded doorway close by and palmed it open. Inside was a cell identical to the one they had just left, containing a very groggy Yuzen sprawled across the bed. From his belt the stranger produced a vial and held it to Yuzen's nostrils for a moment. It produced the desired effect: the Martian sat up sputtering.

The Maung repeated his spiel while Attanio helped Yuzen dress. Now all three were identically garbed, and Attanio at least could pass for a native. Yuzen's height unfortunately made him stand out, but equally tall Maung were not unknown.

After traversing another empty corridor they emerged in a more public space with considerable foot traffic, and even a few *saei*. This was their first and last glimpse of Srasuri's normal life. They were in no mood to appreciate it. Their anonymous benefactor guided them through the crowds to a small storeroom where rows and rows of clothing hung, and here they made another costume change. This time it was knee-high boots, soft caps with trailing earflaps, and long-sleeved jackets. A tool kit slung over the shoulders completed this ensemble.

The nondescript young man stood back to study their incognito, nodding his approval. "You'll do. Now we have a few minutes to spare before the shift changes, so listen carefully. My official job here in Srasuri involves assigning crew and arranging timetables for the weekly shuttle to Vadhuz—that's an island in Phra Viharn, the only place where ships from Luo Viharn are allowed to land."

"Allowed?" Yuzen echoed.

"I'll explain in a moment. Anyway, you two are this week's crew; I've got it all worked out with port comp. You'll be lifting off in twenty minutes on a regularly scheduled run. The ship flies by itself; so there's no need for any lessons in piloting. But here's the tricky part. This run is going to experience a major systems failure: it's already in the cubes. Instead of heading straight for Vadhuz the alternators will misalign and crash you in the Bay of Xai, just north of Vachien. You will abandon ship, the shuttle will sink, and you will swim to shore. Your trajectory has been calculated to bring you within a few kilometers of Taa Phreng, where the Oruri holds court. Your destination is the imperial palace: just identify yourselves and you'll be granted immediate audience."

"Wait a minute," Attanio said. "You're saying our names are household words at the Imago's court?"

"That's right: the Queen herself has engineered your escape. I'm just one of her agents."

This raised more questions than it answered. "Who else have you helped escape?" Yuzen asked hopefully. "Has a Martian named Teoru Mashibara passed through here?"

The Maung shrugged. "I'm not alone in Srasuri but even I don't know who the Queen's other agents are. You two were described to me in detail, so I've been looking out for you for several weeks. I haven't personally aided any other outsystem detainees, but that doesn't mean someone else hasn't."

This was discouraging. "What do you know about the Martian ship that was captured recently, out near the Aab-Oort system?"

"Just rumors. I've heard the crew included a Martian wizard and a few alien Adepts, and that they're confined to the Vriuan Tower under the tightest possible security. With my clearance I'd never get near them."

"In other words *we* were relatively easy to spring." Yuzen pondered. "How did you identify us?"

"Well, actually it was you I was waiting for," the young man replied, indicating Attanio. "You see, I'm a telepath, trained at the Imago's school in the Glass Hills. Telepathy is the only practical means of communication for the Oruri's spies. My contact at Taa Phreng gave me a very clear picture, although your hair looks different now. You wore it in stripes before, didn't you?"

Attanio almost burst out laughing—it was all too bizarre. Who knew him in Taa Phreng? But the Viharnese agent cut off any further questions with a glance at his chronometer.

"It's getting near time. The off-shift comes on in five more minutes, and that's us. Let's go."

At the other end of the wardrobe room a door opened onto a lift, which carried them down to the upper level of the docks. Here they lost themselves in a milling throng of port employees dressed exactly as they were. Without hesitation they crossed the huge open space to a lofty portal guarded by several warriors; their guide produced an identifying medallion and they were waved through. A sleek shuttlecraft awaited them in the extrusion bay, poised for launching.

Few sights had ever been more welcome.

3

The Viharnese ship was fishlike in design, with smooth sweeping lines and paired fins. In preparation for liftoff its stubby wings were retracted, and an oval port stood open at the head of the gangway.

"Ten minutes to go," the anonymous Maung said quietly. All three made for the entry port: but just across the threshold they met a major obstacle.

Two Maung warriors were waiting for them with leveled nullbeams.

"So! Chumeong!" one of them exclaimed, as friendly as can be. "My hunch paid off. I'll have you to thank for my promotion."

"What are you talking about?" Chumeong managed exactly the right blend of confusion and annoyance.

"Don't play innocent—just come quietly. There's no reason for anyone to get hurt."

Apparently Yuzen disagreed. With an inarticulate yell he hurled his tool kit at the second warrior's head and dove for the first man's weapon. Chumeong was right behind him in the fray. The first man lost his gun, and a moment later his consciousness, thanks to a well-placed blow from Yuzen. But the second one twisted sideways to avoid the flying tool kit, and almost by reflex pressed the firing stud of his nullbeam.

Chumeong was in the way. He tumbled backwards down the ramp, limp and silent.

His killer followed a moment later with a broken neck.

Without pausing for second thoughts Yuzen bound and gagged the surviving Maung with articles of clothing and rapidly scanned the shuttle bay for someplace to hide him, along with the two corpses. Nothing presented itself.

Attanio meanwhile was recovering from shock. This was the first time he had seen Yuzen in action against human antagonists: his speed and deadly efficiency were frightening. Definitely a good man to stay friendly with.

"Yuzen," he said urgently, "we've got five minutes before this thing takes off."

"I know. But what do we do with this man? He's still alive.

If he's in the shuttle bay when the air evacuates he won't stay that way."

Parmenio-bred, Attanio was genuinely puzzled by Martian ideals of chivalry. "Maybe we can stick him in a pressure suit?" he suggested doubtfully.

"Good idea. You do that while I check out the shuttle-craft."

In the next few minutes Attanio feverishly located a suit and sealed the unconscious man inside. At every moment he expected a security detail to burst in and put an end to their freedom but the seconds ticked off and nothing happened. He finished the job by attaching his captive to some convenient brackets on the bulkhead, to hold him secure during liftoff. The corpses he left as they were.

In the shuttle's command module Yuzen was busy scanning shipcomp's menu. He glanced up as Attanio climbed in and said, "Now the big question is, how long before these men are missed?"

Attanio shrugged. His stomach was a whirlpool.

Suddenly the craft's audio crackled into life. "Liftoff in sixty seconds. Onboard personnel, please acknowledge."

Yuzen was a quick study at security procedures: he did so with all due formality. Then, without any sensation of movement, they were spaceborne. They exchanged smiles of profound relief.

Hours passed, and the lacey fairyland of Srasuri disappeared behind them as Phra Viharn's crescent grew. There were no signs of pursuit; but after all they'd been through in the past few days Attanio found it impossible to relax. From time to time he thought of Chumeong's pale contorted face, marveling at how the man had lived and died before their eyes—all in the space of a half-hour.

Yuzen, however, had been subjected to a much wider range of interrogation techniques than Attanio, and had been allowed far fewer lucid intervals. As soon as the stimulant wore off, he fell sound asleep.

To distract himself Attanio fiddled around with onboard comp, summoning up views of the planetary surface. Eventually he stumbled on an encyclopedic feature and was inundated with a flood of data about their destination, which he eagerly absorbed. Until then he had been nine-tenths ignorant of conditions on Phra Viharn.

In some respects the planet was incredibly Earth-like: almost the same size and density, with a similar axial tilt and a thirty-hour day. To its original human explorers it must have seemed paradise. Second planet of a small yellow sun, Viharn received slightly more solar energy than worlds like Old Earth or Parmenio, and being largely oceanic it had no polar caps and little seasonal variation in climate. Frost was unknown anywhere—but temperatures rarely mounted higher than 25°C, except at noon in an equatorial summer. With abundant vegetation, an oxygen-rich atmosphere, and no large land animals, Phra Viharn positively invited colonization.

But no pearl is without its price. As a temperate water-world, less than ten percent of its surface was dry land—seriously limiting colonial population and economy. Moreover all that land was volcanic in origin, and while this made for fertile soils and dramatic landscapes, it also meant periodic earthquakes and eruptions. The climate too had its drawbacks. Usually benign, with convenient prevailing winds and just the right amount of rainfall, it could also deliver devastating hurricanes and tidal waves. Thus in spite of its attractions Viharn would never have become a major power without its ideal location in the heart of the Antares Reach: and, above all, its proximity to the Xuun system.

The Xuun were one of the three alien spacefaring civilizations that humans had ever encountered. Yet they had never learned the secret of Puncturing the Veil: their travels were limited to real-space jaunts between the twin suns of Mnai and Xuun. Masters of biotechnology, the Xuun actually grew their own ships and powered them with a biochemical reaction that human science had never been able to duplicate. They could make a return voyage between Xuun and Viharn in a little more than five standard years. Thus at some early date in their astronomically ancient history they had established a colony on an island of Phra Viharn: and here the first human explorers met them.

It was a case of mutual fascination. A research station was immediately founded, soon developing into a colony. The Xuun had no objection to human settlement on the thousands of unoccupied Viharnese islands. What they did forbid were human landings on their own homeworld, but with Viharn as a meeting-ground, that proved unnecessary. The Xuun were glad to export drugs, fine fabrics, biotechnics, and perfumes, literally giving these treasures away as gifts. All they asked in return was a treaty with the Sun Company guaranteeing Xuun complete autonomy and non-interference, plus military protection in the event of alien invasion.

Apparently they had forged a similar agreement with the Tzokol, eight million years earlier.

As he perused these records Attanio recalled Bezoza's colorful theories on Xuun–human relations. Something about a revelation of the divine? Here in these Viharnese memory cubes all was cut and dry, with no hint of such wonders. Then again, shipboard comp offered only the most skeletal information, to be fleshed out in any number of ways by the imaginative reader.

What did become clear was that the Viharnese trading colony had rapidly developed a culture of its own, quite distinct from the prevailing modes of galactic society. In a step unprecedented in human history it instituted an artificial language, Ptok Prime, containing absolutely no vocabulary from any natural human speech, and within two generations made it the birth-tongue of every human being on Viharn. Once the colony's economy was in full swing—and incidentally producing battleships and defense systems far in excess of the Sun Company's quota—a declaration of independence followed. There had been a brief struggle, never ever touching the Phosphorus–Hesperus system, in the course of which the Fujiwaras decided they were overextended and could afford to let the colony go.

Thereafter ensued the decline of the Sun Company and the rise of the Greater Maung Co-Prosperity Sphere. The Viharnese, however, never sought to extend their authority beyond the Antares Reach, content with encircling the Xuun and Maung Systems with a buffer zone of client worlds. According to the computer's archives, a few thousand years passed without war, dissension, or change of dynasty. The Queen Mother, or *Oruri*, ruled benevolently from her palace at Taa Phreng, offering her patronage to the arts, distributing the wealth of the land amongst her subjects, and receiving peaceful embassies from Xuun. Earthquakes and other natural disasters periodically disrupted life's placid round, without inflicting any lasting damage.

But here and there Attanio found hints of discord, tantalizing in their vagueness. There were references to Luo Viharn and Phra Viharn as two separate nations, with noncooperating governments; there was talk of the "Schism" and the "Embargo," of the "Interdict of Phra Xonong" and the "refusal of the false sacrament." It all pointed to a split between the people of the orbital cities and those of the wave-girt islands downworld. From what he could deduce, this schism was of recent date, say within the past few hundred years, and it definitely seemed to involve religion. Luo Viharn had chosen to follow a more secular path while Phra Viharn had remained orthodox and devout.

But what was the religion in question? The archives took it for granted that everyone knew.

The Oruri herself arranged our escape, Attanio reflected, and she seems to be the supreme pontiff of the Viharnese cult. So whatever this religion is, it can't be all that bad; and meanwhile the city fathers of Srasuri are giving atheism a bad name. Nothing to do but wait and see.

Having exhausted comp's possibilities he settled back for a nap, his mind finally lulled into quiescence by three hours of security. But just as his eyelids began to droop—just as visions of white beaches and tropical gardens began to dance through his head—comp comm let out a shriek.

Both men were wide awake in an instant, rushing on adrenalin.

A voice addressed them from the console's speaker. "Attention *Kuun Meo* shuttlecraft. Request immediate vocal and visual contact with onboard human personnel."

"I don't think so," Yuzen muttered, studying the array of controls before him.

The voice repeated its demand. "You are flying without clearance on an unauthorized route. Unless you make immediate contact with Srasuri Control you will be fired on."

Yuzen decided it would be a good idea to stall. He had discovered the manual override sequence and was confident of his ability to fly *Kuun Meo* on an evasion course. "Attanio—talk to them," he ordered. "Say anything."

So for a few minutes Srasuri Control and Attanio Hwin exchanged non sequiturs, while Yuzen explored his options. Comp offered him a visual scan of near space, coupled with a schematic of the Maung defense net; since they were about to pass out of satellite range things didn't look too horrendous.

He initiated his evasion sequence.

Cluj alternators shielded them from the wild effects of acceleration as they looped and spiralled: but nothing could fend off the particle beams slicing at them from all directions.

The craft shuddered. Small objects flew around. Suddenly it was very hot.

"We're hit." Yuzen swore loudly in High Martian. Attanio groaned. "But wait—we're not finished yet—the hull is intact." He ran a quick series of scans, then turned to face Attanio. "But we're going to have a problem landing."

"You mean like Ynenga?"

"Close. Except here we've got a nice big ocean to fall into—it shouldn't be as devastating."

Attanio nodded. What could he expect, after all? Galactic refugees never have it easy.

Fortunately, a matter of a hundred seconds carried them beyond the satellite perimeter. They had been at risk for only a brief interval; though still spaceborne, they had passed out of the jurisdiction of Luo Viharn and entered the Imago's realm.

For the next hour Yuzen used what maneuvering power he had left to bring them as close as possible to Vachien. The Queen's island lay in the midst of a densely populated archipelago; presumably if they reached any part of it they'd have clear sailing. But if they splashed down in the open sea, far from any landfall, they were in deep trouble.

By degrees the Cluj alternators gave out and left them in free fall. They plunged into a dense cloudbank, plummeting blindly, tossed about by gale winds that screeched and roared. Then, about four kilometers from the surface, they broke through into clear skies: Yuzen managed to bring their nose up and ride the wind. Although well east of their target, some tree-woven islands lay within reach.

"We just might live," Yuzen announced. His face was haggard and his voice matched.

Spinning cocoons of webfoam they waited uneasily for splashdown.

XIII. Sea of Dreams

Sea and sky: cloud and wave. The whole universe was a watercolor done in tones of violet and aquamarine. Drifting masses of cloud overhead mirrored the play of sunlight on wave—ceaseless, quivering, hypnotic. Their escape from the foundering shuttle already lay far behind them. Now they were just flotsam on the world-ocean of Viharn.

Without fresh water, under the bountiful rays of golden Mnai, they would die within a matter of days. There had been no time to salvage anything from the wreck. In fact they were lucky to have even these few scraps of foam to cling to; otherwise exhaustion would claim them far sooner than thirst. And yet, in spite of their delicate position, neither Yuzen nor Attanio were the least bit unnerved. They had already succumbed to the planet's spell.

The breeze that caressed their faces and the salt water buoying them up were almost the same temperature, perhaps four degrees lower than the human body. The effect was as luxurious as bathing at a spa. And though the sun was high, ivory clouds tempered its glare, screening them from sunburn or heatstroke. Even lost at sea they felt enveloped in the world's kindness.

Before splashdown *Kuun Meo*'s comp had identified this vast benign ocean as Miong Teai, the Sea of Dreams. They were adrift somewhere in its northern reaches, very close to the Ngok Archipelago, around 35 south latitude. Yuzen's unerring sense of direction told them that the closest island lay due west. But when and if they would reach it was a story only time could tell.

In the still silence it was even possible to talk without raising their voices; however there was really nothing to say that hadn't already been said and said again, so they held their peace.

Until the sail appeared.

They first spotted it from the crest of a wave and immediately began shouting for all they were worth. For the longest time nothing happened, so they screamed till they were hoarse. Then at last came the blessed sound of a horn blowing three times, and the boat changed course to intercept them.

It was built low to the water with a slender outrigger and one lateen sail dyed saffron. Picking it out against a background of sea and sky was no problem, suggesting peaceful owners. As it came closer they could tell that it was made entirely of wood, with no visible backup engines, and that it carried a crew of five. Two of them abruptly dove in the water and began swimming their way.

"Ho! Are you alive there?" The first swimmer came within hailing distance, a woman as sleek as a seal.

"Yes, yes," they croaked, "just tired and thirsty." And they abandoned their float to strike out for the sailboat.

Strong arms hauled them aboard. Smiling faces greeted them: two men and three women, all young and vibrant, honey-colored and smooth, with jet-black hair arranged in complex tufts and whorls. They wore nothing but loinclothes; their bodies were voluptuous rather than slender, supple as eels and rounded with flesh. Folded nets and great baskets of squirming fish revealed their occupation.

A jug of water quenched thirst. Then came the questions, a good-natured chorus.

"What happened? Were you shipwrecked? What ship? What island?"

Attanio drew a deep breath and glanced at Yuzen. For the first time in their wanderings it felt safe to tell the truth.

"Yes, we were shipwrecked. She was the *Kuun Meo*, out of Srasuri." Puzzlement, disbelief, and amazed comprehension chased each other across five faces. "It was a ship of space, not a ship of the sea. We're fugitives from Luo Viharn."

Silence fell; somewhere in the distance wood creaked and water lapped against the hull. One of the women, the same who had swum out to meet them, nodded slowly. "We saw a bright light flash in the sky—like the sun, except that it came from the south, while the sun was still in the east. We sailed out to see what it could be: and you are what we found. I think now this is a matter for Po Dhai." The others murmured assent. A subtle tension gathered in the boat's confines.

Then a woman with jade pendants dangling over her forehead touched the first speaker's arm and protested. "We've no reason to think these poor men are dangerous, do we? Look at them." She turned to Attanio. "You certainly don't seem to be Luo Maung. Your accent is strange, and your hair—" She grinned and touched his straight unadorned locks as if she couldn't imagine even a castaway at sea without braids or beads.

"Yes, we're offworlders," he confessed. "I'm from Parmenio, and my friend Yuzen is from Mars."

This broke the tension; there was laughter and headshaking. "Aliens falling from the sky! It's like a tale from ancient times. Tell us!"

So they did, as briefly as possible. The islanders listened spellbound.

"And now," Attanio concluded, "all we're sure of is that we must go see Talithai Oruri herself."

More nodding, more exclamations of wonder. "But Vachien is very far," put in the woman with jade beads, who was called Yathei. "No ships from our island ever make the voyage."

"They could find passage in Teveng," suggested the man named Lu Taz.

"For a price!" cried his brother Tachik.

"Po Dhai will know what to do," concluded Ko Luang. And that ended the discussion.

So they sailed on in the radiance of noon, as prevailing winds drove them steadily westward. The fisherfolk accepted their presence without further ado; one might think rescuing aliens from sunken spaceships was something they did every day. Cheerful hospitality seemed as natural to them as suspicion and cruelty were to the men of Srasuri.

Leaning close to Yuzen's ear Attanio whispered, "These people are too good to be true. Maybe our troubles are over at last."

"Don't speak too soon," the Martian cautioned him.

With that reminder of fortune's whimsy Attanio suddenly thought of his pouch and its precious contents. He had tied it to his belt back in Srasuri, without opening it; now he felt to see if it had survived the dip. It had: but except for the Tzokol pyramid it was empty. The jewel from Suut was gone.

He told Yuzen. "I'm not surprised," the Martian said. "You're lucky the Luo Maung didn't take your little souvenir too—I'm sure they would have if they'd thought it was valuable."

Attanio shrugged. They were penniless now; but somehow he didn't think these new friends would let them starve.

The fisherfolk's native island appeared first as a smear of green on the horizon. Muun Chai, the islanders called it: the Flowering Cliffs. When the misty image resolved, they could see that this was no poetic hyperbole. Line after line of steep hillside plunged into foaming surf, every square centimeter densely overgrown with vegetation. Most of it was rich green but some blossomed in all the colors of the rainbow. Over the salt-fishy tang of the ocean came the smell of pungent earth, mingled with more delicate aromas of lavender and cinnamon. Attanio felt a lump rising in his throat.

Rounding a headland, Yathei pointed out a jumble of tall roofs clinging to the slope. "Sunfish House," she announced. "That's where the five of us live. But for now we're taking you to the main town, to see Po Dhai." And without ceremony they moored at a weatherbeaten old pier and disembarked.

No village or dwelling of any description was visible here, but a number of paths led up the slope in various directions. The party split: both native men and one woman took the trail heading back to Sunfish House, while Yathei and Ko Luang, fish baskets slung over strong bronze shoulders, accompanied them up the main path leading into Laphang Town.

This was the outworlders' first experience of terra firma since leaving Ynenga—and two planets could hardly be more unalike than the barren homeworld of the Tu'u and this verdant paradise. Phra Viharn positively overflowed with life: even the rocks were swathed in moss, softer to touch than a feather pillow, while the frequent swampy areas blossomed with tiny wildflowers, beneath long trailing willows. Wherever drainage and topography permitted, cycad, gingko, magnolia, coconut, bamboo, and pine all thrived together in wild profusion, alongside other exotica without counterpart anywhere else in the galaxy. The very air they breathed was redolent of cinnamon and spikenard, of intoxicating resins, of a thousand smells unnamed in the human lexicon. And the fauna was just as rich: they glimpsed lizards, crawling and flying insects, glittering snakes, and even Birds of Paradise fleeing the sound of their footsteps. It was plain that many of these organisms were relicts of Old Earth, while the rest were either native-born or the product of artfully tailored genes.

They reached a hilltop and paused to catch their breath. Behind them boiled the vast Miong Teai; before them, like a painted scroll, lay the Vale of Laphang. It was a long narrow valley sheltered by fantastically weathered hills. Most of its area had been terraced into rice paddies, but on higher ground there were clusters of houses, wooden-built with upcurving thatched roofs, tall carven roofcombs, and airy verandahs all around. These sat in the midst of orchards and vegetable gardens whose arrangement was as aesthetic as it was functional. In fact throughout the valley it seemed that nature's unfolding had been guided by human hands, with the most fortunate results.

"Pretty, isn't it?" Ko Luang grinned. "And they're just a bunch of farmers." She reshouldered her burden and began the descent.

Once on the valley floor they crossed the rice fields over a network of causeways. Here they saw men and women at work, naked to the waist and wearing tall conical sunhats—though for the size of the fields they seemed too few. Individual paddies were in all stages of growth, from planting to weeding to harvesting. For the first time they saw evidence of machine technology, in the tiny powered plows some farmers guided. But these were of discreet design, running in silence, so that Laphang's bucolic charm went untroubled.

In other fields they saw something much more disturbing. At first glance Attanio thought his eyes were playing tricks, for it seemed like the soil itself was crawling. Then he realized the truth. The human farmers before him were only a small part of the total labor force; they were merely the foremen of huge work crews composed entirely of gigantic hexapods.

Each one measured almost a meter long. All worked in ceaseless unison at repetitive, highly specific tasks. In some fields they planted the young shoots at precise intervals, with a cleverly adapted proboscis, while in others a slightly different version used long mandibles to pull weeds. In still others, great processions of them cut the mature plants and placed them in neat stacks for humans to bundle in sheaves.

Occasionally one would rise up on its hind legs and click

its mouth parts together in the direction of the foreman; then the human would touch it lightly with a short wand and the bug would go back to work, as if reassured.

Ko Luang and Yathei noticed their horrified fascination. "Those are the *saei*," the latter said. "You act like you've never seen one before. Don't the people of Srasuri use them?"

"I suppose they do. . . ." answered Attanio, with a distracted air.

"We saw very little of Srasuri," Yuzen amplified. "We were prisoners."

"Oh yes, you did explain that." Yathei wrinkled her forehead. "I suppose you must have unpleasant memories. But really, our farmbugs are quite harmless."

"I even think they're sweet," said Ko Luang.

"Sweet . . . yes I suppose so. But where in the galaxy do they come from?"

The women were puzzled. "They just breed," said Yathei. She pointed to a tall pyramidal mound in the middle distance, decorated with bits of cloth and scraps of metal and glass. "That's one of their hives; I think it belongs to a harvester family."

"But they're not native to Viharn, are they?" Yuzen persisted.

"Oh! I see what you mean. No, they were gifts of the Xuun a long, long time ago, way back when men first settled Phra Viharn. I couldn't imagine life here without them."

It developed that the *saei*—which came in an assortment of types, from spinners through farmhands to chemosynthesists—were a sort of distant cousin to the Xuun, bred especially for human service. They were the ultimate in biological robots. Humans communicated with them by means of scent wands. Each foreman carried several such wands, each one imprinted with a different cluster of pheromones to convey a particular message or command. In appearance they were like huge beetles, with hard greenish-brown integuments. They were not, in fact, true insects, belonging rather to the Xuun order of pseudohexapoda, but for non-Maung they carried the same psychological stigma.

"You don't keep them as housepets, do you?" Attanio asked, still a little worried.

The Viharnese women just laughed.

2

It was now midafternoon and the work crews were breaking up for the day. The humans headed home for a siesta on the front porch and the *saei* trooped back to their hives for something similar. A few farmers called out casual greetings to Ko Luang and Yathei, nodding as well to the two outworlders in a neighborly manner.

By now these four had reached the edge of the causeways and were climbing a steep path up the hillside. Their destination was a complex of small buildings beside a waterfall, overhung by five exquisite pines.

"Po Dhai's compound," Yathei explained. "She's the Eldress of Laphang Town, a deputy of Inao Sret herself." But in spite of her standing the lady's house was no grander than any of the others dotting the valley, and exuded an air of slightly seedy comfort.

Like all the Maung structures they had seen downworld, this one consisted essentially of a series of steeply pitched roofs supported by clusters of slender pillars. There was no outer wall; instead an open porch surrounded the screened-off interior. It was apparently designed as a refuge from sun and rain, not a bastion against wind and cold. Clearly this was the land of eternal summer.

They went around the side of the house through a small fruit orchard. Birds with long crimson tails looked down on them from the upper branches, heads cocked curiously to one side. Against a comfortable tree trunk, an old woman dozed. Next to her an overturned basket spilled its bounty of fruit over the grass.

At their approach the old lady started and opened her eyes. At once she was wide awake and smiling, greeting the young fisherwomen by name.

"I seem to have undone my morning's work, haven't I." She ruefully surveyed the scattered fruit.

"We'll fix that!" Ko Luang cried, setting down her own basket and deftly gathering up the yellow spheres. Her three companions joined in.

"We've brought you a present," Yathei announced, pointing to the packages of fish.

"Oh?" The old lady positively cooed, her eyes disappearing in a grin. "But what about these tall young men? Aren't they presents too?"

"No, they're more like problems." Ko Luang handed over the refilled basket and sat down next to Po Dhai. "We fished them out of the sea. They say they fell there from the sky."

Po Dhai's eyes grew very wide, amber as flame and as clear and bright as the noonday sun. Her face was creased with a labyrinth of wrinkles and her slender body showed the fragility of age, but her hair was still thick and lustrous, and her teeth, which she showed often in smiling, were all intact.

"From the sky, you say!" Her eyes traveled up to the fantastic play of clouds. "Do tell me about it, young fellows." And she clasped her hands expectantly.

The pair of them sat down and started in with their tale, trading off in the narration as they pleased. Po Dhai nodded frequently without interrupting; Mnai moved a little further across the sky.

When they were done she said simply, "We'll have to get you to Taa Phreng as soon as possible."

"Then you believe us?" Attanio cried.

"Why certainly! That is, most of the time." She addressed Yuzen. "Take your story, for example, my Martian friend. You said something about 'bearing no animosity for the lords of Srasuri,' but merely wishing to 'ensure Lord Teoru's safety.' Now that part wasn't strictly true at all—you'd love to take vengeance on those men, wouldn't you! And you, my mad Parmenite: your sins were of omission. I can tell you left out a lot at the beginning of your story, and when you described that strange building on the desert world you were definitely hiding something." She smiled benignly. "But these are details. As for being who you say you are and intending what you claim to intend, that's all as plain as the nose on my face." And she crossed her eyes to gaze at that particular organ.

"But what about Queen Talithai?" Attanio insisted. "Do you have any idea why she would sacrifice an agent to help us?"

"That is a mystery," the old lady admitted. "But it's obvious that she knows about you, and that you're important to her. It's also plain that at least one of your comrades is already in Taa Phreng; that's the only way her Adepts could have transmitted your image to that poor young man in Srasuri."

Attanio wondered which one it had been, though he already had a good idea. "How can we get to Taa Phreng, then?"

"By sea, of course." Po Dhai pondered a moment. "I don't suppose you have any money?"

"No chance."

"That does complicate matters. Vachien is far away . . . but I have it. First we must get you to Teveng City, on the main island of the Archipelago, and there you'll seek an audience with Inao Sret. She's the Prefect of Ngok, acting on the Imago's behalf in all things. She can talk to Taa Phreng by radiophone and verify your story. Then I'm sure the Imago will make arrangements for you to continue your journey all the way to the royal court."

Yuzen and Attanio exchanged mystified glances. "Couldn't we simply call Queen Talithai from here?"

It was Ko Luang and Po Dhai's turn for confusion. "How could we do that? There are no radios in Muun Chai."

"But—why not?"

"We have no need for them."

Though the two men came from vastly different homeworlds, neither one could imagine civilized humans limiting the use of available technology.

Po Dhai saw their confusion, meanwhile, and did her best to dispel it. "Long ago the Imagoes decided that instantaneous communications create a sameness everywhere, and that this robs life of its appeal. So devices like radios, airships, and powered ocean vessels are all in the hands of the Oruri and her prefects; their use is strictly regulated. It causes no problems that I can see."

"We meant no criticism," Yuzen assured her.

But privately Attanio thought that the planet was already beginning to sound a bit hivelike. Queen bees and faceless workers, indeed! Aloud he said, "How will we manage this trip to Teveng City?"

"That's easy enough. I have many friends among the ship captains plying these waters, and a few of them even owe me favors. In fact, I think I could have you on a ferry bound for Teveng by, oh, sundown tomorrow."

She waved off their effusive thanks, protesting that she was only doing the Queen's business. Then she invited them to share a little refreshment on the verandah. They sat around a small circular table on low seats, while a child with huge green eyes served them cups of fruit juice. It was pulpy, sour-sweet, and pale blue: the islanders called it *tzat*.

"Po Dhai," said Yathei sometime later, "isn't the White Ship coming soon?"

"Indeed it is," the lady replied with a twinkle. "Ganri Hin will begin in Teveng on the second of Kithao, and continues over the next five days. Then it's on to Vorung for a day or two, then Lella, and Tzong, and finally Muun Chai itself. In fact there's a pilgrim ship setting out from Koko Bay tomorrow, the very one I thought our friends might take."

"You lucky buggers!" the fisherwomen cried. "You'll see Teveng during the festival. Even we've never done anything so grand."

"What exactly are you talking about?" Yuzen asked politely, as Attanio pricked up his ears. "What is Ganri Hin?"

"It's only the best holiday in the whole year," Yathei declared. "It happens in different places at different times, all according to the White Ship's sailing."

"Perhaps you know that we share this world with the Xuun," explained Po Dhai. "In fact, Phra Viharn is their gift to us—the very words signify 'earth-gift' in our tongue. The Xuun have kept one island for themselves and allowed us to take all the rest. Now every year the White Ship sets out from that same island, which is called Phra Xonong, and stops at all the major ports in the world. Its cargo is Ganang Zal, the Nectar of Xuun, which it freely dispenses to all Phra Maung."

"The Nectar of Xuun. . . ." Attanio mused. In Ashbeck it had been legendary, reputedly surpassing even flicker and angels' tears in potence, though of course no Parmenite had ever tasted it. "Just what does it do?"

Po Dhai smiled. "It makes us happy."

Ko Luang and Yathei nodded in agreement.

"That's all?"

Everyone laughed.

"I mean . . ." Attanio groped for words. "What if someone didn't want any? Is that allowed? Or is it like a—" And he realized that there was no Ptok word for *religion*.

His questions occasioned considerable discussion. "Why in the world would someone abstain from Ganang Zal?" wondered Ko Luang.

Then Yathei had an inspiration. "I remember when you used to teach us history, Po Dhai, right under that redfeather tree. One day you told us about the Discord—"

"—the Heresy!" breathed Ko Luang.

"—the Schism between Heaven and Earth."

"Of course," said Po Dhai, nodding. "Clever girl. That's exactly the answer we're seeking." She turned to the Galactics and assumed the role of schoolmarm. "Our Oruri Talithai has reigned for some five hundred-odd years now." This was over 350 standard years, as the outworlders discovered after rapid calculation: apparently Lumiphat wasn't the only fountain of youth in the Antares Reach. "Her predecessor was Thuanat, whose reign however was quite short.

"In Thuanat's day there was no enmity with the sky cities, and the Oruri held court in Srasuri and Prathamim as often as in Taa Phreng. People traveled freely between the two realms. In fact I think all Phra Viharn was a sort of royal preserve, to which the Queen's favored servants retired. In those days the White Ship even sailed through space, to carry nectar everywhere that Maung subjects lived.

"As a nymph Thuanat took a lover among the first families of Prathamim. His name was Chen, I believe. He was an extremely passionate man. Even after Thuanat had ended things—for you understand that Queens never stick with one lover, but flit about like butterflies in a garden—Chen still pursued her and made himself quite tiresome at court. To get rid of him the Oruri promoted him to an admiralty in the Maung fleet and sent him on a mission out past the Coalsack. He was gone for years.

"Now, in all the time of their starfaring, neither Lord Chen nor his crew tasted the Nectar of Xuun. This changed them in strange and subtle ways. And when Chen returned to Viharn, with a cargo of rare elements and precious stones, he continued his abstinence. In time he used his influence to turn this peculiar folly into a fashion throughout Luo Viharn."

"How were Chen's followers different from ordinary Maung of the time?" wondered Attanio.

"They asked a lot of questions," Po Dhai answered wryly. "And they were discontented. They criticized the Oruri. It is even rumored that many of them pursued odd sexual practices, seeking pain instead of pleasure; certainly a few of them turned to the horrible pastime of *murder*."

"You mean to say that before this time no Maung ever killed another?" This seemed incredible to anyone raised in Ashbeck.

"That's right: nor is there any *murder* done here on Phra Viharn in the present era."

Attanio was speechless. The Nectar of Xuun was far more powerful than he had dreamed, and raised far more complicated issues.

"How did the Oruri Thuanat respond to these dissidents?" asked Yuzen.

"For a long time she ignored them. There was no precedent for such behavior among Maung, and it seems Thuanat was not a particularly imaginative woman. Finally, after one of the heretics calmly disintegrated twenty citizens chosen at random from the crowds thronging the Emerald Terrace of Srasuri, she was forced to take notice. But before acting she went to Phra Xonong to confer with the Xuun. She was gone for two stations of the year." Po Dhai sighed in disapproval. "In her absence Lord Chen used violence to seize the reins of government and proclaimed himself Overlord of Luo Viharn."

She paused for effect; her listeners were impressed. "His first act was to forbid the docking of the White Ship at any port in the orbital zone. His second was to institute a criminal code specifying serious punishments, up to death itself, for all crimes of violence."

Both Galactics had to smile at the irony. "And Thuanat?" Yuzen wondered.

"Thuanat chose the Glass Hills. She ended her worldly life and left Talithai as her successor. Talithai, in turn, accepted the division of earth and sky, for this had been the Xuun's advice. She relinquished all control over the Maung starfleet and the orbital cities, restricting her authority to the planetary surface itself. Her only condition was that ships of Xuun be allowed free passage to and from the surface; in exchange the sky folk could retain a base in the volcanic islands of Vadhuz. So it has been ever since."

"A successful *coup d'etat*," Yuzen decided. Privately he thought both sides suffered from the schism, but it was certainly better than protracted war.

Attanio was drawing other conclusions. "The Nectar of Xuun," he said slowly, "is then the basis of your whole social order. It's what makes Viharn what it is—without it I suppose these islands would degenerate into a new version of Parmenio. You'd fall from grace and be like ordinary sinners."

Po Dhai nodded. "That's why we're so thankful to Xuun, for sparing us that misery."

Having satisfied her guests' curiosity she turned briskly away from the subject of history. "Zazu, squeeze us some more *tzat,* would you dear?" And the green-eyed child jumped up from her comfortable sprawl to disappear in a flurry of pigtails.

The old lady regarded her guests affectionately. "Now it occurs to me that you two are no strangers to this thing called murder. And yet you seem like such nice young men."

Attanio blushed; Ko Luang and Yathei were wide-eyed. Yuzen alone retained his composure.

Po Dhai laughed, dismissing the subject with a wave of her fingers. "I'd be a fool to judge outworlders by the standards of Phra Viharn, so I won't. In fact I was going to invite you both to spend the night under my roof."

The fisherwomen immediately protested. "We found them," they chorused, "so let them stay with us!" Yuzen and Attanio were quite flattered by their popularity, which persisted even after their exposure as deviants; they accepted with thanks.

It was agreed that they would return to Po Dhai's house the following day just after siesta time, and she would accompany them to the waterfront to secure their passage on the inter-island ferry.

The lady bade them a warm farewell. "Men from the stars!" she exclaimed, embracing each one in turn. "And in my lifetime!" They set out in great good humor.

Yathei shook her head, smiling, as they headed down to the rice paddies. "That Po Dhai. She's mother to this whole valley."

Mother, Attanio thought. I hardly knew mine, and Yuzen is a clone.

3

They crossed the empty fields and climbed up into the hills again, passing cool waterfalls and luxuriant stands of flowering trees. Overhead the clouds never ceased their polychrome mutations, mellowing Mnai's brilliant light to a gentle wash of dull gold. Before the day was much older they had come to Sunfish House.

By now it was late afternoon, and Yathei and Lu Taz decided to start preparing the evening meal. In honor of their guests they wanted it to be a feast. Since Tachik was meditating this left Ko Luang and Suvei to entertain.

"You must teach us how to behave like ordinary Maung," Attanio said, "so that as we voyage to Taa Phreng nobody will notice us."

The women found this amusing. "Where will we begin?" demanded Suvei. "There are an ocean of changes to make. Your accent, for example—"

"And your hair!" Ko Luang cried. "That's where we'll start, Su—we can talk while we braid."

This proved agreeable to all concerned. In fact, braiding parties were a favorite means of whiling away the long lazy afternoons of Viharn, occupying the same position that video games or cards might hold on other worlds. In no time the women had their guests' hair wetted down and were in the process of weaving bits of coral, crystal, and jade into it. In the meantime they kept up a constant stream of talk about how one behaves in casual society, frequently interrupting their work to jump up and demonstrate a gesture or a dance step.

The Galactics learned that on Viharn one never discusses the weather, except in typhoon season—and right now it was late winter. However, it was perfectly polite to inquire the age, occupation, sexual preference, and marital status of complete strangers. Refusing the offer of a cup of tea or *tzat* was a grave insult—but then all insults were quickly forgiven and forgotten among these cheerful people.

"By the way, what is *your* marital status?" Yuzen asked.

"We're all married," said Ko Luang.

"All five of us, that is," Suvei clarified. "To each other." It developed that conjoint marriages were more common than monogamy—but that the Sunfish House folk were unusual in that they lived permanently with their marriage partners, rather than with their birth-clan.

"No children?" Attanio wondered.

"Not till next year."

"How do you manage that?"

"There is a root the men chew to make their seed infertile."

"And you trust them to keep chewing?"

Suvei laughed. "It stains their teeth."

"So you must always find your lovers in daylight," Ko Luang explained, "and make sure they smile."

"Then it would never work in Ashbeck," Attanio quipped —but no one else got the joke.

Sooner or later the conversation came round to spiritual matters. There were more references to Ganang Zal and Ganri Hin, but in spite of Bezoza's theories the everyday devotions of Phra Viharn had little to do with the hexapods. They were, in fact, a development at several removes of the incredibly ancient teachings of one Gautama Buddha, a mortal man of Earth, dead these seven thousand years. In Ptok the Great Teacher was known as Pho Tak, and his teaching the Chimango or Eightfold Way. It stressed loving kindness and measured delight in the ordinary events of life, rather than asceticism or otherworldliness as in some Old Earth sects. The discipline of daily meditation was, however, a central part of the teaching, and nonviolence was as fundamental to the Viharnese as to any other followers of the Enlightened One.

But the Chimango was more properly a personal philosophy than a devotional religion: its temples were merely gathering places for collective meditation, for performance of music and theater, and for the great banquets held in conjunction with cremations. And there was no priesthood at all.

"Our mothers teach us to meditate on the Way, just as they teach us to use latrines and keep our hair in order," the women said, and that seemed to sum up the average person's views on spirituality.

Mnai was kindling the western hills by the time Yuzen and Attanio's coiffures were judged presentable. Tachik came out to light the three alabaster lanterns on the eastern terrace, followed soon after by Lu Taz and Yathei with huge trays heaped high with food. The ensuing meal was the best Yuzen had tasted since before Tharsis fell to Xil, and the best Attanio had ever had in his whole life. It consisted of twelve different courses, some eaten simultaneously and others in succession, but each one with a distinctive flavor ranging from sweet through spicy to downright bitter. Rice was present in the form of boiled grains, wafer-thin cakes, and creamy puddings;

sixteen different kinds of fish appeared—some raw, some pickled, some smoked, and others steamed. There were sea vegetables and bamboo shoots, stewed bracken and boiled leeks, pressed salads and delicate soups, and to finish it off an assortment of fruits cut and arranged to mimic flowers. The nearer moon had already set before the banqueters abandoned their labor and sat back with cups of sparkling wine.

"This is paradise," Yuzen murmured in tones of awe. "If I stay here long enough I just might forget Mars completely, and the honor of the Shinjuku along with it."

But Attanio gave no reply, having fallen asleep sprawled over Ko Luang's lap.

4

Bird song awakened them. The rising sun had transformed Miong Teai into a caldron of molten bronze, while the old house bustled with preparations for a day at sea.

Suvei came over to where Yuzen and Attanio still lay in a tangle of cotton quilts, squatting down to give them morning tea. "I'll stay with you today," she said, peeking shyly through the fringe of braids that shaded her eyes. "We didn't want to leave you all alone here. And I'll enjoy the holiday."

So after the others had left, after all the embracing and well-wishing, Suvei gave them a tour of Sunfish House and its environs. Her first stop was the wardrobe: a corner of the main hall whose rafters were hung with exquisite fabrics printed in colorful geometric patterns and as fine-spun as gossamer. She named the various articles of clothing there—the sari-like vinga, the baggy trousers known as choi, and the ornamental belts, without which no outfit was complete, called kteng.

"These are festival clothes," Suvei explained. "Some of them have been handed down for generations."

Then from the family's supply of ordinary cotton garments she chose two complete outfits. "Last night Yathei said to me, 'If they're going to see the Queen they can't wear those poor rags we found them in. Make sure they're properly dressed before they leave us tomorrow.'"

So she dressed each man in a pair of knee-length choi, a

few crisscrossing kteng, and a couple of armlets. With their braided hair and bare feet they now looked quite authentic.

Siesta hour came and went, and then just as they set out for Po Dhai's it started raining. Suvei paid no heed; they continued along the soggy path leading down to the valley without a word of complaint. Light showers like this blew up, and then away, more afternoons than not—even in the so-called dry season. The Viharnese simply ignored them. True to form this one was over before they had arrived at Five Pines. A rainbow gleamed in the eastern sky for a few gaudy moments, and Mnai shone once more over steaming rice paddies.

Po Dhai greeted them from her front porch with a shout and a whistle. She positively radiated affection. She had just risen from some complex game played with colored tiles: her companions were green-eyed Zazu and another child even younger. "How did you sleep last night?" she sang out cheerfully.

"With full bellies and empty heads," answered Yuzen, in a typically Maung turn of phrase.

"Good for you! I gather the Sunfish House crew make excellent hosts." She nodded, then her face darkened a little. "So in all your merrymaking I suppose you missed the fireworks in the sky."

There were hisses of surprise. "What are you talking about, Po Dhai?" demanded Suvei. "Don't keep us in suspense."

"I wish I knew." The old lady sighed, but her eyes still crinkled with humor. "In the middle of the night Zoyin here woke me with a bad dream. I sang him back to sleep but then I was wide awake myself, so I took a turn through the garden. It was a fine night: the sky was clear as Koko Bay in midwinter. Thinking of our otherworldly visitors I amused myself trying to spot a falling star or two. Well, I hadn't waited longer than it takes *michi* tea to steep when I saw the most amazing lights over the northern hills. Great bursts of orange flame, and bolts of pink and purple so bright they hurt my eyes. I could tell somehow that they were very far away, very high up in the sky. It was all over in twenty heartbeats: so sudden, you know, that afterwards I could hardly believe it happened. But as sure as I'm standing here it was no dream. Nor was it like anything I've ever seen in eleventy-odd years of watching the night sky."

Attanio shivered. Yuzen grimaced. Suvei simply looked confused.

Inevitably, the specter of Xil disturbed Yuzen's thoughts; however a twenty-second skirmish in close orbit didn't sound like Lord Appucc's style at all. If the Pleiades ever invaded Viharn they wouldn't find out about it the next day.

In any case it was clear that the forces of history were in motion. And there was no escaping their own entanglement.

"I understand it no better than you, Po Dhai," Yuzen finally confessed. "The starlords' motives are a mystery to me."

"No matter then," the lady said briskly. "What will be will be. Meanwhile we must be getting you on the Teveng ferry."

She retrieved a walking stick from somewhere inside and draped a floral-print vinga over her shoulders. Then she indicated two bundles lying side by side on the verandah. "These are for you, my friends—some provisions for the trip." The two men hefted them with appropriate thanks.

Calling to the children Po Dhai led the way seaward. "By the way," she said as they strolled along, "I've decided to go with you into Teveng. It will make things easier for you, especially when it comes to meeting Inao Sret. And I'll certainly enjoy the festival."

Yuzen and Attanio had no complaints over this new development—in fact the old lady would make a delightful traveling companion. Still Attanio managed to sniff out an ulterior motive: in effect Po Dhai was keeping them in custody. They were offworlders, deviants, untamed by the gentle influence of Ganang Zal; since they had turned up in her territory the lady felt responsible for them, and was reluctant to turn them loose, unchaperoned, on an unsuspecting world. He found it rather touching.

Meanwhile Po Dhai was making arrangements for the care of her young wards during her absence. "I'll be back for your name-day, Zazu, never fear!"

Once at the weatherbeaten docks they waited some time for the ferry to come, lighting lanterns as twilight drew on. Finally the triple sails appeared, ghostly in the dusk: the ship, a catamaran some thirty meters long, fairly flew over the water to its brief mooring. Voices shouted; passengers disembarked; Po Dhai called out to the captain, a woman almost as old as herself. This formidable lady brushed a few glyphs in her passage book and their arrangements were settled. "All aboard then," came the hoarse bellowing of the steward. It was almost as exciting as lift-off.

Farewells were necessarily brief. "I'll bring you wonderful presents from Vachien!" the Eldress promised. Suvei grinned and blew kisses; the children wept. Then the ship cast off and took to the vast dark sea.

XIV. The White Ship Sails

Altogether they spent seven days sailing westward through the Archipelago of Ngok. They called at a dozen ports on five different islands, discharging and taking on passengers at every stop. For Yuzen and Attanio it was a simple matter of *dolce far niente,* or as the islanders say, *san cho zazao:* "doing nothing is enough." They traveled under the aliases of Tanyo and Yao Zin, posing as Po Dhai's nephews.

Having heard of Attanio's musical talents the lady had thoughtfully packed a pair of rosewood claves and a bamboo flute, with which they whiled away many dazzling afternoons and drizzly nights. More often than not they were joined by other pilgrims playing a grab-bag of instruments, from the classical seventeen-string zither to impromptu orchestras of whistles, gongs, and castanets. Attanio was a quick study at interplanetary musicology: once he had heard a few Maung folk airs he could deduce their characteristic modes and play the simpler tunes like a native.

Po Dhai often sang along, in a voice like old china: a bit cracked but no less beautiful for its wear and tear. Her songs were of false lovers who took to sea, and the tearful maidens they left behind; of water elementals and sea goddesses who seduced unwary sailors; and of the undersea palaces wherein they sojourned, unsuspecting, for centuries that passed like carefree days. At night Attanio's dreams were all of blue waves in endless motion.

Still the voyage was no excursion into mindless tedium or lazy bliss. Their first night out, somewhere toward dawn, shouting on deck woke the three of them. Half the passengers and all the crew were staring slack-jawed heavenward. There above them a scene identical to the one Po Dhai had described was being reenacted in blazing color.

No question about it: someone was fighting up there, with

lasers and particle beams, somewhere between the orbit of the inner moon and the edge of the stratosphere. It was over almost as fast as it had begun; but afterimages lingered, both in the retina and in conversation.

"What can those cloud dwellers be up to?" wondered a fragrance peddler. "Is it war? Are they killing each other off?"

Others were quick to weave the incident into existing folklore. "It's the Phoenix Lord at work in his laboratory, concocting the elixir of life," maintained one grandmother. "It's the Coconut Prince throwing dishes at his wife," insisted another. "No, no, it's the Oruri herself coupling with the Lightning God—that was their climax!"

Such explanations, however entertaining, revealed just how far the islanders were from any concept of galactic civilization.

"They live here outside of time, as innocent as children," Attanio whispered.

"I envy them their isolation," Yuzen whispered back. "What glorious dreams it breeds."

And it was true. Cut off from most forms of advanced technology, using only the arts and crafts common to all mankind before the invention of steam engines or Cluj alternators, they had transformed Phra Viharn into one vast garden of delight.

"But now reality intrudes on those dreams," Attanio murmured. "How will they survive the awakening?" Thus beneath all the laughter and music of those days at sea ran an undercurrent of disquiet.

2

On the third night of the voyage there was another display of aerial pyrotechnics, prompting more speculation and ribaldry. But it proved to be the last such disturbance, and was quickly forgotten—except by the three pilgrims from Laphang Town.

On the seventh morning the ship approached Teveng City's bustling harbor. They were forced to wait a good two hours at the great water gate before being allowed in, however, for Ganri Hin had already begun. When they eventually sailed into port it was in the midst of a floating carnival.

Hundreds of tiny pleasure craft with bright sails and sculptured prows thronged the waters. Clouds of incense spiraled into the sky; ensembles of drums and gongs filled the air with pulsing music. At the center of it all was an enormous ship making stately progress through the waves, sheathed in white enamel and showing no sails whatsoever. She was the first powered vessel they had seen on Viharn.

"The White Ship!" Po Dhai cried happily. "As often as I've set eyes on her she never fails to enchant." Yuzen and Attanio echoed her fascination.

The ship towered over them like the cliffs of Muun Chai. There was no emblem or insignia visible anywhere on her, nor any crew in sight. Blank, enigmatic, she cut a wake through the harbor waters as arrow-straight and inevitable as the course of time itself. Her destination was plainly the larger of two islands lying in the middle of the narrow bay—the site of an ornate structure of white marble, wildly baroque with its countercurving roofs, multiple colonnades, and five soaring towers. "The House of Life," Po Dhai declared.

White ship drew abreast of white temple and all man-made noises ceased. A gangway silently extruded from the hull, close to the waterline, and touched the island's flower-choked shore. Then from one of the temple courtyards three bronze gongs sounded in succession, filling the harbor with a shimmering chord. Figures appeared on the gangway—some tall and human, wearing lofty headgear and gauzy veils, others squat and multilegged, with huge bulbous abdomens. "The Ganang *saei*," whispered Po Dhai. "They bear the nectar itself. Those humans attending them we name Xonong Ru. From childhood they dwell among the Xuun, and alone of all humanity learn the true language of Xuun and *saei*."

These beings were only the advanced guard of an extremely long procession wending its way out of the White Ship's cavernous hold, on into the halls and courts of the House of Life. Another hour passed before the last replete hexapod waddled into the temple and the gangway solemnly lifted. Once more the bronze triad rang out.

Now there was mass confusion as all pleasure craft simultaneously made for the docks. Right of way became arbitrary, delays lengthened, but no one seemed to mind. Po Dhai set an example for her companions by calmly trimming her toenails in the midst of this nautical chaos.

For their part Yuzen and Attanio were content to study the

boats, the holiday-makers, and the city around them, rising above the bay in a series of irregular terraces. Its houses were half-timbered of lacquered wood and stucco, painted in soft tones of lemon and apricot, lavender and rose.

On their way to the ferry slip they passed close by a magnificent barge. A gilded phoenix served as its figurehead, and its tailpiece was likewise gilded, curving back over the main deck like a snake. Beneath a silken canopy, surrounded by a handful of richly attired attendants, a woman sat talking casually as a young girl plucked the zither. In fact the vessel's entire complement was female: fifty maidens pulled at fifty ebony oars in all the glory of their nakedness.

"Is it the goddess of love come down to earth?" Attanio asked playfully, out of any native's earshot. Yuzen shrugged: but Po Dhai informed them that this was the Lady Inao herself, Sret of Teveng, the very same whose favor they sought.

"She doesn't seem inclined to grant us an audience just now." Attanio's grin was rueful. "We're in the right place at the wrong time."

"Never fear," Po Dhai said. "Lady Inao welcomes all supplicants in the White Temple's inner gardens." And she smiled blissfully in anticipation.

3

With some difficulty Po Dhai found them a room for the night, where all three slept in a companionable heap despite the revels outside their window. The next morning saw them crowding into a harbor ferry bound for the House of Life.

Sunlight dazzled their eyes, reflected off a thousand wavelets, and the odor of the harbor assailed their nostrils with a compound of salt, rotting seaweed, and fish. The boat was so full that it barely stayed afloat. Still the pilgrim throngs were in excellent humor, chattering gaily, breaking into traditional songs whenever the mood struck them. Both offworlders surrendered to this mounting euphoria.

Holding hands with Po Dhai they stepped off into the temple's cool gardens, swept along with the crowd through a series of courtyards and monumental gateways. Music followed them everywhere. As early as they were, hundreds of celebrants had been there before them. They now sat in small groups on long marble benches, faces shining in the afterglow of communion.

"Sweeter far than mother's milk is the Nectar of Xuun." Po Dhai echoed the words of a folksong centuries old; for some reason it made Attanio's skin prickle. He found it harder and harder to separate his own personal intentions from those of the multitude surrounding him. A particular scene struck his fancy: among the groups of post-communicants he saw a tiny girlchild no more than three standard years old, straying off a little from her mother as she sang to herself in a feathery voice:

> . . . Tza chuan vidhyu
> tei teai na mhru . . .
> 'After its long journey through the clouds
> the raindrop returns to the sea.'

Over and over again she repeated the words, as a child will, making it into a sort of mantra. Pho Tak could have expressed it no better himself, seven thousand years earlier on the banks of the Ganges.

Now they left the outer courts behind and entered the temple proper. Attanio expected a huge cavernous space but found instead a cell-like chamber with many exits. It seemed carved of a single block of alabaster: no joinery was apparent, and its translucent walls glowed softly with filtered sunlight. Lavish calligraphic inscriptions in Ptok suggested the circuitry of a memory chip.

The clamor hushed. In sudden silence they heard a deep all-pervasive drone, like the buzzing of distant wings. Abruptly the crowd seemed thinner, and Attanio realized that their fellow pilgrims were already filing one by one through the low doorways that led to the rest of the temple. He was reminded of the Great Cube of Ynenga. But where that had been a dark labyrinth, this was an airy house of wax, home to creatures of sun and sky. He wondered how closely this sanctuary mimicked the legendary hives of Xuun.

"Where will we find the Lady Inao?" whispered Yuzen.

"Oh, we have a ways to go," Po Dhai said. "She sits at the heart of the temple like a Xuun Imago." And she led them toward one of the exits.

Caught by an irrational impulse Attanio resisted. "Po Dhai!" he hissed.

"Yes, child?" Her startled amber eyes were as guileless as a baby's.

"You have something up your sleeve, something you're not telling us."

Her face crinkled. "I thought it would be obvious. The only way to reach Inao Sret is through the chambers of the *saei*. Only those who have dissolved their worldly cares in the Nectar of Xuun may seek her favor."

Now Yuzen bridled. "You never told us that. Why can't we just wait till the festival is over, and seek her out in her own palace?"

Po Dhai shrugged. "That's six days in the future. I thought your mission brooked no delay—I've done my best to speed you along."

They considered their options. On the one hand, six days seemed like nothing, after all the time they'd spent wandering through the drylands of Ynenga, and crossing interstellar space to Viharn. On the other hand they were potentially only an hour away from this crucial interview. It seemed foolish to let paranoia delay them, especially over something even little children did with impunity.

But still a voice cried out in Attanio's mind—don't do it! Don't sacrifice your will!

Yuzen meanwhile reached his decision. "I'll go. I see nothing to fear in one taste of the nectar. You seem untainted, Po Dhai."

She winked at him. "And you, my friend?"

Attanio frowned, still perplexed. "In Ashbeck I thought nothing of sampling offworld drugs. I suppose I shouldn't be squeamish now." And so—however reluctantly—he followed them down a narrow passageway that twisted and turned back on itself like a bumblebee in flight. Doorways curtained in websilk appeared at close intervals.

"Each one must go alone," Po Dhai said softly. As she explained the simple procedures of the ritual Attanio's heart sank. Nevertheless he chose a door and pulled back its fluttering curtain.

The communion cell, she had named it. It was white and luminous, a fantasy of heaven; it called to mind chapels, shrines, confession boxes. Inside on a low dais squatted the

Ganang *saei*, a swollen iridescent thing like an effigy in blown glass. Plainly it was waiting for him. Did it sense his revulsion, perhaps share the feeling?

He knelt and lifted his face to the monstrous visage.

This was the hardest part. Just as Po Dhai had told him he leaned closer still and stuck out his tongue, fighting back horror, struggling to keep his mouth from trembling. The *saei* responded by extruding a long hairy tube between its mandibles. The discharge came as a fluid shock—

> *warm, golden,*
>> *too fast for flavor—*

and his senses are flooded by the smell and feel of a woman.

He lifts his face from the moistly pungent lips, bearded all around with ebony down, and sees her golden body stretched out before him in an afternoon glow. Smooth belly, round breasts, eyes closed in blissful languor, she is a saint with legs spread wide in benediction. Eyelids flutter, unveiling emerald fire, mouth parts like a sliced mango, shaping warm words. "Life to life, marrow to marrow, end to end." An incantation to console the ache in his spirit.

She pulls him closer, takes him in deep, deeper. There are no boundaries any more. He enters her up to the last centimeter of his flesh and feels himself a stranger in a strange new body, merging completely, vibrating and reechoing with a new name that becomes the password to a fresh creation. Now he can see as she sees, in memory, tumbling back three thousand years to a humid peninsula of Old Earth; yes, a most ancient land, studded with *wats* and *stupas* and reverberant with the memory of the Compassionate. Her origin, her homeland—but who is she?

He need only ask to be answered. She is Pushpa Rangsit, Flower Maiden of Ayudhya, Archon of the Reach of Antares under Suzaku XII, first human to penetrate the hives of Phra Xonong, inventor of Ptok Prime, architect of all that would follow...

And now he frolics through the picture gallery of her mind, sharing her insights and perceptions, glimpsing scenes from a life passed long millennia before his own birth. He sees the indescribable opulence of Suzaku's court, feels overwhelming pride at the news of his/her appointment to Antares, smells the heady perfumes of the gardens of Xuun, trembles in the awesome presence of the Imago herself, a huge quivering pearl resting in webwork of silken silver. For the nectar offers memory: passed from tongue to tongue, proboscis to proboscis, all the way back to that first blissful taste of the Queen Mother's juices.

Now it is plain to him, crystal clear, ringing like a bell, all doubts dispelled. They are godlike, the Xuun, bodhisattvas, creatures who have reached the threshold of enlightenment but choose to remain in this material world in order to guide lesser mortals toward the light. The Xuun, the First Parents, who have distilled their loving kindness into a sweet nectar that even now courses through his veins: guardians, teachers, all-wise, all-compassionate . . . his emotion crests and he explodes with gratitude for that sacred love. . . .

Po Dhai's cool hand on his forehead welcomed him back to consciousness. "Attanio? Are you still with us?"

"Yes, yes," he mumbled, surprised that he was still kneeling, more surprised that he was still dressed. He glanced at the placid *saei*, which somehow had come to resemble an old friend, and then, leaning on Po Dhai's wiry arm, left the cell.

For a few minutes they walked in silence. Each one seemed lost in pleasant reverie. For Attanio it was like waking from a wonderful dream which he couldn't quite remember— he clutched at stray recollections in a futile attempt at reconstructing his vision. Something about a woman. . . .

"Po Dhai," he asked suddenly. "Is it different for everyone?"

"Oh, yes!"

"Have you ever been shown the First Imago?"

She was scandalized, though still vastly amused. "My dear Attanio! You must realize that this is a subject we don't discuss. Small children, perhaps, might whisper of it to their mothers, before they're old enough to know better, but grown-ups never."

He hurried to apologize.

"No harm done, none at all—of course you don't know our ways." She shook her silver head. "What matters is the feeling it leaves with you, and I can tell just by looking at your face that it was the same for both of us, yes, for all three."

Yuzen raised an eyebrow. This was something they'd have to talk over later, in private.

They were outdoors again in a formal garden. At the far

end a woman sat beneath the drooping blossoms of a *teltzil* tree, in much the same state as they had seen her the previous day—for of course she was Inao Sret. Groups of people milled around but none seemed to be dominating her attention. They approached casually and bowed low.

"Blessings of the day upon you," she said pleasantly. She was a handsome woman in middle age, whose ample curves had grown with the years. Attanio found her oddly familiar.

"Here are good honest men," began the Eldress of Laphang Town, "well known to me. Their lips are sweet with the Nectar of Xuun." And with this time-honored preamble she launched into a presentation of their case.

After the first few sentences Lady Inao's eyes widened; a moment later she waved her attendants out of earshot.

"You are the first offworlders ever to set foot in this garden," she said. "I feel the aeons shifting around me." And she made them sit before her, and ordered tea. One by one they rehearsed their tales.

The lady's curiosity was as profound as her questions were exhausting. She demanded clarification on every point. Thus Yuzen found himself obliged to describe Martian political economy, and Attanio to detail the pleasures and perversions of Ashbeck. He even showed her the Tzokol pyramid, which she understood no better than he.

"The Queen will know about such things," was her frequent response.

As he spoke, the Parmenite had a strange feeling of distance from the events he chronicled. It was as if they had happened to someone else, someone he hardly knew. Perhaps it was an effect of the Ganang Zal; he found it didn't really matter to him just now.

Midway through the telling Inao Sret whispered some lengthy instructions to a bejewelled attendant. She disappeared into the temple and was gone so long they forgot her. The day was old before their narrative brought them up to the present.

For a while Lady Inao bided her silence, studying the play of light over a filigreed tower. "You bring me tales of broken worlds," she said at last. "Everything outside this walled garden of Phra Viharn sounds fragmented and diseased. Challenging, yes, and thought-provoking, but also frightening and full of sorrow. The shattered cities of Mars, the zombies of

Loei, the withering deserts of Ynenga, even the proud lords of Srasuri, who prefer torture to mercy: your galaxy seems a vast and terrible place. Yet if your warnings be true its terrors are something we can no longer safely ignore."

The court lady in satin and pearls coughed delicately. She held a whispered conference with her mistress, who looked up at the two offworlders with even more respect than before.

"While we were talking, my lady-in-waiting called Taa Phreng on the short wave," she said. "She managed to speak with the Oruri herself. You are eagerly awaited at court."

Po Dhai did a little dance. "My work is done, my work is done—and what a fine conclusion! Now I can get back to my grandchildren."

Attanio rejoiced along with her. But his joy wasn't half as strong as he expected.

4

The next afternoon they sailed out of Teveng in a floating palace named the *Tipherit,* after that long-gone Imago who first owned the five gemstones of Suut. Since they were under the Queen's special favor she was a powered vessel; normally she carried cargo, but occasionally took on select passengers like themselves.

Their course took them directly into the sunset. From an upper deck Attanio leaned over the taffrail, his hair flying madly in the wind as he looked out over burning clouds and sun-brazen water. Since the previous day he had been trying to sort out his mind's jumbled contents. But his attention kept wandering; his senses kept yearning to rest on the glories all around him, to ignore the disquiet brewing deep inside. This in itself was clear evidence of how the nectar had rearranged him.

One feeling persisted: that of the impermanence and insubstantiality of the world, as if at any moment it might dissolve into smoke and blow away. This must be how the Phra Maung constantly perceived their universe. It was like Chuang Tzu and the butterfly, a dream within a dream within a dream.

All his hostilities toward the Xuun and their six-legged servants were blunted, encapsulated. He raged against this enforced reconciliation. Moment by moment he strove to regain his critical stance, and hour by hour it returned.

Yuzen came over and stood beside him. "I see thunder-clouds gathering behind your eyes," he said lightly. "Why such furious concentration?"

"I'm trying to recover my nastiness."

"Hah! It's coming!"

Attanio tried not to laugh. "The nectar didn't affect you the way it did me. Why were you so lucky?"

"I suppose I have built-in defenses against any kind of mind control. My heredity, you know, and my training in Za."

Attanio scowled—a good sign. "My lessons on Ynenga were too brief."

"But you did learn a great deal from your vision—surely you of all people can't regret that."

"I suppose not. But it seems like we're prisoners in the Land of Lotus Eaters. Even our minds aren't free! Don't you see how Ganang Zal makes these people happy and stupid, content to toil over rice paddies and play pretty tunes? Where are the rebels? Who among them would dream of scrawling nasty slogans on the White Ship, or wailing dark songs about how it hurts to die? Who would long for the stars? That's what bothers me—there's no one here like me, and if the Phra Maung had their way, I'd change too."

"But the people here are content. They live in beauty, and no one suffers for it: what could be wrong with that?"

"There has to be a price," Attanio muttered. "They're drugged; they're missing out on what they really could be."

Yuzen shoved him playfully. "I suppose you think Ashbeck is where true freedom thrives."

"I didn't at the time," he admitted. "It was definitely a mess—but now I suspect that you can have too many sunny days for your own good." And he turned back to the fire on the horizon, thinking over and over, no one lives in dreams forever.

XV. Taa Phreng

Although the great island of Vachien lay some 1100 kilometers due west of Teveng City the *Tipherit* first sailed northward to Suru. Her silent engines carried her along far quicker than the wind's vagaries ever could. They crossed the Sea of Phoro, a stretch of open water unbroken by any islands, in little over three days—and on the fourth morning they beheld Suru's long southern peninsula riding the horizon. Here and there columns of smoke rose into the sky from green hills: the captain said they were active volcanoes.

Tipherit docked at the port city of Jupalzin and spent the day unloading blocks of dried seaweed and huge amphorae of the Archipelago's rice wine. Ingots of iron and tin took their place, for Suru was mining country. Then it was southward again across the watery desert to Laoi, a storybook island with mountains shaped like breasts and thatched villages clustered like fruit. Here the cargo was birds: fantasy creatures of assorted genera, some with towering crests, others with bright purple beaks, a few with tails almost two meters long. All had iridescent plumage that put gemstones to shame. These were bound for the gardens of Taa Phreng, where they would spend their days strutting and fretting about as living ornaments.

They broke through into the placid Bay of Xai on the ninth day. To the north, invisible in the distance, lay the wild island of Zemzin, home of the fighting spiders so prized by sportsmen and gamblers. To the south, practically within spitting distance, was Vachien. From here on *Tipherit* hugged the coast. They sailed past marshes, jungles, sandy beaches, limestone cliffs, pastel villages, and fleets of fishing boats. On the eleventh day they stood before the colossal sea-gate of Taa Phreng, capital of this entire world.

There was a saying current on Vachien: "When the gods are tired of heaven they come down to see Taa Phreng."

For the city was a world unto itself. It encompassed more than ninety small islands covering two hundred and fifty square kilometers, and held six million people: more than the entire population of the Isles of Ngok. Two thousand temples lifted their pinnacles into incense-laden skies; eight royal palaces, each with extensive gardens and parklands, graced the eight major sectors of town. Theaters, restaurants, teahouses, libraries, palestras, and brothels all found a place within its limits.

On the morning of *Tipherit*'s arrival the city was wrapped in a fine mist, from which only ornamental roofcombs, tree-covered hilltops, and temple towers emerged. At the docks the ship's steward engaged them a private gondola. With lanterns hung fore and aft (and much bell-ringing) it carried them along the ghostly channels toward their final destination: the fabled court of the Imago. Attanio was as taut as the top string on a classical zither, so full of anticipation that he was speechless. Now and then he grinned stupidly at Yuzen, who seemed almost as eager. Both stared into the swirling fog and peopled it with visions of the future.

"Do you feel like yourself yet?" Yuzen teased.

"No! I'm too happy."

They docked at the imperial quay and climbed shallow steps of green marble to the palace precincts. The mist began dissolving; all around them the island-city materialized in vivid color, dreamlike in its clarity and silence. The palace itself was impossible to take in at a single glance, especially from such a close perspective. All they saw was a profusion of roofs and gabled towers and long low garden walls. At the top of the green staircase a chamberlain greeted them and conducted them with all seemly haste to the Queen's chambers.

A triple doorway led within. They glimpsed varicolored pillars and faded mosaics, overhung by a stained-glass dome. Directly before them, on a modest throne, sat Queen Talithai, appropriately bare-breasted, braided, and befeathered.

The chamberlain called out their names and accompanied them to within a few meters of the throne.

Then a major earthquake rocked Attanio's world. He remained standing only with considerable effort. His mouth moved spasmodically and peculiar noises escaped his throat. For there before him, chin resting sidewise on well-manicured hand, iridescent plumes drooping from nephrite headdress—

the very picture of languid elegance—sat Sringlë.

She gave a half-smile at his obvious stupefaction. "I look familiar, do I?"

"How is it possible?" Attanio squeaked.

"Science," she replied. "But I'm not who you think I am."

"You're *not* Sringlë?"

"Actually no one is." She laughed—that same unmistakable cascade of sound that had first captivated him at the Succubarium. "No, I'm Talithai Oruri, none other, and we've never met before. You have me confused with—I suppose we can call her my daughter."

Both Yuzen and the Queen's chamberlain were listening to this exchange with varying proportions of baffled amusement. Attanio suddenly felt incredibly foolish. "I beg indulgence, Your Highness. I'm a person of low estate, ill-suited to civilized company."

"Nonsense," the Queen said. "You've weathered many hardships and don't deserve my cat-and-mouse games. Please sit." Chairs were waiting. "Now I'm sure both you and your worthy Martian friend are full of questions. Ask away."

They did, to their hearts' content. Finally they had a willing informant with all the answers.

Naturally their first inquiries were about Sringlë and the rest of *Samuindorogo*'s crew. "Are they here in Taa Phreng?" Attanio asked eagerly.

"Only the woman whom you knew as Sringlë of Phayao, and the two Myinti named Kkrih and Hsseu. As you have probably guessed by now Sringlë was a Phra Maung operative—her real name is Chuyin Vaoi, and she is the child of my body. When Chel squadron disabled *Samuindorogo* on the fringes of the Aab-Oort system, Lord Teoru, the four Myinti, and my daughter Chuyin were all taken prisoner to Srasuri. With the help of other Phra Maung agents, Chuyin broke out of her prison and even managed to loose two of the Myinti. They hid in Srasuri's warehouse district for a few days and then stowed away on a surface-bound shuttle. Unfortunately Lord Teoru, Fsau, and Yaaish remain in Luo Maung hands."

"Then how did your agent manage to rescue us?"

"The fact is that the lords of Srasuri weren't particularly interested in you. They had already interrogated Lord Teoru and the Myinti and obtained a treasure trove of information. Realizing that other passengers of *Samuindorogo*—namely yourselves—might still be at large somewhere in the Reach, they offered a bounty for your capture, meanwhile circulating accurate descriptions of the Martian princes and Master Attanio Hwin. This they did reflexively, as a matter of course, without any sense of urgency. Several weeks passed before you turned up, and by then you were considered superfluous. Consequently you were poorly guarded."

After digesting all this Yuzen asked, "Can you tell us anything about those aerial battles we saw a fortnight ago?"

"Yes . . . that." Talithai sighed and shifted position on the wooden throne. She was the picture of radiant youth; but both her guests knew she was more than three centuries old, and for the first time they had a glimpse of her true age in the faraway set of her eyes. "The past has begun to catch up with the present," she said softly. "No doubt you've heard tales of the schism between the sky cities and the landsmen. I myself played no small part in that conflict. At the time I took steps to ensure that Phra Viharn would never be vulnerable to attack from the Luo Maung. Before the treaty went into effect, and quite unknown to them, I rewrote the programming of the satellite network. I made it impossible for those weapons ever to be aimed at the surface—they would autodestruct first.

"Centuries have passed since then; centuries of peace. Just as I planned." She gave her languid half-smile. "The whole Antares Reach has pursued its downward spiral quite unimpeded. Then the Martians arrived with news of galactic war. . . ." She laughed. "And you two young men, out of all the galaxy, in your mad flight from Srasuri to Phra Viharn— you were the first to trigger those fatal energies. And when you did the Luo Maung finally discovered my tampering, for the satellites failed to respond as they should have. For three nights after your escape they tried to unravel my sabotage. All they managed to do was destroy the whole network. You saw some of it, didn't you? What an extravaganza!

"We're quite defenseless now, you know. The Luo Maung are terribly worried." Though Talithai didn't seem to be, not at all. In the pale sunlight streaming through the dome she seemed as untroubled as a flower.

"Do you have any plans to spring Teoru and Fsau?" ventured Attanio, after a moment's respectful pause.

"Chuyin is working on that now," she replied. "And I'm sure you're eager to see her. Yes?" She stirred from her languor, summoning the chamberlain. "Bring these gentlemen to the Indigo Tower, to the presence of Chuyin Vaoi." And as unceremoniously as it had begun the audience was over.

As they left Attanio marveled at how much Talithai and Chuyin-Sringlë were alike. Not just their looks but their moods, their mannerisms. Sringlë had always seemed to hold a mocking attitude toward the Martian clones: but now it was clear that she was one herself. In fact Sringlë, Talithai, and Lady Inao were all merely echoes of the First Imago herself, Pushpa Rangsit of Old Earth, whose memories he had briefly tasted in Teveng City. This knowledge did nothing to still the pounding of his heart.

Perfumed arbors, shaded walks, all passed by unnoticed as they drew near the steeply gabled Indigo Tower. From a balcony several stories up a raven-haired woman leaned out and called to them. Her voice was music.

"Attanio! It's you! And is that Yencho? I can't wait to hear your tales!"

Seven flights of stairs only added to Attanio's breathless anticipation. They burst out onto the top landing and he flew into Sringlë's arms.

A few inarticulate sounds were exchanged. Then the Parmenite was babbling, "You siren, you sorceress, you trickster! What a chase you've led me! I never knew your name, or your homeworld, or even your hair color! Look at you now!"

Indeed. Sringlë had resumed her true colors at last and was far more beautiful than he remembered. Viharnese fashions exquisitely suited her Amazon glory. Quetzal feathers streamed from elaborately knotted hair, accentuating the emerald sparkle of her eyes, and her naked breasts were sprinkled with flakes of mica. Her *puun* was of spiderweb fineness, floating around her hips in a floral print of black, violet, and verdigris. Talithai had suggested a delicate afternoon breeze: Chuyin-Sringlë was a dawning gale.

She held Attanio at arm's length with undisguised admiration. "You're a survivor, Attanio Hwin—though I suppose you, sir, have had something to do with his continued good health." This last she added in Yuzen's direction.

For a few moments the Martian warrior had been quite ignored, but now Chuyin-Sringlë turned her attention on him. "You're not Momozon, and you're not Yencho either." She frowned.

"We've never met," Yuzen explained. "I was in stasis until Ynenga."

"Ynenga? Lady Inao didn't tell us much in her radio broadcast. I'm afraid we have a lot of catching up to do."

So they spent the rest of the morning in the tower room doing just that. Sringlë was amazed at their tale: "You were born under a lucky star, Attanio," she told him again and again. And to Yuzen she said, "Of all Prince Myobu's sons, I think you are the finest."

Her own adventures since Loei were much less colorful, comprising merely her escape from Srasuri and her homecoming at Taa Phreng. "I've had to learn how to behave like a princess again," she confessed. "Court life seems a bit stale after my days in space. Though there is a great deal to be said for civilization. . . ." Her tone of voice plainly implied that Taa Phreng was the only civilized place in the galaxy.

Watching her, listening to her, absorbing her presence, Attanio found this latest version of Sringlë the most irresistible yet. She was a vortex that pulled him deeper and deeper into a flood of emotions far stronger than the ones that first engulfed him in Ashbeck. At the same time he thought of Yuzen, recalling the constancy of his love and the long familiarity of their companionship. Against the Martian's straightforwardness he weighed Sringlë's teasing, her evasions, her proliferating disguises. But the heart has no logic. Sringlë drew him with the force of a singularity.

As he expected, she pounced on his description of the Great Cube of Ynenga. And when he produced the tetrahedron she was dumbfounded. "That's a Tzokol Riftstone," she breathed. "Attanio—how did you ever get it through the Veil?"

She went on to tell what she knew about such artifacts. "The Xuun have preserved a great deal of lore concerning the Lizard Kings, which they impart to selected humans. I've spent a few seasons in Phra Xonong studying whatever they would teach me. They—"

Attanio interrupted. "You weren't one of those pathetic children carried off in the White Ship, were you?"

She smiled. "Close, but not quite. I managed to avoid the pointed turban and the vows of chastity. No, all close kin of the Oruri are sent to the hexapods to round out their education. Naturally I was fascinated by the Tzokol question. This stone, now. I suppose the Ynengans taught you something of the Alien God, and the Dark Prison? Well, the Tzokol manufactured objects which served as foci—perhaps catalysts might be a better word—for a trance state, in which they projected their minds into the Void and communed with their nameless god. That's what this pyramid is. It's quite a small one, you know—suitable for a child. But you were saying that the Cube contained much larger ones, correct?" She drew a deep breath. "In that case we may be on to something. Because these Riftstones can project more than thoughts. Watch."

She took the stone in her hand and assumed a relaxed, meditative posture. Her eyelids drooped; her breath came slow and shallow. For some time nothing more occurred, and Attanio found himself listening to the liquid song of a bird nesting in the eaves. Then Yuzen touched his arm.

Sringlë was flickering. *Now you see her, now you don't.* On the "don't" part of the cycle sunlight passed blithely through her, and there was a rush of displaced air. This phenomenon lasted only a moment. Then a crooning sound escaped her lips, her head nodded, and the pyramid tumbled out of suddenly limp hands. Yuzen caught her before she could fall.

"How was that?" she asked weakly.

"Quite a trick!" said Attanio. "Maybe you'll teach us someday."

"Oh, it's easy." She was already recovering. "So much for my excursion into the Void. It's quite beautiful, you know—like drowning in an ocean of light. But the point is that with a large enough Riftstone you could move a whole world. That is, you couldn't, I couldn't, but among the Xonong Ru there are circles of Adepts with that much power. And with things as they are we need all the power we can find.

"So how would you like to pay a return visit to your friends on Ynenga?"

"I'm yours to command," said Attanio.

"Sweet boy. But I'm being a little hasty; a move like that requires planning. We'll see."

"Sringlë." Attanio caught himself. "Or should I call you Chuyin? These aliases are confusing. Tell me—are you a telepath? You've just proved that you have some form of psionic power, and I've always suspected you of reading my mind."

She laughed heartily. "What a silly question! Your mind is an open book to me, and light reading at that." Attanio lunged playfully for her throat.

"I apologize! And I lied. No—I lack that gift. Though as you've seen, the Xuun, and the Lumis too, did manage to teach me a few parlor tricks. Actually my specialty is prognostication."

"You're a prophetess!"

"Not exactly. But it *is* a truism that through a complete understanding of the present one can make accurate predictions of the near future. I have a strong intuitive grasp of current possibilities; with enough information I can make an integration which points toward the most likely future. That's how I found you, Attanio: when I saw you at the Succubarium I just knew that you'd be the one to help us. And look how far you've come."

"True, true," Attanio said modestly. "But you didn't do so well on Loei."

"I beg your pardon! Who kept saying, 'Let's get out of here fast'?"

A comic altercation seemed imminent, so Yuzen stepped in. "Let's get back to the subject of Teoru. You were saying that the Queen's agents recently discovered—"

"Yes. He's been moved, though we're not sure why. A few days ago he was flown from Prathamim to Phra Viharn itself, to a remote Luo Maung outpost in the Vadhuz sector."

"Then what are we waiting for?" Attanio demanded.

"Earthquakes and typhoons."

2

In fact Sringlë had already devised a plan for liberating the Martian lord. It hinged on the geology and meteorology of the western hemisphere, where Vadhuz lay. This region was so prone to earthquakes and volcanic eruptions that it contained no permanent settlements whatsoever. Teoru was being held in a makeshift prison on the island of Pao, site of a particularly active volcano; and while it was winter at the latitude of Taa Phreng, in Pao it was full summer—the season of storms.

"We Phra Maung are as skilled in the prediction of earth movements as we are in forecasting the weather," Chuyin said. "It's a simple matter of survival. Furthermore we have among us certain individuals who can actually control the forces of nature—I mean weatherworkers, lightning masters, earth movers. These are arts which the sky-dwellers have lost and probably forgotten. But my mother the Queen employs dozens of Adepts who can change the course of hurricanes and still the shaking earth. These past few days, ever since I learned of Teoru's move, I've been planning an expedition to Pao. With an airship and a few weatherworkers we should be able to pull it off easily. I still need the Queen's approval for my requisitions—though now that you've arrived with that Riftstone I think I'll have more leverage with her."

"You mean she overlooks you sometimes?" Attanio found this hard to believe.

"Certainly. I'm just one of the crowd. You see, when I call her my mother I'm using the term a bit loosely. I carry most of her genetic material but I'm not the product of her womb. No, all of us *sret* and *vaoi* are . . . manufactured. Yuzen understands, I see. There's a huge laboratory, or factory if you will, where the Queen's offspring are conceived. We're implanted in surrogate mothers, born in the normal way, and raised in the palace creche. It occupies its own island on the fringes of Taa Phreng."

"Then how many daughters does the Imago have?"

"In the course of her lifetime, hundreds. At any given moment—maybe fifty or sixty living offspring. There's a distinction between near-duplicates, like myself, and women with a broader mixture of heredity. Inao Sret is an example of that—you could think of her as Queen Talithai's sister. But no matter how closely we resemble the Queen we're all carefully designed with a particular end in mind. Then as we mature, she keeps an eye on us, to see how well we fulfill our promise. If we're good girls we're rewarded with positions in government. If we're just ordinary specimens we revert to the mainstream of society and follow a profession. Some of the Queen's daughters have ended up as tavern keepers, ship captains, farmers, or even seamstresses."

"How are you doing?"

"Oh, very well indeed." She grinned. "But I have some fierce competition."

3

Over the next several days Yuzen and Attanio became well acquainted with the intrigues of court life. The Imago's daughters—the *vaoi*, or nymphs—presided over a glittering round of banquets, salons, levees, evenings at the theater, cabinet meetings, water parties, clandestine interviews, and love trysts. From the start Chuyin-Sringlë used them both to further her own interests. First she insisted that Yuzen remove the black dye from his hair, so that his silver Martian mane was revealed in all its glory; then she prevailed upon Attanio to restore the zebra stripes that he had flaunted in Ashbeck. Thus she emphasized the alien glamor of her two new proteges.

For Chuyin was at the center of Taa Phreng's interplanetary movement. Talithai herself had set her on this course when she was just out of adolescence, by smuggling her offworld and sending her on a long *Wanderjahr* among the worlds of the Reach. The Queen was considering a revision of her isolationist policy; she had the unique capacity of dividing herself into several different viewpoints, through the agency of her clone-children, and then examining every side of a particular issue. Thus Chuyin was the leading exponent of interplanetarianism: she favored detente with Luo Viharn and an extension of Viharnese cultural influence throughout the Reach. Her position had been strengthened by the appearance of the Martians, whose account of the Xillian invasion brought home the futility of isolationism. From opera house to market square she was surrounded by admirers eager to hear her opinions.

However, the fact of Teoru's imprisonment, along with the continued hostility of the Luo Maung, complicated matters to the point where there was no single obvious solution. Chuyin-Sringlë's ideas weren't the only ones clamoring for the Queen's approval. During her long absence from Viharn some of her other sisters had risen to prominence in court circles, particularly Tiao and Aeian.

Tiao was the diplomat of the lot. She had more angular features than Sringlë and went around draped in antique vingas. Politically, she supported the status quo, opposing any expansion into space, and was rumored to be the Queen's favorite. Aeian, on the other hand, took no interest in politics whatsoever. Of all the royal house she had spent the most time in Phra Xonong and was the most skilled at Xuun-derived psionics. If anything she would prefer a deeper immersion of Viharnese society into the Xuun hive-mind: certainly she was indifferent to the other worlds of the Maung Cluster. Her personal style was dreamy and detached.

Yuzen found this *haut monde* of Phra Viharn an extremely frivolous collection of types. He remembered the refinements of Tharsis and Olympus Mons, and while Taa Phreng lacked nothing in delicacy or good taste, there seemed a great void underneath it all. There were no social tensions, no pressing issues of philosophy or morality, no sense of the future. The pursuit of pleasure went along without the slightest hitch, with the Nectar of Xuun thrown in once a year to keep everything lubricated.

It really was the Land of the Lotus Eaters. Rather than rage against it the two Galactics decided to join in, at least until the Imago decided their case.

4

About a week later Attanio and Sringlë were riding in a gondola bound for Three Bridges, where the lady had an appointment with an old geographer. These days most of her waking hours were spent preparing for the mission to Pao.

"I never dreamed you could be this cold," Attanio was saying. He was in a sulk; his face was all scowls and his hand trailed listlessly in the canal.

"Don't be tiresome, Attanio." Sringlë had her nose in a book. She was doing her best to ignore him.

"Tiresome? How should I behave, then? Would you prefer a trained spider doing somersaults? What does it take to hold your attention? Since I've been in Taa Phreng we've had one night together—one single night—and all the rest of the time you've acted like I don't exist."

She put down her book. "You must realize, my dear, that this isn't Ashbeck, and I'm not some little party girl drooling over my man. Of course I care for you. But it just isn't the custom for royal ladies to be involved in exclusive relationships like the one you have in mind." She spread her hands helplessly. "It's not in our nature. Can you understand that?"

"It doesn't seem human," he said, as if to himself. "Why did I ever get involved with all you pedigreed clones?"

"Oh Attanio!" She laughed, not unkindly. "What about Yuzen? He's as dependable as the law of entropy, and you know he loves you. How can *you* be so uncaring as to ignore that, and hurt him by chasing me?"

"But *I* love *you!* I loved you long before I ever met Yuzen." And his voice held no anger, no accusation—only pain.

She relented a little. "My poor pumpkin," she said, taking him in her arms. "This city is full of distractions. Surrender to it—don't keep your heart fixed on me."

"I'll try . . . oh god, this sounds like one of those awful old love songs, the kind people always wanted me to sing in Ashbeck but I never would." Irony was some consolation, and so were the lady's arms: he brightened a little. "You know, Yuzen has already been following your advice. He's been having an affair with that guardsman in the Queen's retinue—"

"Aha!"

"—so you see he's not as dependable as you think."

"He's just realistic, that's all. He knows you'll come around sooner or later, and meanwhile he sees no reason to pine away. You should do the same." She disentangled herself, but kept hold of both his hands. "And as for that I'm not rejecting you either, not ultimately. I'll come around too—you know I have my moods. Just take what comes: that's how we do it here in Taa Phreng."

Attanio nodded. "Maybe I should pay court to one of your sisters. You know, I was formally presented to Aeian yesterday. She's quite a charmer."

"Aeian? Charming?" Sringlë seemed to find this unlikely. "You did mention something about that. Talithai wanted you to show her your Riftstone and brief her on Ynenga, right?" Now he had her attention. "How did that turn out?"

"It was hard to tell—neither one of them say much. They're very similar, aren't they."

Sringlë frowned. "I've noticed the same thing since I've been back. It wasn't like this before I left. I must confess, it *is* a bit hard on my identity having all these mirror images walking around . . . and then discovering that I have less in common with them than I thought. I used to imagine I was the Queen's true heir, but now I have my doubts. Aeian was interested, though, wasn't she? Mental tricks are her obsession."

"Yes, she was interested, but only in an abstract sort of way. She said she'd like to have a few years at her disposal to study the Great Cube—and then went on to say how impractical that would be, given the political climate."

Her frown deepened. "How did my mother react to that?"

"She didn't."

Sringlë shrugged. "She's bound to come to her senses soon. Yuzen has already given her the gory details of the Xillian invasion, and his version was a lot more compelling than my secondhand description. She knows we can't go on as we have."

They had reached the Three Bridges, tall graceful arches spanning the intersection of five canals. Their craft docked and Sringlë stepped out. "Take a holiday, my love. Go chase Aeian, for all I care. Go to a whorehouse." And with that sweet farewell they parted for the afternoon.

5

That evening Attanio went along with Yuzen to a marathon performance of classical drama, presented in an outdoor theater beneath strings of painted lanterns. The players wore elaborate masks and moved in the most stylized postures, and the accompanying music had a cumulative, hypnotic effect. In spite of some moments of real theatrical power Attanio found himself nodding.

With an apology he left his seat to take some air in the nearby gardens: given the great length of Maung productions this was a common practice, perfectly acceptable. In fact it often added to the excitement of a night at the theater.

He was on his way back to Yuzen's side when a girl of ten or eleven approached him. She was elegantly dressed and carried herself like a lady of the royal house. With a practiced curtsy she handed him a note; then without waiting for his reply she turned away, smiling coyly over her shoulder, and ran off like the child she really was.

The note was perfumed. Its handwriting was distinguished, and decidedly feminine. "When has night been more beautiful?" it read. "The nearer moon has set but the farther moon still shines, never wholly obscured by clouds." Its signature was simply the character for "wistaria."

Attanio was both intrigued and entertained. He almost laughed aloud—but then caught himself, for perhaps the poetess was hiding somewhere nearby and even now had her eye on him. It had to be some court lady—but who? Was there some clue in the reference to Viharn's two moons?

He looked up and saw that in fact the further moon was alone in the sky, half-veiled by passing clouds. Then he noticed a blue wistaria in the garden he had just left. He walked back. Sure enough, there in the shadow of its trailing branches stood the figure of a woman.

He bowed in her direction. "The further moon has hours to go before retiring; must she hide behind clouds till the night is spent?"

The lady stepped forward into the lamplight. She was rather small, with a round voluptuous figure; her face was concealed in the folds of a purple vinga. "Perhaps if the night wind blows hard enough he will carry off the clouds, and then moonlight will rival dawn itself."

Attanio finally did laugh, throwing his head back merrily. Here was the distraction Sringlë had recommended, right on cue. This mysterious lady already had him in her power.

Without a word she led him down through the garden to the canal, where a gondola waited. The little messenger was already aboard, sitting next to a boy a few years older. Attanio begged their permission to send Yuzen a note—explaining that he'd be back the next day—and persuaded the child to act as go-between one last time. When she had accomplished this much they cast off: the boy poled them along like a professional.

Attanio was surprised when they headed away from the palace district. "I thought you lived at court."

"Once I did. It didn't suit me."

Their destination was one of the many residential quarters of town, neither slummy nor grand. They moored at the edge of a garden and climbed a small hill to a slightly tumbledown villa, the children walking ahead with lamps. The villa's upper story was a pillared terrace, furnished with tables and couches, and here the lady kissed the two children goodnight and dismissed them. Then she turned toward Attanio and pulled him close. Only moonlight intruded on their shared embrace. Gently he removed the veil . . .

He gave no sign of his surprise. She had Sringlë's face, of course.

They spent the night in mutual pleasure, sleeping late the next day. Her name was Xaiya. She was one of those errant nymphs who had failed to meet the Queen's expectations, and had retired from court some twenty years earlier. The boy and girl were her children by two previous lovers.

She supported herself as a screen painter. Her work affected the air of dreamy melancholy so much in vogue here, and she did well.

But after a day or two Attanio found that her life mimicked her art. Her moods were as changeable as the wind, tending toward neurasthenia; she had squandered her emotions on a string of lovers who always left her before half a year went by. Moreover it took no prying to learn her romantic history: the subject came up in almost every conversation, much to the Parmenite's dismay.

It was obvious that Sringlë had set her up to this particular tryst, which had all the earmarks of a cruel joke. For after three nights of the lady's company Attanio found that she bored him. Her resemblance to Sringlë was simply not enough to hold his interest, and in fact began to seem grotesque.

He made his farewell with a poem.

"Once more the further moon has risen alone: how many nights hereafter will she wax and wane, and look through this same garden after me—in vain?" Not the kindest thing he could have said, or the most original, but then that was Attanio.

On returning to the palace he sought out Yuzen. "I'm sick of Taa Phreng," he announced. "It's a womanish place, and all the women are either teases or melancholiacs. I feel like going back to Ynenga!"

Yuzen regarded him quizzically over a cup of morning *tzat*. "I see your diversion has already gone sour. So has mine: it's not just the women, Attanio. These people are great gamesters of love. We're no match for them."

"They have it reduced to a science," Attanio agreed sadly. "I feel like I've just been the subject of a very calculated experiment. Sringlë has taught me a lesson, all right . . . but not the one she intended. I still want her as much as ever."

Yuzen sighed. "Even the Nectar of Xuun can't cure our hearts."

XVI. Talithai's Choice

Instead they decided on a rice-wine binge. Even the staid Prince of the Shinjuku got as drunk as a skunk and sang obscene love songs, while the palace staff giggled behind their fans and stayed out of the way.

Then, two blurry days later, a summons arrived from the Oruri herself:

> Your attendance is desired at a meeting of state on the Emerald Terrace, this afternoon, just before the Hour of the Phoenix. Sobriety is encouraged.

After a swim in the royal lagoon they attired themselves in snakeskin and satin and arrived punctually. Chuyin, Aeian, Tiao, and the rest of the Oruri's intimate circle were on hand; seating was informal. As flutes sounded the hour the Queen swept in.

Her vitality seemed amplified a hundredfold: she was like a star come down to earth. Without preamble she began speaking in a ringing voice that Attanio had never heard her use.

"Through the teachings of Pho Tak and the compassion of Xuun, humankind has flourished on this planet for three thousand six hundred and ninety-six years. We have seen the motherworlds crumble while our own civilization endured. For centuries we believed that we were the principal remaining outpost of humanity in the whole galaxy.

"Now word has come—" she nodded toward Yuzen—"that a military state has risen in the Pleiades. It is expanding toward the Core and can be expected in our own Reach any year, any day. We Phra Maung are not alone in this knowledge; our kinsfolk in the orbiting cities have received the same intelligence and even now are planning their defense. However, their leadership is divided, their armaments insufficient.

221

"You may wonder what concern any of this can be for us. The star patterns at the outset of my reign decreed that this era would be one for the earth and the sea, for the tending of vines and the laughter of children. We left behind us the game of starships and death; we forsook all imperial gestures.

"That era has ended. From this day I Talithai Oruri resume my sovereignty over all Maung, whether on land or in the sky. In two weeks time my daughters Tiao and Chuyin will lead an embassy to the lords of Srasuri and inform them of the new order." She paused; Chuyin-Sringlë and most of the others tried hard to stifle their amazement.

"Human authority in this region of space has always derived from Xuun. A few centuries past a movement arose denying this basic truth. There was bloodshed and destruction; everywhere humans lived in a state of confusion. But the reigning Imago decided to let the heresy run its course, concluding that it would eventually die a natural death—whereas persecution could only prolong the agony. Discontent and even madness now run rampant in the sky-cities, while the serenity of Phra Viharn continues untroubled.

"Now this threat of invasion from the Pleiades gives us the perfect opportunity to reassert ourselves over the heretics. In accordance with the Chimango we will achieve our ends bloodlessly, without any military conflict whatsoever. For the lords of Srasuri are slowly realizing their helplessness in the face of attack. Only the technology of the elder races can protect them—and only the disciples of Xuun have access to that technology. As a flower turns toward the sun so will the Luo Maung turn to us for their salvation."

There was applause, which Queen Talithai acknowledged with the slightest nod of her befeathered head. Attanio, however, was baffled. It seemed to him that the Oruri had spoken in almost mythological terms, with far more optimism than the crisis deserved. But this apparently was the prevailing style of Viharnese speechmaking. Now, as the gathering broke up into conversational groups, the Queen moved among them to confer with this or that individual. Here was where the real meeting began.

Sringlë caught his ear. "Did you notice Aeian's composure during the whole speech? None of that came as a surprise to her."

"I did notice. I suppose that means she enjoys special favor these days, yes?"

Sringlë frowned. "So it seems. I don't understand. The Queen has just formally embraced all the programs that I've been urging, but meanwhile she's hardly spoken to me in days, and she's given me no public credit at all."

Attanio couldn't contain his amusement. "You royal ladies do enjoy your games, don't you."

Her reply was cut off by the Imago's approach. She drew Sringlë aside and spoke for quite a while. There was some disagreement at first, at least as far as Attanio could tell, but in the end both seemed satisfied by the exchange.

Finally Yuzen and Attanio's turn came. "I think I know what's uppermost in your minds," Queen Talithai began. "I've decided to give my approval to Chuyin's projected mission to Pao, with one minor change. Chuyin herself intended to lead the rescue: but now that we're in the process of normalizing our relations with Luo Viharn, and now that Chuyin will be one of my chief negotiators, I hardly think it politic. Instead Prince Yuzen will command. You'll have a team of weather-workers at your disposal, plus a handful of picked warriors."

Yuzen thanked her in his best Shinjuku manner. For his sake Attanio was glad: he knew how much this official recognition meant.

"You realize how important it is to be discreet," the Imago went on. "There can be no witnesses to our intervention; I don't want to give Chelzin Tep any grounds for mistrust or noncooperation."

They allowed as they understood. Then Attanio politely asked, "What are your intentions concerning Ynenga? In your address you mentioned the wisdom of the elder races: did you mean the Riftstone?"

"Indeed I did, and I have you to thank for that. My daughter Aeian is departing for Phra Xonong this very evening to charter a Xuun starship for a voyage to Ynenga. Her mission is to bring back a few of the larger Riftstones. A great deal hinges on her success."

"But that means she'll be rending the Veil," said Attanio. "I thought Xuun starships couldn't do that."

"Strictly speaking, they can't. But we Imagoes have always maintained a few veilship drives, camouflaged in

Xuun hulls, in the spaceport at Phra Xonong. It's a well-kept secret." And with a polite nod Queen Talithai moved on to her next interview.

The two Galactics indulged in a little back-slapping. "What more could we ask?" Attanio exulted. "But I wonder what Sringlë's thinking. She's the great starfarer, and here the Queen's just given an interstellar command to Aeian."

Yuzen shrugged. "If you had known the intrigues of the Shinjuku none of this would surprise you. Rulers always play off heirs against each other: everything they do is a test."

"Then poor Sringlë. No wonder she treats me the way she does."

2

Time had become Yuzen's enemy. They had spent four days now flying over the Tzrin Teai in the airborne palace Queen Talithai called a fighting ship. It was easily capable of speeds exceeding 600 kilometers per hour, but since they had located the infant typhoon three days past they had crawled along at only 800 kilometers a day—exactly the speed of the typhoon itself.

One of the beauties of Chuyin-Sringlë's scheme was its ingenious method of camouflage. They had only to find a typhoon brewing in the open sea and match its progress with their own, keeping all the while to the zone of calm weather at the eye. By staying within a kilometer or less of a powerful electrical storm they effectively screened themselves from any long-range detection instruments on Pao.

Meanwhile Pzu Cheng the lightning master guided the storm's movements with the effortless ease of a Wiwa tribesman riding an *ihya'at*.

By late afternoon of the fourth day they were within reach of Lord Teoru's island prison. Yuzen was itching to strike, but still they must wait a little longer, till the eye was almost brushing Pao's shoreline. For hours now the island had borne the brunt of the typhoon's onslaught: torrential rains, winds powerful enough to uproot saplings, heavy coastal flooding, inland mudslides. In spite of his impatience Yuzen found time to worry about his master's safety amid such havoc.

Nor was this his only concern. The very day they left Taa Phreng, intelligence had reached the Oruri concerning Lord Appucc of Xil. Talithai had one invaluable agent privy to the transactions of the Council of Lords in Srasuri, who reported on the session which had so inflamed Prajit La. So now the Oruri knew all about the Xillian armada lying off 73 Imniot. She made no secret of the news; thus her whole court shared the burden of uncertainty and dread. Every second of the way from Vachien to Pao Yuzen was haunted by memories of Mars and forebodings of some new horror here on Viharn.

It could happen at any moment—and worst of all there was nothing he could do to stop it. Wherever he looked the horizon was dark, though a blazing sun burned overhead.

"Prince Yuzen." One of the lesser Adepts sought his attention. "Vahat Sen is ready to enter trance. Will you attend?"

He would. "Cease forward motion. Hover at present altitude till I give word." And with that Yuzen left the bridge and followed the young Adept to a stateroom on the upper deck.

Vahat Sen the earth mover was surrounded by four or five members of her order. She was very young, of an age with the boy who had just summoned Yuzen; her breasts had barely begun to show and her face was plump and unsubtle. She glanced dully at him as he entered but made no other acknowledgement. Her eyes were already half-closed, her body slack.

With a little help she lay down on the polished floor, starfish-style, an Adept at each of her five extremities. Almost immediately she shuddered and moaned. Her converse with the volatile spirits of the earth had begun.

This trance was no limp passive thing: she writhed, struggled, and whimpered, challenging the considerable strength of her five assistants. At times it seemed like every bone in her body was broken, so distorted were the postures she assumed. Sweat bathed her face and breasts; her color was as pale as foam on the Tzrin Teai.

Finally she emitted a great bloodcurdling wail that Attanio would have been proud of, and it was all over. Yuzen almost expected a baby to start hollering somewhere. She floated up to consciousness, radiant, whispering, "It's done. I've wakened the monster."

There were no seismographic instruments on hand, but Vahat Sen assured them that Pao was now in the grip of a major earthquake. It was time to move in.

They angled steeply for the upper air, trying to avoid the worst of the storm, meanwhile using all the speed they had. Then, at the apex of ascent, they dove down again blindly, relying on dead reckoning to find their target in the churning maelstrom below.

Close to the surface they flew more sedately through a grey curtain of rain. Forked lightning flashed continuously; the hills of Pao were littered with broken branches and uprooted trees—where the topsoil hadn't been entirely washed away. Even through the gloom a baleful red glow flickered from the direction of Mirunga, the island's principal volcano. Incandescent rivers of lava had begun their slow passage down the cinder cone; the stench of sulfur was everywhere.

Pao's single village was in ruins. At first glance there was no sign of life, which gave Yuzen a few uncomfortable moments: but then Pzu Cheng glimpsed a knot of refugees huddling under some shredded sailcloth. Apparently they were all that remained of the garrison. The ship circled and came to a halt a few feet above ground, whereupon Yuzen bawled out questions.

"Have you any casualties? Will you evacuate? Who is your commanding officer?"

They posed as a scientific mission blown off course by the typhoon, but these wretched survivors could have cared less. All they thought about was getting off the island.

Teoru was not among them. "Are there any others?" Yuzen demanded. At first no one would say, but then the senior officer confessed that there was another contingent assigned to a tower halfway up Mount Mirunga. "But they're dead men," he said. "The earthquake must have wrecked the tower and killed most of them, and the eruption surely got the rest."

Yuzen only glared at him and ordered the whole detail aboard. Moments later they were heading for Mirunga.

As predicted the wooden tower was half-collapsed, but since it stood on a rocky spur it had escaped the lava flow. Crouched in the shelter of some fallen pillars was a bent figure with silver hair. It could only be Teoru.

Yuzen leaped off before the ship had fully stopped. Clouds of steam billowed up to swallow him as rain vaporized on hot lava, with a sound like a thousand hissing snakes. He struggled his way through this boiling fog to Teoru's side.

There was no time for an emotional scene. Teoru seemed at

the end of his resources; Yuzen lifted him bodily and carried him back to the ship, where Attanio waited to pull him aloft. Yuzen followed and the airship shot away from Mirunga like an arrow.

Moments later the volcano blew. Its concussion was so violent that it knocked several of the crew unconscious and deafened the rest for a quarter of an hour. But the pilot at least kept his wits: soon they were outracing both the shock wave and the ash and debris that choked the atmosphere in an expanding radius. Vahat Sen had wrought well indeed.

3

Altogether it was hardly an auspicious moment for the Shinjuku clan's reunion. Teoru was installed in the best suite and put to bed at once, for he was on the brink of exhaustion. Yuzen and Attanio stood by to serve him. Looking at the man stretched out before them they could hardly believe their eyes: Teoru had become a stranger.

"You notice a change," the philosopher said dryly. "The Luo Maung are great healers, you see. They've cured me of all my ills."

Even Attanio, who remembered Teoru as he was before the *nong khla* therapy, was shocked. For the Martian Adept had suddenly grown old. He was frail, visibly shrunken, his face a maze of wrinkles, his flesh hanging off the bone in creases. Even his eyes were dimmed, and his voice only a cracked memory of the magnificent instrument it had been.

"At first they treated us quite courteously. From the start the so-called Sringlë of Phayao was separated from us: I suppose she had done her job and was being relieved of duty." He shook his head as if in regret. "I see my biggest mistake was to trust her."

Attanio would have interrupted, but Yuzen silenced him with a gesture.

"They found the *nong khla*, of course, and guessed who was using it. They offered to cure me of the addiction but I declined. Then the tortures began. I'm sure I was the easiest subject Chelzin Tep ever interviewed. All he did was wait until the current symbiot was moribund, and I was clay in his hands.

"You'd have been ashamed of me, Yuzen. By the code of Shinjuku I should have suicided at my first opportunity. But there is something in the furthest limits of pain that crushes the will. I was powerless.

"They learned everything, both the things I would gladly have told them and the things I would have kept hidden. I only hope the knowledge does them some good. At the end I was given into the care of the excellent Doctor Lusu and his six-legged assistants. Oh, we became fast friends, though we disagreed on the diagnosis." His chest rattled in a ghastly imitation of laughter. "I'm convinced that Maung pharmacology has no equal anywhere in the worlds of men. In a matter of days the doctor had restored my body to its natural state of health. I was free of the *nong khla* and, better still, my wounds of the Xillian conflict were healed. I felt whole again —for a span of perhaps twelve hours. Then it became clear what else the doctor had cured."

He gestured at the ruin of his body. "It seems that the *dwedo* of Lumiphat induces a self-propagating virus in the human organism. Most humans can't tolerate the intrusion and die quickly, while a very few adjust and go on to live indefinitely. *Dwedo* is tenacious: to survive it must keep its host in good health, and so it does, century after century. But Doctor Lusu expunged the virus from my body, all unwitting, and left me victim to the natural processes of age. In the first weeks it was horrifying: catching up for all that lost time, you see. More recently the decline has stabilized. I should last at least another whole year."

Yuzen protested but Teoru simply waved it off. "I'd be a fool not to appreciate the peculiar justice of it all." He sank back on his pillows. "But I see how senility has addled my brains already. Here I've been accepting your presence on Phra Viharn as the most natural thing in the world, when in fact it's little short of miraculous."

So Yuzen sketched their sojourn on Ynenga and their dealings with Damashek and Bezoza.

"We ended up in the care of Doctor Lusu, just as you did. But we managed to escape. Tell me, my Lord: what is your impression of the Maung political situation?"

"Byzantine, convoluted, tradition-bound."

"What about conditions here on the surface?"

Teoru was puzzled by his line of questioning. "In spite of

all the propaganda to the contrary, it appears to be yet another instance of a world that can't support human development. The Maung civilization is based in space, not on the surface of Viharn. Oh, I'm told there's some sort of high priestess down here, with a few temples and acolytes, but her office is symbolic and her followers inconsequential."

Yuzen nodded and caught Attanio's eye. "It seems the Luo Maung love to rewrite history." And he proceeded to describe their own experience on Phra Viharn.

When he was done Teoru simply held his head. "What a race of liars. And I believed what they said about Sringlë, how she was just a common agent assigned to keep an eye on Outreach intruders and inveigle them into capture. I've cursed her name a thousand times."

"She'll forgive you."

But Teoru made no reply. Attanio could imagine how much he was remembering, how little he was predicting of his relationship with the Viharnese exquisite. And all the while the ship carried them steadily closer to Taa Phreng.

"How did you manage to be installed on Pao?" Yuzen asked after a time.

"I was of no more use to them. They kept me separated from the only friends I had, the Myinti, so that my whole world was a luxurious prison in one of the highest towers. It was wearisome in the extreme. I asked to be sent downworld: if I'm to die, at long last, I'd rather do it beneath a blue sky with earth under my feet. I suppose they pitied me, for they did grant my wish. As far as the lords of Srasuri are concerned I'm out of the picture."

"Especially now that Pao is too," Attanio observed.

Awhile later, over the Sea of Phoro, the Martian lord came out on deck for a breath of air. Yuzen helped him into a lounge and all three sat talking once more.

"I see I need a great deal of reeducating," Teoru said with a trace of rue. "For example, the Xuun seem to have done much that is good for this world, according to what you've told me, and yet the Luo Maung constantly vilified them. I'm particularly curious about all the branches of the *saei* family. The sky-folk don't use them much, except of course on their guests."

So they spoke of the spinners, the delvers, the planters and harvesters, the legendary builders who had raised the Glass

Hills in a single day. In spite of his afflictions Lord Teoru's intellect remained lively.

"Like the other peoples of the Antares Reach the Luo Maung tend to paint a sinister picture of Xuun," he said. "But they did tell me one story which should provide you both some food for thought. For millennia, human scholars have puzzled over the enigma of Tzokol: where they came from, where they went, what their artifacts mean. As you must already have learned, more than one alien species has a clearer picture than we do. The Luo Maung even preserve Xuun traditions of the true location of the Tzokol homeworld." He smiled slightly, the first smile they'd seen on that ravaged face. "It's Viharn."

"Impossible!"

"Not so. You forget that eight million years can change even the face of a planet. According to Doctor Lusu's tale, Xuun, not Tzokol, was the first starfaring species in the Orion Arm. They never pierced the Veil but their biomorphic drives were capable of the real-time haul between Mnai and Shu. On Mnai's second planet they found a primitive reptilian civilization, ten, fifteen million years back. The Xuun were completely fascinated. Not only were these creatures individual personalities, rather than hive-units; they had also developed an effective material technology instead of genetically modifying their own bodies, or the bodies of some subject species, as the hexapods had done. The Xuun established peaceful relations and studied them for thousands of years. Then, with the knowledge they acquired, they began manipulating.

"It was under Xuun guidance that the Tzokol reached the height of their civilization and spread out into the stars. But they weren't mindless puppets; in fact they were an extremely creative and idiosyncratic race. Still, everything they did somehow served the interest of Xuun. For example they excelled in devising defenses against all forms of warlike incursion."

"What about their extinction?"

"That was their ultimate rebellion. After a few million years the symbiosis faltered; new religious movements rose among the Tzokol, ideas that they were locked in a prison, that evil demons ruled their lives. But they were a completely nonaggressive species, so it never occurred to them to wage war against the Xuun, or even to thwart them in any overt way. They never rattled the bars of their prison. Instead their path was inward. As always they chose ritualized self-destruction as their tactic: it was a twist on the old theme of potlatch, which they called *m-zilk-ff-zm* or 'destroying what is most perfect so that it no longer suffers pain.' It was their way of expressing intolerance of an inimical world, in a slow attrition over millennia.

"Finally they decided on the supreme act of potlatch. They culled Viharn of most of its land animals in successive waves of artificially tailored plagues. Then by exciting the planet's core they induced cataclysmic crustal movements which submerged most of its land masses, leaving only the scattered islands we see today. The western hemisphere still hasn't settled down."

"To put it mildly."

"Meanwhile all the remaining Tzokol had taken to interstellar space in what ships they still kept. There in the emptiness between stars, using some device long lost, they opened a passage out of this universe and went through."

Attanio thought of the tiny Riftstone he had carried from world to world and shivered.

"How did the Xuun react?"

"They were puzzled, and quite helpless. Interstellar communications had collapsed; they had only their own ships to carry them from Shu to Mnai. Naturally they were paranoid about invasion from space, now that their protectors had disappeared. But they had to wait seven million years before a new race came applying for the job."

"So Viharn was bait. A seemingly virgin world begging for colonization. Only now we know the virgin was a whore."

"Apt, if crude."

"Does the Nectar of Xuun play any part in this story?"

Teoru stroked his chin. "In fact it does. It was something the Xuun developed to keep their symbiots happy, so that nothing like the Tzokol suicide would ever recur. That's why the Luo Maung reject it. They want to be free to rage against their confinement."

"Except they don't."

"No, they just do things like tear the wings off flies."

With this new angle Attanio felt he finally understood Phra Viharn: all the pieces fell into place. But the picture wasn't appealing.

There still remained the problem of what to do with the Luo Maung warriors they had rescued. Killing them was unthinkable, but so was bringing them back to Taa Phreng, where they would raise all kinds of diplomatic wrangles. The solution was to drop them off, over their loud protests, on an uninhabited islet well east of Simkok. There they could live in comfort and eventually even build some kind of boat. Meanwhile, as far as Chelzin Tep could discover, the island of Pao had been devastated by natural forces which none of its residents survived.

XVII. The Armada of Xil

The reunion of Teoru and Sringlë was a private affair, from which the lady emerged quite devastated. Irrationally, she blamed his misfortune on herself. Teoru of course would hear nothing of the sort; but as a result it was impossible for the two of them to endure each others' presence. All of this gave Attanio a bitter insight into the offhand way she treated his own suit.

He spent an evening in the palace gardens with her a few days later, sipping flower tea while a woman entertained them on the flute from a discreet distance. Yuzen rounded out the company.

As Suvei's slender crescent brushed the treetops the conversation turned to antique myths.

"There is a story of the moon goddess," Sringlë was saying, "how she loved a mortal man and begged her father, the lightning god, to grant him immortality. Only her father was cruel, and clever: he gave the mortal unending life but withheld the gift of eternal youth. And so her lover grew old but could not die, and shrivelled like an insect. In sorrow, the goddess transformed him into a cricket, to sing for her on moonless nights." The flute trilled; a tear or two sparkled in her eyes.

"We had the same tale in Tharsis," Yuzen said. "I can glimpse a parallel—but surely you don't intend to put Teoru in a cricket cage?"

She shook her raven head. "No, no, but I've urged him, so far unsuccessfully, to take advantage of the Queen's *saei*. To go back to the insects, in fact. He may mistrust Maung pathology but we *can* work wonders, even against old age. Look at the Queen."

"But Sringlë—can you really help Teoru now? He's resigned himself to death."

233

"It's a complex issue, I agree. Teoru has lived long and suffered deeply. I can understand his acceptance of mortality. I suppose it's only my own selfishness that wants to prolong his life now. But no matter what happens, the Maung worlds have many difficult years ahead, and I'd like to have him around to help us through them."

"Then your *saei* really could restore his vigor?"

"They could, if he wants it."

2

Aeian's message reached the Queen on the following day and set the whole hive buzzing. Her mission was a huge success: her ship, the *Sril*, was even now in the outer reaches of the Mnai system, hurtling homeward with its precious cargo of Riftstones. Now the endgame began.

Srasuri sent challenge after challenge to the renegade veil-ship, which continued on course unheeding. "We are un-armed," Aeian signalled the Luo Maung. "If you wish we will dock in one of the Triple Cities." This was acceptable; thus she acquired an escort of Maung Scorpions all the way in.

In the meantime Chuyin and Tiao set out for the Xuun spaceport at Phra Xonong, to charter a surface-to-orbit vessel for their own embassy to Luo Viharn. At Attanio's insistence he and Yuzen were included in the party, disguised as members of the honor guard. Teoru remained in Taa Phreng.

They spent no more than a few hours in Phra Xonong. Still it was enough to send Attanio's senses reeling, for it was like a voyage to another world. Past the glassy landing field and the veined integumenta of the starships he glimpsed acre after acre of manicured gardens, blue as the sky, and improbably pointed hills of pale violet. No aspect of the landscape was safe from Xuun artifice. Flimsy towers that seemed carved of diamond shimmered on the horizon, arranged in complex fig-ures that teased his perception. Even the air seemed heavier, more tangible, filled with odors he had no name for and no desire to remember.

They dealt exclusively with the turbaned Xonong Ru—but always on the fringe of things lurked the delicate shapes of the Xuun themselves.

"I never thought I'd say this," Attanio said softly, "but

they're beautiful. Not what I expected, not bugs at all."

"No, my dear, they're creatures of the air. Once I saw a pair of Alates perform a Sun Greeting: ever since then, even the best human dancers look like cripples to me." Sringlë smiled. "And they can grow flowers that recite poetry."

Of course their language was all scents and flavors anyway; but still Attanio caught himself wondering if there really could be such a thing as a superior race.

3

Chaong Cycle: every fighting man and woman in Srasuri waited tensely on alert. Fifty vessels of the Spider class wove a defensive web around the city as two Xuun starships matched orbit. Both had an escort of Scorpions, but the lords of Srasuri were cautious men. Four hundred and fifty Viharnese years had gone by since any Xuun ship had approached Luo Viharn; no one knew quite what to expect.

"I couldn't have planned this better myself," exulted Tiao Vaoi, aboard the *Mezd*. It was a standing joke between her and her sister.

"That's right—we really have to hand it to the old bag." But Chuyin-Sringlë's laughter rang false even in her own ears; humor couldn't hide the fact that they were frightened.

Because Queen Talithai's scheme was anything but foolproof; half of it rested on the outcome of Aeian's voyage to Ynenga—which fortunately had proved successful. Now the second half depended on another uncertain quantity, namely Chelzin Tep and his fellow Lords Councillor. So the Queen's three daughters, riding in orbit aboard *Mezd* and *Sril,* were simply waiting for Luo Viharn to force their hand.

"Here it comes," Tiao said. The voice of Srasuri Control chattered parrotlike over their headsets. "They're ordering Aeian to dock."

"Stand by screens!" Chuyin called out.

"No, Your Excellency," Aeian's disembodied voice was saying, "let my sisters confer with you in person while my ship remains in independent orbit. They will be a surety for my own nonbelligerence, as I will be for theirs. You can believe we have no hostile intent."

But the lords of Srasuri were accustomed to having their

way. "You will dock at Bay Number Seven and prepare for a boarding party," Control demanded. "Otherwise we will be forced to open fire."

Still Aeian's tone never lost its calm insistence. "By the will of Pho Tak and all the articles we subscribe to," she began—

And that was their signal.

"Up screens!" As Chuyin shouted, her ship, *Mezd,* acquired a halo of refracted light: but *Sril* vanished without a trace.

All Luo Maung channels erupted in confusion. "Central Cluj alternators nonfunctional—city in free fall—Scorpion drives impaired." And all over Srasuri, whatever wasn't bolted down started floating off in the sudden absence of gravity. Most of the population was shocked and helpless; the city itself faltered in orbit.

Tiao immediately took command of the crisis, even as Luo Maung nullbeams flared against her screens. Safe within her Darabundit field, *Mezd* was unaffected by the dysfunction plaguing Srasuri.

"Do not be alarmed," she broadcast. "We are taking defensive measures only. Cease fire. Repeat, cease fire. Your Clujpulse failure is merely a side effect of the enhancement of a Tzokolian artifact on board *Sril.* If you agree to a truce, the artifact will be deactivated."

In fact Tiao was bluffing, because whether Luo Viharn accepted the truce or not, there was no way of conveying the news to her sister aboard *Sril.* Ship and crew were beyond the reach even of telepathy. Nevertheless, Chuyin-Sringlë had achieved an extremely clear integration to the effect that the Luo Maung would cooperate anyway: thus Aeian was simply waiting a prearranged unit of time before relenting.

Seconds ticked off. From Srasuri there was only silence as Chelzin Tep deliberated. But his decision came just as Sringlë foresaw.

"We grant you one-tenth of a rotation to explain your violation of the Treaty of Vadhuz."

More seconds passed before Aeian's limit expired. Then in an eyeblink *Sril* rematerialized: everywhere in Srasuri objects resumed their normal weight, sometimes with drastic consequences.

Both downworld ships now conferred with Luo Maung authorities about the proposed negotiations. The cloud-dwellers were sufficiently impressed by Aeian's demonstration to be agreeable.

It was conceded that Aeian would remain aboard *Sril* and that Tiao would enter Srasuri as primary negotiator. But the Oruri's daughters had one more condition which puzzled the Council of Lords.

"As you can see, our ships bear no conventional armaments whatsoever. On account of this strategic disadvantage we therefore require a hostage for the Lady Tiao's safety, a civilian whom we will name."

This was acceptable: but only because Chelzin Tep never dreamed whom they would choose.

"Send us the Lady Prajit La."

The exchange was made. Tiao proceeded to the Council chambers with a small Phra Maung detachment—all Amazonian females for maximum effect. Simultaneously Prajit La was ferried out to the *Mezd*, quite alone. Chuyin-Sringlë welcomed her aboard.

"It's an honor to meet you," she said warmly, conducting the lady to one of the ship's sumptuous drawing rooms. "Our agents keep us well informed of your public appearances."

Prajit La, mistress to the Overlord of Luo Viharn, acknowledged her modestly; meanwhile she missed no detail of Sringlë's jewel-encrusted costume or of the room itself. They traded pleasantries for a moment or two.

But then it was down to business. "We know how cumbersome the Council of Lords is," Sringlë began, "how long it takes to formulate policy. We also know that the invaders from Xil may strike within a matter of days. Now, Talithai Oruri has already conceived a plan that can save us all; my sister is no doubt presenting it to the Council right now."

"More likely in an hour from now," Prajit La said dryly. "I'm sure they're still examining her credentials."

"That's exactly my point. The lords of Srasuri are moving too hesitantly. In fact, my sister's embassy is just a formality: we know very well that *you,* not Chelzin Tep, are the most powerful person in Luo Viharn. That's why you and I will do the real negotiating. Right now."

Of course nothing suited Prajit La better. Five hours later they had a working agreement.

4

For the Luo Maung forewarned meant forearmed. In this they
had an enormous advantage over the unsuspecting defenders
of Mars. Furthermore their battle computers had been programmed by no less a strategist than Fsau of Myint, already a
veteran of the Xil War, master of a thousand ploys and gam-
bits. Five hundred ships englobed Viharn in a series of defensive shells that grew ever denser as they neared the planet's
upper atmosphere. Since the first sighting of Lord Appucc's
armada the ships of Viharn had circled tirelessly in the void,
waiting for the blow to fall.

And true to form the Xillians struck like a sledgehammer.

Simultaneously, from every quadrant of heaven, half the
fleet rained down in a blaze of firepower. The outer shell was
pulverized—but since these were mostly robot craft, pawns
on the second row, they were no great loss. Penetrating deeper
into the sphere the Xillians found themselves harried on all
sides by Maung craft which matched them in armaments and
outclassed them in speed. This first wave of attack quickly
degenerated into a chaos of individual skirmishes.

They fight like dogs, Lord Appucc thought contemp-
tuously. They won't take the offensive—they only bite when
cornered—they come on us in snarling packs, never one on
one.

His body occupied a couch on the flagship's bridge, but his
mind, in direct sensory hookup with ship's comp, ranged
through the battle theater like a wraith. He bathed in the trans-
uranic flames of wrecked destroyers, rode particle beams
home to their elusive targets, felt Darabundit overloads as a
tingling in his own flesh—all the while calculating the armada's gains and losses with enhanced powers of analysis.

The Luo Maung had attempted to wage psionic war alongside the steady barrage of nullbeams, pulse bombs, and anti-
matter projectiles. But they met their match in the Pa-chwa
Adepts, whose barriers negated all sendings as an ocean swal-
lows sparks. The battle therefore was confined to the material
plane, for all that its vicious energies sometimes strained the
fabric of reality itself.

For now the inner shell held fast. Phra Viharn was safe

from the frenzy in the sky, although a few dying ships entered terminal orbits and burned up in her atmosphere. Tzarit too was protected behind conventional screens, the only remaining sky-city in planetary orbit: but Lord Appucc was confining his wrath to the Maung fleet, sparing planet and city so they would make better spoils.

In the first thirty minutes of combat Xil lost seventy-seven ships, Viharn one hundred and three. In the next ten minutes Xillian casualties rose steadily, while the Maung held their own. Fsau's defense was paying off.

Perceiving this Lord Appucc immediately withdrew and regrouped. Half his ships had yet to see action, whereas every single Luo Maung vessel was heavily involved. However much the initial foray had cost him he was still confident of victory: in fact his blood sang with it, his nerves flashed with a consuming will to conquer.

The Armada of the Pleiades was a precision instrument. Within an hour it had reformed into four conical divisions and once more plunged into the fray, spewing lethal energies all up and down the electromagnetic spectrum. And now, incredibly, the Maung gave way. Wherever Xil struck they parted ranks to let the enemy pass—and then fled. Upward, outward, arrowing toward Appucc's reserve divisions where they circled in wide orbit, they left the brilliant sphere of Phra Viharn naked before his onslaught.

They were handing him the prize. They had conceded victory! What dogs, what worms—they were worse cowards than he dreamed. Lord Appucc knew the ecstasy of complete success—for one brief moment. Then his enhanced sensorium told him that something was very, very wrong.

He had just enough time to see it coming but not enough insight to figure out what it was. And then it was too late, for schemes, for countermoves, for regret.

The events of the next few moments can be described only in the most approximate and conjectural terms. Sequence itself was blurred, along with probability and the rest of the props reality depends on.

In the attacking Xillian divisions all sensors and shipdrives ceased functioning. Simultaneously the Maung homeworld vanished from the continuum like a candle flame blowing out. Beginning with the space it had just vacated, a wave of annihilation spread outward, its progress visible only in the wreckage it created and then swallowed without a trace.

Tzarit was engulfed, and both moons. Never again could lovers in the gardens of Taa Phreng make trite comparisons with the beloved's luminous charms. The inner divisions of the Xillian Armada itself were consumed in a matter of seconds: not even dust, not even ions remained.

The fleeing ships of Luo Viharn managed to keep one step ahead of this expanding singularity. Then just as Appucc's reserves began firing on them the continuum shuddered yet again, as three hundred-odd Maung vessels pierced the Veil in almost perfect unison, escaping from the nightmare at their backs.

Gravitational anomalies and probabilistic distortions left the surviving Xillian ships so much scrap metal. There was no way they could maneuver effectively in real space, much less repeat the Maung's trick. Sharing their fate were a handful of Viharnese destroyers which had failed to achieve Puncture in time, and now wallowed in free fall next to their enemies.

But not for long. Before the heat-death of the universe came more than a few seconds closer, the all-consuming void brushed these derelict hulls too, and they were lost. In one instant the Armada of the Pleiades was dismembered, disintegrated, and dematerialized. All the savage warriors of Xil, all the subtle philosophers of Pa-chwa came to the same abrupt conclusion; and with them ended the dreams of Lord Appucc of Xil.

5

On an island very near the south pole of Viharn, two men and a woman sat quietly in the glow of a wood fire, bundled in quilted robes against the damp. They were Yuzen, Attanio, and Sringlë. Above them the sky was as black as the abstraction of all blacks, an absence of light so profound that its contemplation was best avoided. Only a few minutes ago that same sky had glittered with the stars and auroral displays normal to the long polar night: but precisely when Tzarit had been swallowed, and the invaders disintegrated, a curtain had fallen over the world. Now the three humans clasped hands and looked to each others' eyes for comfort.

On the other side of the island, invisible behind a range of hills, one of the enormous Riftstones of Ynenga had been erected four days earlier in precise alignment with Viharn's geomantic currents. Its polyhedral counterpart had similarly been installed at the north pole. From these two focal points Aeian Vaoi, a Xonong Ru delegation, and a multitude of lay Adepts directed their planet's defense, overseen constantly by a pair of Xuun ontologists specializing in the manipulation of the plenum.

The Riftstones' field had delivered Viharn from invasion; its interface with normal space/time, extending further into the material universe, had nullified the enemy fleet; but now the problem remained of restoring the world to its accustomed plane. Already the Mnai system's gravitational balance had been upset, making reentry a vastly more delicate operation than departure.

"Now you see how the Tzokol species managed to disappear from history," Sringlë said.

"I hope we don't join them." Attanio risked a glance at the emptiness above.

"The purpose of these artifacts is to facilitate extinction. Working them in reverse is tricky business."

"We could end up in the heart of the sun, right? Or adrift between galaxies. . . ."

"No point in worrying. Besides, I trust the Xuun."

Yuzen found this last a multileveled statement. Trust the Xuun to what? Aloud he said, "Something has been bothering me all along. What would Queen Talithai have done if Attanio hadn't showed up so conveniently with that miniature Riftstone?"

Sringlë pulled her robe a little closer. "I can only guess— but I have a suspicion that she would have abdicated in favor of one of her heirs and left the problem in *her* hands. Talithai has lost all interest in the real world, just like Thuanat before her. I'm afraid world-weariness is an occupational hazard of Imagoes."

"The blood's run thin," Attanio muttered. "But what about Xuun? Would they have stood by for the rape of Viharn?"

For a long time he got no answer, and a cold wind keened through the rushes. Finally Sringlë said, "Yes, they would have. If we can't save ourselves then Xuun has no use for us."

"But what about their love and compassion for the people of Viharn?"

She laughed, a strange hollow sound. "Compassion can't ward off particle beams or shock tubes. No, if Viharn fell, I think Xuun would have worked something out with the conquerors from Xil. They can be extremely persuasive when they want to be."

So Yuzen's question was answered. The Xuun could be trusted to protect their own interests, and not much else. The sky continued as black as the Coalsack.

"Why don't you sing for us, Attanio?"

"What do you want to hear?"

His question met no reply, for in that same instant the stars switched on again. In spite of herself Sringlë began murmuring, "In the name of Pho Tak, the Merciful, the Compassionate. . . ." while Yuzen and Attanio simply cheered.

6

It was dawn in the green hills of central Vachien. Thick mist carpeted the upland valleys, luminous in the sun's first rays; a thousand birds sang invisibly through liquid throats. The air was pungent, inspiriting, heavy with portent.

Days earlier the remnants of the Luo Maung fleet had limped home, with Fsau and the rest of the Myinti leading. The last surviving Xillian squadron—fortuitously stationed in the zone of planetoids—had long since fled, bearing news of Lord Appucc's defeat to the Pleiades. The sky cities of Srasuri and Prathamim had returned to their accustomed orbits around Viharn, unaccompanied now by lost Tzarit or the two vanished moons.

A glittering assembly was gathered here before the Glass Hills, known also as the Tombs of the Queens, to greet the new day in Vachien's rural fastness. Lord Teoru was at hand wearing the formal robes of Shinjuku, looking much fitter since his first session with the royal *saei*. Ranged around him were the valorous Myinti, and at his right hand was Prince Yuzen in iridescent scaleplate. Attanio stood a little apart, self-conscious in borrowed finery: he now held a rank at the Court of Taa Phreng, an honor however which seemed all but meaningless.

Also a little separate were the impassive Xonong Ru, as alike as castings from one mold. They stood in for Xuun: for the hexapods themselves avoided human gatherings.

Luo Viharn however was well represented in the persons of the various Lords Councillor, including the Overlord Chelzin himself. And Prajit La flashed with outworld gems like a super-nova.

Naturally all the Sret and Vaoi of the realm waited attendance, draped in antique silks and sporting tall feathers of peacock, quetzal, and raggiana. Even Xaiya had stirred from her melancholy to join these more worldly sisters, taking her place beside such notables as Aeian, Tiao, and Inao. But of all that multitude none could compare with Chuyin Vaoi, alias Sringlë of Phayao—she seemed reborn in glory, like a butterfly fresh out of the chrysalis, or a snake with new skin.

And at the center of everything was the Imago. She stood like an icon before the tall portal of the tombs, wrapped from head to toe in a white vinga. Behind her rose the crystalline spires of the Glass Hills, reared in a single day by builder-*saei* in a miracle of biomorphic engineering. As the rising sun showered her with light she seemed to shine forth of her own volition: a white flame, a pillar of pure energy, poised between earth and heaven in one taut moment of equilibrium.

"It is done," she said. Out of the long silence her voice cut like a sword. "The illusion has outworn its novelty. I leave you to the whims of a new dreamer."

These brief cynical words marked the end of a reign. She stood a moment longer, silently watching the generations assembled before her, feeling their curiosity, their incredulity, their awe. Then she turned without a backward glance and strode through the tall gateway where eight previous versions of herself had passed.

Like them, she was never seen again among the mortal beings of the galaxy.

Now the tenth in an unbroken lineage stepped forward to address the gathering. "By the grace of Pho Tak I am chosen Oruri of Viharn." Chuyin-Sringlë bowed to her subjects, and they answered in kind. A perceptible wave of relief spread over them. "The new era has already begun. Never again will the people of Viharn keep themselves aloof from the rest of the galaxy, denying their wisdom and withholding their gifts. The sky has been opened. Henceforth, Maung veilships will voyage everywhere in known space, not as conquerors but as defenders, sharing the technologies of Xuun and Viharn with all beings. For Xil has been repulsed but not defeated. We cannot rest until all the galaxy is free of the warlords' threat."

For Teoru this pledge was the long-awaited fulfillment of his mission, the final declaration of revenge on the destroyers of Mars. For Attanio it was empty rhetoric—and still he wept silent tears. Because Sringlë was lost to him; she had ascended to the stars, she was a goddess incarnate. He had prepared for this moment ever since he learned of the succession a few days past. Now it had come and it tasted of ashes.

The world's charms had faded. He found himself wondering how much of Parmenio had survived the invasion from Xil.

XVIII. The Coconut Dynasty

"Attanio darling you were brilliant!" Silk Effanse adjusted her cowl to take a sip of hot *shekk*. "Your adventures have only improved your style—after all, you always used to say how uplifting pain can be."

"Did I?" His mind drew a blank. Even after three days, so much of his former life in Ashbeck seemed a dream. "So you think there's still a future for cabaret here, even with Makhlouf and the drug barons out of the way?"

"Well. . . ." She frowned melodramatically. "Things are bound to change—but didn't you say there was going to be a war, and that Parmenio would be a major link in the supply line? Just think of all those bored soldiers passing through—they'll need entertainment! Like in the old cubes."

"True." After a brilliant gig at the Succubarium Attanio was still wrestling with his options. "What about the Nectar of Xuun? What will happen when Maung ships start landing here once a year offering Ganang Zal to all takers? Maybe people will want less jarring forms of theater. I've seen what that stuff does, Silk—it turns people into vegetables."

Silk laughed uproariously. "Look around you, honey—we're not exactly in the company of geniuses." In the dark crowded club people hunched over tables, leaned against walls, clutched drinks and gazed out of hollow unfocused eyes. Flicker was not as easy to come by as it used to be, but blood crystals and shindust were still plentiful.

"Attanio," she said, "it just sounds like you're trying to find excuses. If you want to stay in Ashbeck there's definitely a place for you. Stars above, if you wanted you could buy the Succubarium yourself and start a whole new movement in theater. You've got the bloody Queen of Viharn on your side now—it's not as if you're a struggling young artist anymore. You could turn Ashbeck into a . . . whatever you wanted! People still remember you, oh yes. You left at the peak of your career—and pulled off the robbery of the decade in the process! Attanio Hwin is still a name to conjure with on the Flicker Circuit."

"Yes, I suppose so. . . ."

Later the two of them shared a bowl of rice at the Coconut Dynasty. The Pinkflash, Attanio's other favorite after-hours haunt, had not survived the Xillian occupation. But then it would have been disappointing if nothing had changed.

"What's happened to Yuzen?"

"He went back to the hotel to get some sleep. You know how clean living those Martians are."

Silk snickered. "Yes, I remember that other group. Dull, dull, dull. But this one isn't so bad, I must admit."

"No, he's not bad at all . . . I think it has something to do with the company he keeps."

She toyed with the battered chopsticks. "Tell me more of your story. I'm still confused, hearing it all in snatches the way I have. It still amazes me to think that the Xillians are . . . gone. Just snuffed out! You can't imagine how horrible they were." She grimaced at some stray recollection. "It seems that they'd never have been beaten if the bad Maung—"

"You mean the sky-dwellers."

"—hadn't decided to cooperate with the good Maung. Sringlë pulled that one off, right? How did she do it?"

"You may remember that a woman called Prajit La had the president of the Council of Lords wrapped around her little finger. Well, Sringlë conferred with her privately and made her an offer she couldn't refuse."

"Which was?"

"Prajit La is beautiful and vain. She's also getting older. Sringlë offered to restore her youth."

"She can do that?"

"Oh yes. But now I've just told you a state secret—because part of the deal was that Prajit La has to conceal her bargain for the next few years, until Luo Viharn and Phra Viharn are firmly consolidated. Then she gets her reward."

"I see. In other words Sringlë foresees trouble:"

"Well, it certainly won't happen as easily as Queen Talithai intended. For now, the Luo Maung accept the Imago's authority only in spiritual matters. The real government is still in the hands of the Council of Lords. But since Prajit La is the official liaison between earth and sky, you can see that Sringlë has things well under control."

"To think I actually met her!" And Silk began posturing like a mad holodrama star, miming the part of a queen with much fluttering of veils. "You know, I rather liked her. She seemed just like an ordinary woman."

Attanio choked on his rice. "Sringlë? Ordinary?"

"No, no, that's not what I meant—I mean she didn't put on airs. She was very down to earth, you know; she was a strong woman who could look you in the eye and acknowledge you as a fellow human being. That's not how I imagine a queen, somehow."

"I suppose not." Attanio ran fingers through his hair. "I loved her, Silk."

"Of course you did." Silk was unimpressed. "That's why you ran off with her, isn't it?"

"Well, yes, but . . . you don't understand. I loved her. And it's killing me that I can't have her."

Something in his voice made the lady sit up and take notice. "You're very drunk, aren't you."

"Yes, but that doesn't change anything. I fell under Sringlë's spell the first moment I saw her. She was like an addiction, an ache, an emptiness I had to fill. It was never like that for me before. And all she ever did was play games with me. She hid behind a dozen masks, she even tried to fix me up with her twin sister, but always I could see beyond the illusion to the real woman underneath. I can't put it into words. . . ."

"Don't try, dear." Silk put a sisterly arm around him and kissed his ear. "Now I see why you can't make up your mind about anything. You've got it pretty bad. How come she's not interested?"

Attanio spread his hands helplessly. "She, she's just not made that way." He was perilously close to tears. "She's got the mind of a three-thousand-year-old woman, in the body of a—a goddess. Men are just toys to her. All she sees is the big picture, the long view. She won't take me seriously."

"Then she's best forgotten."

"That's why I'm here."

At that moment a trio of old acquaintances happened by. "Attanio! We heard you were back!"

"We thought you were dead!"

"What was it like offworld?"

And answers multiplied into the wee hours of dawn. He managed to bid them all farewell only as greyish sunlight filtered over the crumbling city walls.

Outside the Panspermia Silk balanced on a pile of rubble, striking wistful poses. "So will you stay, Attanio?"

"I don't know."

She jumped down. "When does the Maung division move on?"

"Three more days. Yuzen is captain of his own ship, you know."

"I guess he wants you to come along."

"Yes, into war." Attanio yawned ferociously. Spending the night on the Flicker Circuit was as stupefying as he remembered. "They're going into the Myint stars to gather an armada against Xil. New worlds, new wickedness, new disasters."

"So will you stay, Attanio?" She skipped around him, batting her eyelashes like a half-wit.

"It's tempting."

"Or would you rather see the stars again. . . ."

"No. I'll stay." He reached for the glass door of the hotel.

"Won't you miss Yuzen?"

"Okay, I won't stay. I'll go with him."

She cackled.

"I'll stay."

"Sweet dreams, Attanio."

"I'll go."